THE DRAGON'S EGG
THE SAINT GEORGE CHRONICLES
VOLUME THREE

M.L. EADEN

Print ISBN: 978-1-962655-06-4 — Douglas Illusions
eBook ISBN: 978-1-962655-05-7 — Douglas Illusions

Book Cover by Joanne Kwan: linktr.ee/dashalutris

Dragon and Iconography designs by Martin Whitmore: martinwhitmore.com

1st edition 2024

Content Warnings: *Oviparity, on-page sex, magical death involving possible suicide, loss of limb, polyamory (secondary characters), mental health issues, family secrets.*

QUEER STORIES BASED IN MYTH, LEGEND, AND SCIENCE FICTION.

Reader's Note

The Universe you are entering is a contemporary one with magic, myths, and legends living and working alongside each other. There are many sentient and varied species. Some of them are out in the open while others are not. However, everyone knows they existed, knows there's magic in the world, and knows that whether something walks in the light or goes bump in the night, it's as real as the sunrise and sunset.

It's a world where science and magic work hand-in-hand, creating advanced technology and building a day-to-day life where you could easily meet a dragon astronaut, an orc mage specializing in medicine, or a fae working as a tailor. Moonbases exist, sustainable living is a reality, and promises which seem to be mere figments of imagination are woven into the fabric.

Enjoy!

TO DISCOVER MORE:

MLEADEN.COM/BOOKS

CONTENTS

OPENING NIGHT

GREGOR

I turned on the holo in Xavior's den. The red carpet premiere for Jordan's latest movie was in progress and the original plan had been to attend the premiere with Jordan and host the after-party at Xavior's estate. Unfortunately, our egg had other plans.

Considering Xavior's condition, Jordan had suggested a change to an outdoor venue for the premiere, which could accommodate a dragon. While he appreciated Jordan's suggestion, Xavior didn't want to shift the venue, knowing they had arranged for the location while the movie was in pre-production before our pregnancy was even a factor.

Plus, he really wanted to wear the creation he and Jael had made for the premiere. However, fate decided Xavior couldn't put off shifting any longer, so our egg could finish growing. Once he passed the egg, it would incubate for a few more weeks, then we'd be parents. I was nervous and excited. While pregnant dragons can have short tempers, Xav was more uncomfortable and annoyed than anything. This latest change in plans hadn't helped.

The estate was abuzz with the final preparations for the after-party we also wouldn't be attending. When I offered to work with Edward to shift things around and use more of the outdoor space so he could at least attend one event tonight, he declined, not wanting to make more work for everyone.

"It's just shitty timing. That's all. I won't demand changes at the last minute just because I'm missing out," he sighed as he tried pressing on his belly again to alleviate some of the pressure. "I don't think anyone would see it that way. If it was anyone else that need accommodations, you'd make sure they were available whether it was a last-minute request or not." He always liked a good party, especially one he helped plan.

He smiled at me and touched my face. "You're right, but it's also my call. Everything is sore right now. I wouldn't be good company." He looked away, then caught my gaze. "You can go."

"Oh, fuck that. You know I won't leave you by yourself. Not right now." And definitely not while he was in pain. Our connection was the only thing helping him manage it.

"Okay, okay." He smiled, gave me a long kiss before he backed away and shifted. His feathers were bright even in the dim light of his den. It took him a while to get comfortable, but once he did, he made a light chuffing noise and offered me a spot next to him. Once there, we settled in to watch the rest of the red carpet event.

"I've been asked to audition for the stunt teams. Apparently, my training and good looks paid off." It had been a mid-production consultation that ended up with me playing a stunt double for a minor role character in the movie. Xavior made a small noise of agreement, then shifted a little, trying to stay comfortable. I kept talking to take his mind off of it.

"I wonder how many glamours are being used at an event like this." When cameras stopped using mirrors, they stopped breaking glamours. It was one of those odd things that proved to be a benefit of the digital age.

Xavior's large green head rested on my leg, close enough that I could feel his breath, but not so close as to hook me with one of his horns. I gently rubbed his snout until he became annoyed and moved. Until recently, all he wanted was attention and affection. Reassurance that he wasn't alone in all this. As things progressed and he had more discomfort, nothing seemed to help. Things were progressing normally, according to Catherine, so all we could do was wait it out and try not to be too upset with one another.

On the holo, Jordan stepped into view of the imagers tracking the red carpet crowd, looking very dashing, if not subdued, in his three-piece suit. "Xav, Jordan's on." I made a hand motion to turn up the volume. Xavior lifted his head up and turned it so he could get a better view.

"Consort Gohansberg, how thrilled are you about opening night in the US?" someone off camera asked.

Jordan smiled. "Well, I'm very delighted. The movie did extremely well in Europe, Africa, and Australia. We're hoping to have the same reception here this week." He wasn't dressed in the typical flamboyant colors or fabrics he usually wore. Tonight, the three-piece suit was a deep red with a black silk shirt and shoes. His hair was shaded darker, from his normal chestnut brown to a dark brown, with two small braids extending from his temples. The rest of his hair was a curtain around his head, with a larger braid down his back. Even with all of his finery, his cuff links stood out. They were made with a bright ruby, probably six centimeters in diameter. My bet was that the stones were a consort gift. Which explained the dark colors he was wearing. He wanted to make sure everyone's eyes were on the cuff links.

There were other shouts and questions, but one cut through the noise. "Could you introduce us to your lovely companion?"

"She's quite capable of speaking for herself, if she so desires. Isn't that so, my lady?"

Jordan had visited often enough while Xavior and I were in Spain that we thought nothing of it when he would leave for a few hours or a few days and come back. Xavior noted something odd once with Jordan's usual smell, but had chalked it up to the pregnancy messing with his senses.

The woman that stepped into frame wasn't shy. Circumspect would be more accurate. She smiled at the interviewers and stated her name. "I'm Doctor Catherine Alexander."

"What's your specialty?"

"Medical sciences and magic." Dr. Alexander and Jordan had started an affair that we hadn't caught onto until we returned to San Francisco. It wasn't that she and Jordan weren't inseparable, but they spent more time together than either of us had realized.

"They really are a beautiful-looking couple," I said. Xavior chuffed his agreement.

Dr. Alexander looked like she was in her mid-forties, though she was much older and Jordan was definitely older than that. If not for the points on his ears, and the increasingly red flush to his skin as his ice-blue eyes admired Catherine, I would have put him around mid forties as well. Catherine's light brown hair was braided in the same fae style as Jordan's, likely by Jordan's own hands. Once she finished answering questions, Dr. Alexander turned away from the imagers and took Jordan's hand as they continued to walk down the red carpet and the imagers followed.

Her black dress shimmered as she walked. It had deep slopes of fabric draped from her shoulders, framing a scalloped cutout tastefully exposing her back. Thin straps held the cape in place, which attached it to the front at the shoulders. The front of the dress had a similar feature with a deep v-slit that started at her shoulders and went nearly to her navel. Jordan had bragged about designing the dress, explaining that it was nearly all black lace, with diamond chips and sapphires woven into fabric to accentuate Dr. Alexander's curves. Even I could admire the artistry of the garment.

Xavior grumbled quietly, his mood shifting again. Xavior's clothes for the premiere were styled to make him look like a cherub, the way the fabrics gathered around him when he wore it. There was even a sheer panel in the front that showed off his stomach. Annoyed by our pregnancy, Xavior may be, but he was incredibly proud of it too.

"Maybe you'll still be able to wear your robes after you pass the egg?" A disappointed grumble answered my question. "Well, maybe not to the next premiere, but I would be happy to see you in them. Then take them off of you." My playful comment was rewarded with a chuff, the dragon equivalent of a small laugh, which made me happy. "Do you want to swim some before guests show up?"

I stood so I could make eye contact. I saw a flicker in his eyes, the idea tempting him. Likely he was trying to decide if it was worth the trade off now that he was comfortable. "If you go for a swim, I'll come with you. Then feed you ice cream after." The egg had more room to finish growing now that Xavior would be a dragon the rest of the pregnancy. I was hoping swimming would still prove useful during this last phase.

The goal for the last part of the pregnancy was for us to remain as calm and relaxed as possible. Dr. Alexander wasn't sure, but during her last few examinations, she noted that the embryo's heartbeat was slightly off. It was strong; she had said, though sometimes she heard what she thought was an echo or mummer. The more Xavior stayed calm, the less the skip happened. That was the problem with magical beings. There was very little anyone could do while the egg remained in utero. It was better to help the parent instead and hope for the best.

Xavior slowly moved to his feet and headed toward the doorway to the den. When Dr. Alexander suggested Xavior swim to relieve some of the pressure, he moved his den from his bedroom suite to one of the smaller first floor reception halls to make it easier for him to reach the pool. It had a doorway that led to the garden walks and the pool and sauna area.

The late twilight of evening had a pleasant breeze that cut through the day's heat. Dressed in only my boxers, I walked with Xavior out into the early evening air. I would have removed those, but we had guests and extra staff tonight for the party, so I kept some modesty for my sake and theirs. You'd think a dragon focused on walking to the pool wouldn't bother with that minor detail, but he noticed and grumbled softly.

"You have guests, remember? Besides, we're sleeping in your den tonight and based on the amount of heat you're putting out, there's no way I'm going to bed with clothes on." That statement won me another chuffing noise of amusement from him.

The wide steps on one end of the pool were specifically made for a larger body to enter without difficulty. Xavior flapped his wings as he entered, but as soon as he was half submerged, he folded his wings and used his limbs to paddle out further into the water. I followed until the water was up to my neck and swam next to Xavior while he relaxed.

Xavior's muscles along his shoulders and neck loosened up first. Then his hindquarters. Once he was floating, he made slight movements to keep himself in the middle of the pool, but remained still otherwise. I swam to the side on the deeper end and hoisted myself out. The deck was still warm under my ass, but the breeze gave me a few shivers.

All that mattered was that the evening swim still worked. His eyes were closed, face absent of any stress. Unlike human children, whelps came out in an enormous egg. The shell hardened in the last few stages before Xavior's body squeezed it out. All that hard shell pressed into nearly all his organs and had no give to work with. The whole process sounded very unpleasant. Thankfully, the pool had helped and we wouldn't have to wait much longer.

Xavior moved his head to rest on the side of the pool where I sat. I rubbed circles into his scaled forehead while he continued to relax. We didn't realize it would be the last peaceful night we would have for a while.

STUCK

GREGOR

"What do you mean, it's stuck?" Xavior was groaning loudly, and projecting distress I could feel in my bones while his personal physician was telling me that our egg was lodged in his pelvis.

"It's not uncommon in smaller dragons, and given Xavior's age, and the way he conceived. Simply put, the egg is larger, so he's having a hard time passing it."

I rubbed the back of my neck while Catherine waited for me to respond. "Okay, so how do we get it out?"

Xavior's anxiety and pain were nearly overwhelming. Jordan was trying his best to help Xav calm down, using magic he knew, but it was having little effect.

I knew enough about dragon anatomy to know that Xavior was in trouble, and I hated how much I couldn't help him. Watching him suffer was the second worst feeling to watching him die. The difference this time was that I could pick up nearly everything in our connection and had to use all my willpower to stay functional enough to help, even if that was only to communicate what he was feeling to Catherine.

"Well, there are a few options. One would be to stimulate the seminal canal to loosen. Another would be surgical intervention, but that rarely goes well with dragons."

"There isn't a way to remove the egg magically?" Because I couldn't believe that science and magic hadn't figured something out to help parents in distress during birth.

"Certainly, but given the nature of dragon scales, those methods won't work here. Plus, the more Xavior resists being calmed by any means, the more dangerous it becomes for the egg and him."

Jordan came up to us and sighed. "Nothing I've done has worked. I could fetch a potion maker to the house. If we could have him inhale or drink something, he might relax. His anxiety is keeping him from doing what his body needs to do."

A glance at Xavior was proof enough that Jordan was right. He was on his side, curled in on himself with his wings and legs tucked close against his body. He refused to stand or position himself to make it easier for the egg to pass.

"The only time I've ever seen him relax is in the pool." Catherine and Jordan shared a look. "What? What is it?"

"If we could get him to walk there, it would be easier," Catherine said.

"But he's not moving. We've all tried." Jordan looked frustrated. "But maybe we haven't motivated him properly." He grabbed me, spun me around and had me in a choke-hold before I even realized what was happening.

"Jordan," I gasped.

"Darling, I don't think this is a wise idea," Catherine said as Xavior stopped groaning and swung his head to look at Jordan.

"That's right, I have your mate." Jordan tightened his arms. I hadn't realized how strong fae were. I fought against his hold, but Jordan held fast. Even kicking him didn't help. Spots floated before my eyes and my vision narrowed.

Xavior roared. His distress turned to anger and Jordan moved us toward the den's exit. Xavior followed, saliva dripping from his mouth and eyes narrowed on Jordan. I was gasping for breath and wondered how choking me half to death was helping anything. The more I struggled, the more Jordan used his strength and the less air I inhaled. If I got out of this, I would not underestimate Jordan again.

We stumbled out into daylight as we exited the den. Jordan kept walking us to saints knew where and Xavior followed, wings flapping, and teeth bared. His mind was chaotic, and it disrupted our communication through our connection. The only thought that was clear was an overwhelming sense of 'mine' from him.

"Gregor, listen to me. Listen." Jordan move his arm a fraction to let me gain a proper breath and I stopped fighting him as he whispered in my ear. "We're near the pool. I'm going to throw you in, and hopefully, Xavior will follow. If he doesn't, you need to call for help with everything you have. Do you understand?" I tapped his arm twice to let him know I got it. "Good. Wish me luck."

I didn't have time to say much of anything before Jordan tossed me into the pool. A searing heat spewed past me as I hit the water. Had Xavior breathed fire at Jordan? Could you even hurt a fae with fire? Breaking the surface tension knocked what little air I had from my lungs. I sank like a stone until I came to at the bottom of the pool. My vision narrowed as my lungs burned. Before I could orient myself to try and reach the surface, the world grew dark as a large taloned paw reached into the water and wrapped around me. I fought at first, the feeling of being trapped sparking ingrained nightmares. It wasn't until I saw Xavior's face that I realized I didn't have any reason to fight him, then everything went black.

When I opened my eyes, Catherine was there, and Xavior was in the pool, watching. I coughed up water as I felt healing spells work on the pain lancing through my body.

Catherine shook her head. "That fae is going to get himself roasted someday, and I'm going to be left with the ashes."

I chuckled, because it wasn't the first time Jordan had pulled that stunt, as she well knew. "He's in the pool."

"Yes, he is, only because you're alive and still breathing." Catherine concentrated for a moment. "Okay, you're knitted back together. Nothing too serious. Though it might hurt to breathe for a day or so." She got a nod in response until I could take in enough air to respond.

"Is it alright for me to sit up?" I tried to move, and she slowed me down.

"Not too fast. Take your time," she said as I finally made it into an upright position.

Xavior came close and pushed his snout in my face, taking a large sniff. "I'm fine." I said, reaching out to caress his nose. "Don't worry about me. Focus on you so we can see our egg, Xav."

Xavior made a whining noise, and the intensity of the distress through our connection made me tremble.

"I'm right here. So is Catherine." I projected calm and continued to comfort him, though mostly I was tired and scared for us both. As it turned out, the burst of energy he'd used made him tired as well. He moved slowly to prop his head on the steps of the pool and closed his eyes.

We watched for a few minutes while his breathing pattern normalized into a deep, resonating sound, indicating he was asleep. Catherine helped me stand, and we walked over to where Xavior laid his head. "It's the first time he's slept in days."

"This is good. It will let his body adjust hopefully, though I'm concerned about the stress endured from Jordan's stunt."

I shrugged. "He was already stressed. I'm more worried about Jordan."

Catherine rolled her eyes. "If he knows what's good for him, he's in our room." She moved to leave and touched my shoulder. "Save your concern, Greg. I don't think Xavior caught him with a full blast. And as old as he is, I'm sure he had some trick up his sleeve to handle it."

We laughed softly, as people do sometimes after a moment of high stress. While I hoped Catherine was right, Xavior wouldn't forgive himself if he hurt Jordan, even if it was to defend me.

"Do you need anything?" She didn't ask if I was going back inside. There was no way I could leave Xav's side right now, even if it meant I would spend the night sleeping next to the pool.

"If someone could bring me some dry clothes and blankets, that would be good. Maybe food too." We'd definitely be here for a while.

She nodded. "I'll come back once I find out whether my consort is in one piece."

Xavior's soft snoring vibrated the deck and occasionally made bubbles in the water when his head drooped to one side. I sat next to his head and laid back on the warm concrete until one of Xavior's staff showed up with supplies. It was times like these I was very thankful Xavior had people around to help, though it still felt awkward.

According to some histories, dragon families had been large enough to take care of each other. One of the few times they were less territorial was during a pregnancy. Some of the information Xavior and Gavin had discovered hinted that one reason families could stay in the same area was because of powerful pregnancy hormones that kept everyone from fighting.

If several dragons were pregnant through the year, then everyone stayed relatively peaceful toward each other during the birthing season, which lasted anywhere from three to five years, depending on aging cycles. With several whelps in close proximity to pregnant members, the effects lasted longer, allowing multiple family units to cohabitate an area.

As dragons declined, so had their communal nature. There were very few places on earth now that dragons congregated safely, and many of those used a great deal of magic to maintain it. Like Firebaugh Resort. Though we discovered first hand how precarious anyone's safety could become given the right circumstances.

While Xavior's family had been supportive of our choice to continue his pregnancy, we were all worried. As far as anyone knew, Xavior was one of the oldest dragons on record to have a first pregnancy. He hated the distinction while I thought it was rather extraordinary, given everything we've been through. Our whelp was a miracle. Of that, I had no doubt.

MIDNIGHT BLUES

XAVIOR

When I woke, the first thing I saw was Greg laid out on the poolside patio as if he was dead. Glow spells floated around him, completing the tableau while lighting the scene and protecting the body from insects.

He looked pale, translucent in a way that was alarming and yet comforting. We had died. In our pains to become a family, I had succumbed to some complication, and Greg had drowned.

Greg's arm was draped over his chest, and his body was in perfect repose. He very much looked like the poet Shelley monument. The beauty and the loss were profound, but it comforted me that we were together, in whatever this afterlife was that we shared.

Then he snored.

Did people snore when they were dead? The question amused me just as a pain shot through my middle and bowed my back. Water sloshed around me from my involuntary movement. Greg opened his eyes and sat up.

"Xav, you alright?"

I narrowed my eyes at him. The answer to that should be obvious as we weren't dead and my body had not, in fact, died in the process of passing what had to be the largest shit of my life. Why did anyone put themselves through this?

My insides contracted again, which forced another groan from me. Something shifted inside me and I grabbed for the edge of the pool. Greg's beauty and half dressed form darted in and out of my vision.

"Slow, deep breaths. Follow the circles."

He meant the circles he drew on my jaw and forehead with his hands. It was something we practiced to help with my anxiety. It worked most of the time. Sometimes I amused him by pretending to follow along. As he used it to calm himself, it would calm me. Greg being calm was what really worked. It was something I wished I had told him before I couldn't, as I groaned over what had to be real labor for an egg that continued to be lodged in a very uncomfortable place.

"You come through this and I'll never make you do this again. I'll make sure I can't. We'll have a nice laugh between us when Trevor and Faith are pregnant again in another twenty years, and we've stuck to the one whelp. We'll spoil the fuck out of them. Their grandparents will be so possessive they'll fight over which weekends to babysit. Who'll pay for summer camps. Which college they'll attend. What people they'll meet. What flavor of cake will be at their birthday parties. Who takes pictures of their first date. . ."

Greg went on and on and I groaned and chuffed and pushed and groaned some more. My claws pierced the perma-slab on either side of Greg as I felt something split me open and escape. It slipped from me into the pool and I panted from the effort. Greg jumped into the water and waded past me toward the deep end.

He had no idea what other muck was in the pool with him, but that didn't stop him as he came back with an egg-shaped object slightly larger than the size of his torso.

"You did it, Xav." He held onto the egg to keep it from sinking again. "Can you shift so we can move it? I don't know how long it can stay in the water. It needs to stay warm, right?"

Yes, warmth. I reached out with my tail and wrapped it around the egg and moved it under my left wing. I used my wing and tail to raise it from the water, then took the pool stairs slowly so I wouldn't drop it. Greg scrambled to get out of my way as I marched toward my den, entered and carefully settled the egg in our nest. Greg had followed as I wrapped myself around the object and promptly passed out.

I felt a caress along my snout, which got me to open my eyes. The next thing that tickled my senses was roast chicken. I opened my mouth and Greg popped a whole, nicely seasoned bird right in. I chewed while he smiled at me.

"Morning, sunshine."

A query noise escaped me at the odd endearment. He'd never called me that before.

"Don't mind me. I don't think I've slept since you passed the egg. I've been in the kitchen annoying everyone with putting together enough food to help you recover and make sure we have enough ready for when the egg hatches."

This was good progress. Exactly what a non-laboring partner should be doing. Mostly it was instinct, but also Greg had asked a lot of questions. Not of me, but Faith. As my sister and her husband had ten whelps, he considered them experts on the subject. After once, I was in awe of them. How they had managed through the pain and discomfort five times each astounded me.

"Catherine said she'll be down to check the egg as soon as she has breakfast. And you'll be happy to know that Jordan wasn't permanently damaged. Though you singed his hair. He had to cut most of it off, which he's not happy about."

Well, served him right, considering. Now, after everything had calmed down, I felt somewhat guilty. I understand what Jordan did, but he deserved the hair loss for the stunt he pulled. Maybe. Talking about it didn't make me happy either. Greg's prone body along the poolside flashed in my mind, upsetting me.

"Hey, hey, calm down. He was trying to help you, not hurt me. You have to know that." Though I sensed Greg didn't quite believe that himself. He wasn't lying, though the uncertainty was a subtle current under his concern.

I stopped growling in an effort to appease my mate. Greg was still here, whole and alive, so I might eventually forgive Jordan. He rubbed my snout and the simple action along with his scent comforted me.

"Did you want to freshen up before the Doc gets here?" Greg was dressed in old jeans and a t-shirt. I hadn't caught onto that until he pointed out the mess. No birth was ever a pleasant process, and the smell hit me rather suddenly. I was covered in my own feces, blood and whatever other fluids I'd produced last night in the wake of pushing the egg out of my body. I would definitely need to make sure whoever cleaned the pool was given a bonus.

Shifting was the easiest way to solve the problem, though I needed to keep the egg warm as well. We had planned for that and had stacked several stones around the fireplace I'd created in my den just for this purpose.

I moved hot stones to with my talons to the nest and built them up around the egg. The stones were a stopgap solution because Greg didn't have a dragon form to help keep the egg warm. The deficiency bothered him, but the compromise let me leave the den to take care of my hygiene while he stayed and check the temperature. Once the stones were in place, I shifted and the smell coming off me was even worse. "By the elements, I reek."

Greg laughed. "You do, but I still love you." He came close enough to place his hands on my face, then give me a kiss. I relished that contact. It had been weeks since we'd been able to have any real intimacy. "You did really well."

He rubbed muck from my cheek, and my face heated from his gaze. The reverence and longing in his eyes was so intense I had to look away. My mind was there with him, but my body reminded me of what it had been through in the last few days.

I kissed him back. "Let me clean up before the stones cool off. Then we can change the bedding out and clean the egg so Catherine can examine it."

Greg nodded. "If you see Jordan, don't hurt him, okay?"

I took a step back. "When have you been Jordan's advocate?" The annoyance in my voice and emotions that slammed through me at the mention of his name surprised us both. Greg took a step away from me, then stopped and reached out to touch my arm.

"He has a habit of saving our asses. Albeit, in rather aggravating ways." I knew Greg wasn't only talking about the last few days, but also when Greg had a reaction to the transfiguration potion. Jordan was also responsible for keeping us both working on things that occupied our time while we waited for our whelp.

He watched as I shook my head and gave him one more kiss. "Fine. I'll let the fae be. He's lucky that all I burned off was his hair." Greg chuckled and kissed me before he pushed me away.

"Go, quick. The stones are cooling."

Right. I turned and thought I was going to jog away and pulled up short. My groin felt like it was on fire and it was everything I could do not to double over in pain. Greg, thankfully, didn't laugh at me as I left at a much slower pace.

CANDLING

XAVIOR

Once I got back to the den, Greg was already wiping down the egg with a warm towel. He smiled as he worked, which made my heart flutter. I knew he'd be a good parent, but to see the care he took even before the whelp emerged was something I'd hold in my heart forever.

As I approached Greg, he turned that parental smile on me, and I kissed him. I only had a towel wrapped around me since I knew I'd be shifting again soon. The stones around the egg were touchable but still warm. We had a little while, though I didn't want to risk it.

"I cleaned most of the egg that I could reach, but I didn't want to move the egg without your help. I figured I could get the bottom after you shifted again and we changed out the bedding."

"It's a good plan." My stomach grumbled, and we laughed.

"Once we get you situated again, I'll grab some more food for you. And me. I haven't had breakfast yet."

I reached out to touch his face. "Make sure you eat." He made a face as I felt emotions swirling in the connection between us. Commitment, determination, protectiveness all wrapped up in his love and desire to keep me and our egg safe. "Please. I can't have you grow weak during all this. Take the time you need to sleep and eat. Okay?"

Greg nodded. "I promise as soon as Catherine is done with her exam, I'll go pass out." I leaned over to caress his face and kiss him again. He leaned into the kiss and the smell of his desire blanketed me, creating warmth in places that were still angry from the previous night's exertions. If it wasn't for my groin being a center of my discomfort, I know I would have responded in kind. I missed being able to lie next to him and touch him with more than a clawed foot or the flat of my tongue. But I needed to heal, and we had the next week or two of waiting for our whelp to emerge.

It was as if he read my mind. "We've been without for longer. As soon as the doc clears you, we'll make up for lost time."

I laughed. "That's what got us into this mess." We laughed together.

"True, but it was worth every minute, don't you think?"

"Absolutely." I gave him a bunch more pecks on his face and then let him go so I could shift and we could get things moved around for Catherine's exam.

Dr. Alexander looked at the egg, checking it for cracks, which Greg and I had also looked for. Thus far, it was one solid piece, which was good.

"Lightly pebbled surface, no abnormalities. It's somewhat large, but nothing too unusual. Are you ready for me to light it up?"

"Light it up?" Greg's worry tickled my nose. I chuffed in response.

Catherine smiled. "I can light up the egg with a bit of diffused magic. Somewhat like holding a smaller egg in front of a candle to see the developing embryo."

"Oh. Well, that sounds interesting. Can we take pictures of it?"

"Sure." Catherine smiled. "It's like an ultrasound for humans, but in this case, you'll only see the shadow of the embryo instead of distinct details."

Greg pulled out his phone and got into a better position to watch Catherine illuminate the whelp inside. Her hands glowed and once she touched the egg, something extraordinary became very apparent.

"Wait. Am I seeing what I think I'm seeing?" Greg looked astonished. His pheromones were an instant kaleidoscope to my nose.

Catherine chuckled. "I believe so. It would explain why the egg is above average size. Looks like you have twins. And that would explain the odd heartbeat sounds. That's a relief."

Greg's face went through several emotions, and the one it settled on was joy and tears. He was crying as he stared at the egg.

Personally, I was rather proud of myself and secretly hoped that Greg would, in fact, take measures toward a permanent birth control. I was prepared for one whelp, but two was a lot. And I couldn't imagine having a third or possibly a fourth. Not that we'd have to worry about that for some time. Even so, two was definitely enough for me.

I could tell Greg was still processing this new fact because he stood there holding his phone without doing anything. I chuffed to get his attention. He responded with a smile, not realizing he was ignoring Catherine.

"While I can hold this for a while, I'd rather let the whelps rest and get Xavior back in place so he can keep them warm."

"Oh, OH right! Sorry." Greg snapped a bunch of pictures, then Catherine moved and I got into place with the egg and Greg took a bunch more. When Greg finally stopped, Catherine moved up next to him so that I could see her as well.

"Keep doing what you've been doing. Make sure you eat and rest, both of you. We're in the home stretch now. I'll stay until they hatch to make sure everything turns out well. Twins can be a lot to handle, according to my records."

Whether she was referring to my brother and me or Faith's twins, who knew, but I was grateful for her continued assistance. And while I was still annoyed at him, I had to admit I was grateful for Jordan's help, too. Risking myself to help Greg was one thing, risking Greg was unacceptable. The audacity of it made me bristle. Jordan couldn't be careless with Greg again, especially not now. He was tough, but only human. A much more fragile species than mages, fae, or dragons.

"Hey, Xav, you alright?" Greg touched my side, and I took a big breath and huffed. My emotions were all over the place. I had no idea how Faith and Trevor managed during this entire process. I should have asked more questions, but I wanted to seem like I knew what I was doing. Thankfully, Greg wasn't so stubborn.

"Okay, love. I'll take your word for it." He rubbed my side, then rubbed the top of the egg like a good luck stone. That amused me. "I'm going to grab you some food, then curl up with you and take a nap. Sound good?"

I gave him the slightest nods and watched him smile as he nodded back, then walk toward the den exit. Fuck, I really loved him. And we created not one, but two embryos that would hatch into whelps and grow into strong, beautiful dragons.

Life was amazing. I drifted off to sleep as I thought of names and wondered what their scales would look like.

WAITING

GREGOR

"Dr. Alexander!" I caught up with her as she was heading back to her room.

"Hi there. Did you have more questions, Greg?"

"Not about the egg, no. How's Jordan? Is he really okay?"

She smiled. "He's sulking a bit. I've been role playing with him, which has made the short hair more appealing and eased his ego somewhat."

"Role playing?"

She gave me a look like I was being naïve, and maybe I was because I hadn't thought about sex in a while. When I did, things became very uncomfortable fairly quickly, causing my libido to circle around thoughts that should be firmly under control for the time being. "Ah. Right."

Catherine laughed. "It's alright, we're all adults. Speaking of which, I'll come back tomorrow and check Xavior over. Make sure things are healing properly. I don't see why the two of you couldn't be doing some of your own role play soon."

My face must have amused Catherine to no end because she laughed as I felt heat creep up my neck. She patted my shoulder, took my arm, and started us moving toward the kitchen.

"Have any ideas for names yet?"

Names. Plural. Shit. "No. We hadn't really thought about names. I mean, we should have, but now we'll need to think of two, or maybe more since we won't know what they'll chose as their gender identities for a while. Plus, I don't know if Xavior's family has any traditions around dragon names or family names and things like that."

"Well, if they hold to Spanish tradition, it's three or more names, though I've only ever heard the Brantley and Ramirez dragons call each other by their given names. Do you know Xavior's middle name?"

That took me by surprise. Did he have a middle name? We never asked each other. How had we skipped exchanging that information? Mine was a little out there, but in keeping with the children of my mother's family, all having some biblical middle name. My dad liked it because it was also the name of a god that protected forests.

"You'll have time. Something to talk about while the two of you are herding whelps," Catherine said, noticing how much I was lost in my own thoughts.

Just then, it occurred to me that these wouldn't be children, but magical beings that could change into dragons and just fly off. Cause mischief. Disappear. Burn things to the ground. Fuck, what were we thinking?

"Greg, you okay?" Catherine's hand rested on my shoulder. I had stopped walking, leaned up against the nearest wall to catch my breath.

"Ah, no, not exactly." I felt myself break out in a cold sweat. We were parents now, but we really didn't have a clue, and I definitely had no clue how to take care of a magical infant of any kind. "I think I'm might be sick."

Catherine rubbed my back as I bent over and tried not to vomit. "Just breath, Dad. You'll have time to learn everything, and the things you don't have time to learn, you'll catch onto quick. You have plenty of family to support you and Xavior. Besides, most dragons can't fly for the first year or so, or do any kind of magic. So try not to panic, yet." Of course, she had guessed. As a mage, dealing with magical beings and her mage children gave her some perspective.

"Right. One thing at a time."

"Exactly." She rubbed my back, creating a warmth there that was soothing and slowed my breathing. Once I was upright again, we continued to the kitchen, and I grabbed a cart for everything the staff had ready for Xavior while Catherine made herself another cup of coffee.

"You got this." She gave my shoulder another firm pat of encouragement. I nodded. "Remember to send everyone pictures. They'll be happy to know how things are going."

"Thank you, Dr. Alexander."

"Don't thank me. I'll send my bill later." She grinned, and we laughed. Who knows where we'd be if we didn't have her help. I was happy Xavior's family had the Alexander family of physicians on retainer. It was one way to make sure everyone stayed healthy. I don't know if we could have done this without her help, and Jordan's.

By the time I had the food back to Xavior, he was dozing peacefully. Nothing would go bad if he didn't eat immediately. I picked up my plate and settled down in the small spot Xavior had for me near him and the egg.

A normal size egg, from what I understood, was a little bigger than a basketball. Our egg was more like the size of a large medicine ball. It was no wonder that Xavior was having a problem passing it. Though it made me wonder how Xavior's mother dealt with her twins.

Did phoenixes have similar enough physiology to dragons that they were born in the same egg? Or were they a clutch, like birds? Not that it mattered all that much now, since it was apparent that the embryos were dragons, or at least dragon shaped.

I touched the egg again and smiled. Xavior raised his head to look at me. His emerald eyes held affection that I could feel to my toes. I hoped one whelp had his eyes. Or maybe they would have red ones like the ones I had once. I still couldn't believe the pictures sometimes.

Xavior had several photographs from my time as a dragon in a holo scrapbook device on the desk in our suite. He enjoyed looking at it from time to time. I accepted that I'd never look that way for him again. It depressed me for a while, though Xavior distracted me a lot. He would always point to the pictures and remark how handsome I was as a dragon. Then tell me what human features he liked while he kissed each and every one.

It's possible Xavior thought he could restore my dragon. I had heard him talk about it once with someone when he didn't know I was listening. Frankly, I'd rather think it was a onetime thing than hope for it, or maybe even gain it and lose something else. I mostly hoped that it didn't affect the whelps.

Their shapes looked alright inside the egg, but magic was odd sometimes and the effects unpredictable when too many variables were involved.

Once I finished eating, I grabbed a blanket from the pile and curled up next to Xavior and the egg. Xavior moved his wing to cover us. With a full belly, surrounded by solid warmth, I fell asleep for the first time in almost forty-eight hours.

HATCHING

XAVIOR

"What's your middle name?" Greg asked.

We had occasionally discussed first names for the whelps during my breaks from keeping the egg warm. While it was an important topic, we usually ended up doing other things with the limited time we had before the stones cooled. Besides, we wouldn't need to decide on names until after their first shift. Maybe that's why he was asking about middle names.

"Alonso. Hadn't I mentioned it before?"

"No, not the whole time we've been dating."

"You've never mentioned your middle name, either." Greg's gaze slid away. I felt a mild embarrassment through our connection. "It can't be that bad."

He turned back and looked me in the eye, his face daring me not to laugh. "Silvanus."

I tried, but he noticed and hit me with a pillow that was previously part of his bedding in our nest, close to the egg.

"That was definitely Philip's choice. Or Maybe your Grandpa Jack's?" I smiled.

Greg tried to throw another pillow, and I grabbed it from him and tossed it away as I moved in for a kiss. His hand threaded through my hair and the kiss grew more heated. He broke away first, his other hand drifting down my body. I had shifted to clean up and spend time with him and hadn't bothered with a towel.

His hand found me hard, and I worked at getting him out of his boxers as we continued to kiss and stroke each other. I grabbed his hands and pushed them above his head while I pressed our cocks between us, using our pre-cum and friction to get us both off.

"Shit, Xav, I'm close. Fuck, you feel good."

I kissed his mouth, then bent to lick his nipples. I let go of one of his hands and sunk mine into his jet black hair. "Use your hand," I breathed out. "So we can come together."

Greg wasted no time slipping his hand between us, wrapping it around both our dicks. I continued to thrust into his hand as he groaned and shot long, messy gobs of cum all over his abs, our cocks and his hand. He used what was on his hand to slick us up even more while he whispered to me.

"That's it, love. Fucking paint me with everything you have. Mark me, so that everyone knows I'm yours. Just like I'm marking you right now. This dick in my hand is mine, and I want you to show me how much. Xavior, show me how much." I moaned, desperate to show him. "Show me," he whispered over and over again.

The noise that came out of my mouth as I unloaded all over him probably sounded like a wounded animal. I pressed my head into his shoulder and nearly cried from the combination of pleasure and relief I felt. One never feels particularly sexy while pregnant, and the last month or so, I hadn't felt like doing much of anything. Greg and I had tried one time after, while I was a dragon. He decided to be all responsible and even made a condom of sorts out of some pillowcases, so he wouldn't be directly doused. It was nice, but not as nice as it could have been if we'd been able to enjoy the aftereffects like we had before.

I lifted my head and kissed him, which he returned as he smeared our combined spunk all over my back. I kept kissing him, desperate for each interaction because I knew I'd have to shift again soon. The stones keeping the egg warm were growing cold.

A noise echoed in the den.

Greg and I stopped kissing and stared at each other, then looked at the egg. "Was that from the fireplace?"

"No, I don't think so." Nothing in the fireplace would have made a sound like porcelain cracking.

Another snap rang out, but this time, a beak tooth had poked through the shell.

"They'll need skin contact." I didn't explain more before I shifted. Greg wiped his hands off on his discarded boxers, then grabbed his phone and snapped a few pictures. We watched as little by little, they took apart the egg from the inside out and two whelps slowly emerged.

The first one to emerge was mostly green, with a stripe of darker green fuzz down their back, matching the same green fuzz on their tail.

They opened their wings, letting the amniotic fluid slide off as they pushed with their paw and beak on the side of the shell. It broke and spilled them into the nest along with their sibling.

The other was mostly white. It was the same pearl color Greg had as a dragon. Their arms and legs were tucked protectively close to their belly, and their wings were pulled in tight around them. They hadn't opened their eyes yet.

I extended my tongue and licked at the green one's eyes first as they moved, unsteady, inching around the nest, rubbing against the bedding. The pearl whelp hadn't moved.

Greg's worry was strong in our connection. He wanted to help, but wasn't sure how. I gently picked up the green one with my tail and deposited the whelp in his arms. It was barely bigger than a small dog. They responded by instantly curling up and sticking their snout in his armpit. The delighted laugh from Greg bolstered my spirit.

I tried several times to stimulate a response from the pearl whelp, but nothing worked. As Greg watched, I wrapped my tail around the other whelp and brought it to my mouth, gently placing them inside and closing it. No matter how many times Faith had explained this process, Greg and I were still skeptical.

"So you pretend to eat them?" Greg asked.

Faith shook her head and laughed. "No. Sometimes just using the tip of your tongue doesn't stimulate them enough to start their lungs once they are exposed to air. Putting the whelp in your mouth and sucking on them gives them a whole body stimulation. It's helpful when they aren't responding."

Trevor nodded to Faith's assessment. "The twins took both of us working with them. They were stubborn after one of them accidentally cracked their shell, but stopped working to get out. It was like they ran out of energy just as they were getting started."

"So you turned them into dragon lozenges. Only fair considering all the energy they suck out during the entire process," I said, half joking.

"You'll see, little brother. Once they're here, your instincts will kick in and it won't sound so strange."

Faith, as usual, was right. Though she neglected to mention that the practice had applications for unsuccessful pregnancies as well. Gavin had provided that small piece of information. While I was annoyed and tired most of the time, the last thing I wanted was a failed pregnancy. I had asked her why I would need to use my tail to move them, and her reply was 'you'll see.' She was right. They were so small that using my paw risked hurting them with my claws. The only thing I'd risk using my tail was tickling them.

Greg stared at me while a moved the whelp around in my mouth. I was determined to see both whelps survive. I hadn't come this far in the process to lose one now.

"Should I get Catherine?" It showed how worried he was, considering he was still nude and covered in fluids. I knew he wouldn't hesitate, even if it cost him his modesty.

The longer I sucked and licked at the whelp in my mouth, the more concern grew in my chest. When I was about to give up, I felt a wiggle. Then another, followed by a soft vibration across my tongue. The distinct change in taste made me realize it was a fart. I chuffed as I leveled my head with the nest and gently took the whelp out of my mouth as it writhed and stretched before it let go of a massive shit, followed by a piercing cry.

We were filled with utter joy as our whelp screamed. My gaze met Greg's as he wiped snot and tears from his face. The one in his arms moved and screamed too, demanding food as much as the other had. I carefully put both of them near the remnants of the egg and let them feast on it.

They both had stripes on their bellies. The green one had white stripes while the pearl one had green stripes. The other interesting thing was that they both had crests on their heads that reminded me of Greg's dragon instead of horns.

Once the whelps started to eat, Greg retrieved his phone, snapped a few more pictures, then dropped it in our pile of clothes and crawled toward us. I'd wrapped myself around the remains of the egg and watched. It was an important time for bonding with parents and siblings. It kept territorial problems down as they grew. I knew Greg and I would smell like each other; even more so because of what we'd done before they hatched. Which was good for Greg, since he didn't have his dragon for them to bond with.

"Xavior, they're beautiful."

A whelp screeched at his words. I chuffed, and Greg laughed. Both whelps copied me, and Greg grinned. We stayed in our bubble of happiness until I noticed the whelps chewing on pillows. Before I could convey hunger to Greg through our connection, he jumped up and grabbed a pair of sweatpants from the pile of clothes he kept in the den.

"I'm on it. Be back in ten minutes!"

One whelp tried to follow, and I gently brought them back to the nest. They returned their attention to the eggshell and the muck inside, breaking it down and grinding it with their nubby teeth. When Greg returned, the egg was almost gone, and Greg had a cart loaded with replicated meat parts and veggies.

I had no chance of keeping them in the nest once their senses told them they had another food source. Greg fed them whatever they wanted to try, and we watched while they bit through apples, squash, chicken bits, lamb parts and other delights.

"Edward knows and is informing the rest of the house. They are prepping another cart of food for you and the whelps. It should be here in twenty minutes or so."

I gave him a nod and a huff. Greg continued to smile as he handed each whelp various items from the cart, with very few initial rejections. When I was a whelp, my brother and I feasted on a fresh carcass, along with onions and potatoes that were easy to store in my parent's den. I don't miss having to kill for our dinner, nor do I long for onions and potatoes. I might have been envious of the variety our whelps had, but I wouldn't change that for the world.

Greg caressed my snout and in turn, I licked his face. The scent must have drawn them away from their food. They moved toward Greg, carefully touching him and testing this other shape. Intuitively seeming to understanding that Greg was part of them, but not the same. It was during this moment of exploration that they opened their eyes and we discovered that they both had a light golden color that shimmered in the low firelight.

When they finally grew tired, they came back to me and curled up under my wing to keep warm. The whelps wouldn't be able to regulate their body temps correctly for a while, which necessitated having warm places for them to rest and sleep. I the meantime, Greg brought in more food. The hours went by in our small world, catering to two new lives. Eating when we woke, playing and exploring, then napping again, regardless of whether we were tired.

Our tiny bliss, ignoring the outside world for a short time, was an absolute joy. That time alone with the whelps would always be one of the happiest times of our lives. One we would often refer to late at night after a long day, thankful for surviving it, and thankful of the small peace we had as a family, unaware of just how much was about to change.

THE JOYFUL NEWS

GREGOR

My family was asleep in the den, and I was fighting a mix of excitement and exhaustion. I'd been the only one to leave the den, as Xavior was still a dragon and wouldn't shift until the whelps were ready.

He barely lifted his head when I smiled and at him and pointed to the exit. He closed his eyes and went back to sleep. While Xavior could take care of most of the whelps' needs via magic, I preferred to take the time to deal with my hygiene in a more mundane way. It gave me the precious minutes of space to myself that I hadn't realized I would need between feedings and wrangling curious whelps.

In the suite down the hall, I stepped inside and closed the door. It occurred to me I hadn't called my sister to let her know the news. She was traveling through South America on a backpack trip of self-discovery. Or so she said the last time I talked with her.

My plan had been to leave a voicemail considering it was fairly early in the morning. Instead, Katie picked up on the third ring.

"This is Katie."

"Hey sis, how are you?"

"Greg! Shit man, I'm good. How are things with you? Last time we talked, you were all wound up about Philip and Jennifer's anniversary, and your partner. How did your red carpet thing go?"

"Wasn't able to make it. Something important came up."

"Ah, that sucks." I could hear her moving things around but trying to be quiet about it.

It was clear she was distracted or she would have asked me why we missed the red carpet event. "What are you doing up this early? Don't you have a hard start at noon?"

"Ha, something like that." I could practically hear her smile.

"So, what's up with you? Why are you awake?" She cleared her throat as I waited for an answer.

"I met someone."

"No shit?"

Katie laughed. "Honestly, she's great. She can dance circles around me and has a wicked tongue."

Dancing was one of the few things we had actually enjoyed that our mother made us learn. It wasn't the wild swing styles my ex and I picked up. Basic two step and simple ballroom dancing weren't thrilling at the best of times, but for a bunch of kids constantly under pressure to physically perform, it gave us the reprieve we needed from our often grueling training pace. No one expected us to be perfect, just respectable, for whatever that was worth among various hunter groups.

It sounded great to hear her joy over the phone. Katie had always excelled at keeping herself occupied, but it was rare for her to express it so openly. "You sound happy. I'm glad you're happy. You deserve to be happy."

"How many times are you going to say happy, bro? You're sounding like a pop song." We laughed. I was repeating myself. Exhaustion was riding the edges of my awareness. The connection between Xav and me was peaceful, which let me know he was in that state of deep restorative sleep. I pushed sleep off a little longer, not willing to give up the rare moment with my sister.

"You must really like her though, if you are up this early."

"Yeah. I do. I thought I would make her an omelet."

"You checked for allergies this time?" Katie had made an omelet one morning for a guy she was seeing and had no idea he was allergic. He was polite about it, but they didn't see each other much longer after that.

"She scarfed a whole plate of perico the other morning before we jumped on the local transport."

"How long have you two been traveling together?"

"A few weeks. We found a cute rental in Montevideo, so we've been taking our time."

"Wow. Sounds serious. Are you serious?" I could hear the light tones in her voice. Something about her travel partner had her in a wistful mood. Or at least a good enough one to make breakfast for her.

"I'm not sure it's at the serious stage yet, but we're definitely enjoying ourselves."

"I'm glad to hear it, really. You sound really good, Katie."

"Thanks, Greg." There was a pause. "You sound tired, actually. That mate of yours keeping you up late?"

"Well, in a way." I smiled, thinking about the last few days. "Our egg hatched."

"Oh shit, seriously? Congratulations, Greg! No wonder you're tired. Tell me what they look like?"

"They look like twins."

"Did you say twins?"

I laughed. "Yeah. We were totally freaked out about it a few weeks ago, but now that they're here, it's been amazing. Xavior's amazing. I can't believe all these years and everything we went through, and I'm here now, with him and a family. It's more than I ever dreamed." I rubbed an errant tear or two from my eyes.

"You deserve it. After our childhood and everything the two of you have been through, you deserve to have everything you've dreamed of and more." She took a deep breath and continued. "Being part of the anti-hunter crowd hasn't been a picnic. You showed me that there was a different way, Greg. If you hadn't stood up to her and been brave enough to follow your heart, I don't know where I'd be now." She was talking about our mother. We rarely talked about her. Mostly, we actively avoided it. Katie's backpacking trip seemed to have her thinking about the past.

"Katie, you would have figured it out. With or without me."

"Maybe." She was quiet for a moment. "I always looked up to you. And for a while I was mad at you and mother for what happened."

"You had a right to be. It was ugly. I shouldn't have argued with her in front of everyone."

"She wouldn't listen. Her dumb ideology was more important. What else were you supposed to do?"

It's true. I didn't think about it much since I'd left Narissa's house all those years ago. Our argument was over dinner, when she had made some quip about how the other hunter families were turning lax, allowing queer family members to remain part of their hunter groups. I had heard her say these horrible things before and had ignored her.

That night was different. I was a freshman in college and had met a really nice guy I fooled around with, but had asked him to keep it quiet. The look on his face was enough to stab me in the heart. I wasn't out, and he was. After that, he didn't want much to do with me. I couldn't blame him.

I had expected the same exploratory nature I had shared with Jake, who I had lost my virginity to the summer before both of us went to college. It had been a somewhat natural progression of our childhood friendship, with the normal fumbling and odd discussions about what we did like, and how. Even looking things up to help us figure it out. It was odd to think about Jake now. I hadn't thought about him in years.

While I always considered us friends, maybe more, how things ended up was odd. Maybe it was because while we fucked around a lot, we were never that into each other to think it was anything more. Especially with both of us heading to college at the end of the summer. What we had was a lot of trust as friends. Though at some point our first year, Jake's folks moved to Canada, and I never saw him again.

For the first time in my life, I was mostly on my own at college. I was expected to be an adult, decide things for myself, and keep my own schedule. Try out for the basketball team, join study groups, and find a whole new set of friends. The experience was jarring after being homeschooled in such a sheltered environment for so long.

Narissa's words had ignited an anger I hadn't realized was there. So on that particular night, while visiting from school, in front of the whole family, I called her a bigot. Stunned silence followed. Then she started yelling and saying that no son of hers would defend unnatural people. That's when I told her I was gay, and that's when she told me to leave, not just the table, but her house. She didn't care where I went and promptly returned to eating dinner.

I grabbed some of my shit, a cash card that Dad had given me for food or local transportation, and my cell. I called Dad on the way to the regional station and he helped me pay for a ticket home. It was lucky that our falling out happened during winter break. It gave me space to figure out if I wanted to go back to school or not.

Dad helped me figure out how to pay for college after Narissa disowned me completely. The scholarships from the basketball team helped. I finished school and didn't look back until Katie called me to tell me she had left, too.

"I don't know." I surprised myself with that answer. I'm used to having answers. Therapy breakthrough for the win there.

"Exactly," she said with confidence. "Seeing you do it made me brave enough to do the same thing. Hearing about you and your family stirs some of those same feelings."

"Really? The self-proclaimed rogue and wanderer wants to settle down?"

"Maybe not settle, but maybe find someone that wants to walk the road with me. Figuratively and literally."

Her words made me smile. "You'll get there. Just don't push it." I'd hate to see Katie do the same thing I'd done with my ex. Though she's always been smarter than me about relationships to some extent.

"Trust me. I'm taking my time."

"Good."

There was a comfortable pause as she started making breakfast and we listened to each other just exist for a few moments.

"I'll let you get back to your morning plans. I need to clean up and grab food for the whelps."

"Send me pictures when you have a chance. I'd love to see them."

"Can do. Send me some pics too, okay?" She rarely did, preferring to be in the moment. I didn't blame her.

"Sure thing."

"And let me know when you're coming back to the states so you can visit. You should meet my family." I hadn't offered before and Katie had never asked, but it felt right. She knew Xavior was a dragon, but we didn't talk about that much either. The specter of who we were and our upbringing always loomed between us.

"Are you sure?" Her voice broke in a way that I knew I should have asked sooner or talked about it. So much had happened the last few years, and we'd barely spoken to each other lately. It had never seemed the right time.

"I'm sure. Xavior's wanted to meet you. His whole family is amazing. We're also planning on being in Spain for the winter holidays, so if that works better, let me know. We'd be happy to host you."

"Shit, Greg. That's . . . thank you. I'd love that."

"Good." I said, clearing my throat. "Have a good morning, Katie. Good luck with the omelet."

She laughed. "Good luck with your omelets too! Love you, Greg."

"Love you too," I said, then we disconnected. I grinned at myself, happy I talked with Katie and glad we were planning a visit. Whenever that would be. "Omelets. Ha, Xav will get a kick out of that one."

It also reminded me I didn't have that much longer before said omelets would need to eat. I tossed my phone on the bed and went to clean up so I could get my family's day started too.

GLIDING

GREGOR

While Catherine might have been right about flying, even she was surprised that we had the equivalent of giant flying squirrels on our hands. Any chance the whelps had to climb, jump, and glide, they did. At eight kilos each, they were way more mobile than most dragons their age and size.

Xavior and I had given up trying to keep them from the bookshelves. To safeguard his priceless volumes, he changed the main area of the den to the equivalent of an elaborate tree house. The books and journals were relocated somewhere safe, creating a small pang of loss for me when they disappeared. Having access to Xavior's library had helped pass many hours while we had waited for the egg to arrive, then hatch. I realized it might be a while before either of us could read any time we wished.

It was week four in the den, post hatching, and Xavior hadn't shifted because the whelps hadn't either. I facilitated meals, maintained contact with our families, and took the occasional shower. Neither of us had slept a full night, and I could tell Xavior was restless from staying in one place. Each day that passed without the whelps shifting, he grew more concerned.

Catherine, who had moved back to Spain, returned to examine the whelps, and Jordan accompanied her. It was the first time we'd seen his short hair and Xavior had a sudden onset of guilt over Jordan's loss. His waist length hair was gone, replaced with a stylish asymmetrical bob cut.

The dragon and I glanced at each other, then Jordan. The cut made him look young, and then I remembered Catherine mentioning role play and promptly stopped any more thought in that direction. Xavior seemed amused, but he was looking at Jordan when I felt the emotion, so I couldn't be sure it was from the haircut or my odd reaction to it.

As Catherine went looking for hidden whelps in the tree limbs and vegetation, Jordan approached us.

"Is it alright if I'm here?" Jordan asked.

I glanced at Xavior, then Jordan. "I don't think you would have been able to enter the den if it wasn't, Jordan. He feels guilty about what he did to your hair."

Xavior huffed in agreement.

Jordan smirked. "It worked out in the end."

Nope, I refused to understand that statement, and Xavior chuffed his response, which made the whelps chuff.

"Ah! Found them. Do you want a snack?" Catherine asked the dragon shaped tree limb. They reached out and took the offered treat, though I couldn't tell exactly what it was from where I stood next to Xavior and Jordan near the nest. The other whelp followed and took a treat as well.

"Greg, could you help? They are going to want to cuddle up once the calming herbs have a chance to work through their systems."

"Calming herbs?" I grew concerned as Xavior tried to reassure me through our connection. Jordan followed me to where Catherine was standing and explained.

"Standard practice for examinations. Catherine doesn't have a dragon's hide. This allows her to make sure everyone is safe. It wears off in thirty minutes. Didn't Xavior tell you?"

I glanced back at Xavior. "No, he's locked in his dragon form and has been since they hatched. The whelps haven't shifted yet."

Catherine caught part of the conversation. "I'm sorry, Greg. I never would have proceeded if you weren't aware."

"It's. . . it's okay." *Fucking Knight training anyway.* Sometimes I hated what I knew. I trusted Catherine to use the correct doses. If they were the same herbs I knew about, they could render a whelp, even a full grown dragon paralyzed depending on the amount they ingested.

Our green whelp was hanging by a paw and a wing claw, eyes drifting closed. I positioned myself under them so if they dropped, I'd catch them. Instead, they glided down and land on me. Even in their sleepy state, their agility continued to amaze me.

Our pearl whelp had moved away from Catherine and approached Jordan instead. They hung upside-down near the fae and twisted their neck so that they could look him in the face. Jordan smiled, and the whelp smiled in return. They mimicked his facial expressions until they let go of the branch and drifted toward Jordan like a feather, landing on his front as their wing claws gently clasped his shoulders.

Catherine motioned for all of us to go toward the nest so Xavior could observe what she was doing, considering his condition.

"Healthy teeth, wings, and eyes. They physically look sound. Sensory responses are good. It appears they'll have a ridge of pen feathers from their head down to their tail based on what I'm observing." The small thing yawed, staying in my arms as Catherine spoke and her glasses recorded notes about our green whelp.

The pearl whelp had nuzzled their snout into Jordan's armpit and made soft cooing noises. It was something we noticed the whelps did when they were sleepy and happy.

Claws, legs, tails, and head ridges were all checked over. Catherine glanced at their rear ends and looked between us. "Are they voiding waste alright?"

Xavior chuffed, and I responded. "We've been trying to train them to use absorbent padding in a designated area, but their gliding and climbing habits cause them to void like birds wherever they perch."

Jordan tried not to laugh. Catherine gave us a sympathetic smile. "It'll be better after they shift, hopefully. At the very least, you'll be able to contain some messes, though the whelp poop will be a wonderful gift."

"Who wants whelp poop?" It really shouldn't surprise me given my experience with Xavior's family during Christmas last year, yet I couldn't help myself.

Jordan grinned. "To celebrate the births of new dragons to the family. It symbolizes protection and prosperity for the area Xavior's family governs. Though how Xavior plans to have the waste transported to Spain is another matter."

"Well, he's been making it vanish. To where, I don't know."

"Probably a small bubble dimension off of his den." Jordan looked up at Xavior and Xav nodded.

"You can make more of your den?" Xavior vocalized his agreement, and I shrugged. "Okay. Interesting." Which meant somewhere, attached to his den, was the equivalent of a closet full of whelp shit, and possibly other things I hadn't even considered.

"I'm surprised they haven't shifted." Catherine looked up from the whelp attached to Jordan. "Have you seen them try?"

"No. Should we be worried?" Because I wondered about that. Most whelps, from what I knew, shifted within a few days of hatching.

"Not yet. It could be because they are fraternal twins." She frowned. "All the other twins in the family look identical, with only the slightest variations. They aren't following the family pattern."

"Do you think that has slowed their development?" It made me nervous. What were we missing? Did we need another dragon to help our whelps adapt?

"No. From everything I've observed, they're very healthy. Maybe they're waiting for something, but what I'm not sure." Catherine looked concerned, which made me concerned.

Xavior wasn't as concerned. His mind was clearly on being a parent, regardless of whether the whelps ever shifted. The possibility of Xavior remaining a dragon for the rest of my life, and the whelps, wasn't one I had imagined.

"What happens if they don't shift?" I asked.

No one had an immediate answer. My mind threatened to spiral into dark thoughts as Jordan touched my shoulder. "We'll figure it out. It'll be alright."

I knew we were in trouble if Jordan was trying to reassure me.

ACCEPTANCE

GREGOR

"When can we see them, Greg?" Jennifer, my mom, asked.

My parents had seen all the pictures I'd sent them over the last two months since we knew the egg contained twins. We hoped that they would have shifted by now so my parents could visit. The twins still hadn't shifted. Now everyone was worried.

"Dr. Alexander thought we should wait, but if the twins are going to take longer than normal to shift, I'm not sure anymore."

They had seen Xavior, once, while he was a dragon in the few weeks leading up to our egg's arrival and they haven't visited since. I worried they were scared of him. Though my parents, being who they were, sought Dr. Alexander's advice. She advised caution, as mated pairs were generally left to deal with things unless they explicitly asked for help.

While this would have made sense with a pair of mated dragons with territorial concerns, it didn't quite add up for Xavior and me. Xavior was the less territorial of the two of us, amazingly enough. Even so, I couldn't imagine it would be an issue with my parents. I've never had to protect Xavior from them. If anything, they were more protective of us both after we started dating.

"Greg? Are you and Xavior alright? Maybe the two of you need a break." Jennifer suggested.

It wasn't a bad idea, though I wondered if Xavior would even consider leaving the twins for five minutes, let alone an hour. The longer the twins took to shift, the more anxious and protective he felt about them.

Ah, screw it. "Come to the estate. There's plenty of room for you, and I'll talk with Xav."

A few days later, Edward set my parents up in a suite and after they settled in, he brought them to the den entrance and messaged us so I could meet them and guide them through. Once we were inside the entrance, I handed them protective vests similar to the one I wore.

"What are these for?" Philip asked as I helped him into his vest.

"They'll protect your skin. The twins' teeth and claws are developing. They try to be careful, but accidents have happened. Dr. Alexander set us up with healing potions if anything serious occurs. Xavior and I wanted to make sure you were protected."

Jennifer had hers on already. I helped her adjust it so it was snug. "Whatever it takes to see my grand babies." She patted my shoulder, and I smiled, or tried to.

"What is it?" Mom asked.

Tears threated to form, and my parents pulled me into a hug.

"All kids do things in their own time. It's okay to be scared, son. We're here for you and Xavior, you know that," Philip said. I nodded into my father's shoulder and I accidentally wiped my tears on him. Mom rubbed my back. Her small comfort and reassurance eased some tension in my shoulders. I hadn't realized how much I needed to see them, and their reassurance helped. They had always supported me. I'd never be able to thank them enough for their wisdom and guidance.

I wiped my face and pulled myself together. Xavior was concerned, but I reassured him I was alright, just emotional. "The nest is this way." I led my parents down the hall. The walls were still bare of books and various items Xavior normally displayed. Tucked away somewhere safe from teething dragons. I had a hard time imagining his den as it was before. Even the reading nook was absent.

To entertain our very curious offspring, Xavior expanded on the tree house idea and transformed his den into a massive indoor forest. Complete with large trees, small crevices for the twins to explore and lighting disguised as rocks and wild vines.

"We tried to clean up as much as we could. If you need some place to sit, ask Xavior and he'll conjure something for you. If you need to leave, I can walk you back out. It's a little tricky if the den isn't familiar with you. That should change the more you visit."

"You're parents, honey," Jennifer said. "The fact you aren't wearing your lunch is amazing enough."

"I changed before you got here." My parents had a good chuckle until they walked into the open cavern space Xav called his nest.

While my parents had met Xavior, they had never been in his den. It felt like I was leading them to our bedroom, which in some ways, that's exactly what it was. The twins were doing strafing runs as Xavior pretended to miss them as they glided past. My parents watched in awe. "This is one of their favorite games. I try to stay out of the way. From what Dr. Alexander tells me, it's the way dragons learn how to hunt." Though it was a bit early in their development for the skill. They should have shifted first.

We watched as Xavior pretended to swipe at one twin while the other flew past to one of their spots. They were teaming up against him now instead of taking him on one at a time. From what I knew of dragons, that was not normal. Xavior's surprise registered as he realized it, just as the twins attacked him in tandem. He used his wing to block one twin while he snatched the other out of mid-air with a paw. Xavior gave a chuff, followed by a small growl and another chuffing noise as he dropped them into the nest of bedding next to each other. It was the equivalent of telling them 'good job' with a command to stay put and be good. Xavior knew my parents were in his den. The twins chuffed in response and generally made happy noises as they panted from their play.

"We can move closer now." I waved my parents forward, and they followed me. The twins turned their heads toward us as we approached and Xavior gave a tone of greeting.

The slightly smaller of the two twins, the one with mostly pearl scales, hopped toward me. As I picked them up, they quickly moved to hang on my chest as they peered at my parents with their light gold eyes.

"Hello Snow pea. How's my baby? Did you have fun?" They nuzzled into me and cooed. All it took was one cute noise to have my parents completely enamored.

"They're adorable, Greg." Jennifer reached out to touch the twin in my arms. "Is Snow pea a nickname?" It was better than what Katie had suggested, though not by much.

"Yeah." I smiled and bounced the whelp I held. "Snow pea." Then I pointed at our green scaled whelp still in the nest. "And Sweet pea. Our two peas in a pod." Not that either of those peas would be in a pod together, but when have nicknames ever made sense?

"At least that's what I call them. Xavior likes the names well enough." It's something I wished we could have come up with together. Maybe he had nicknames for them, but I wouldn't know until he shifted, and he won't until our whelps gave him some kind of signal that they were ready.

Snow pea turned toward Jennifer and made a cooing noise, then moved away from me toward her. "Hold firm. They'll figure out how to latch on so they feel safe. They're surprisingly good at climbing and gliding, so don't worry so much about dropping them."

Sweet pea came over and crawled up my back to watch their sibling. While I knew they were there, they gave me a gentle head butt as if to remind me. I reached back and scratched their snout while their sibling settled into Jennifer's arms.

Xavior chuffed and moved closer to Philip, who reached out and touched his snout. "They're beautiful, Xavior. You and Greg have done a good job." Xavior made an affirming noise, which made me smile.

"He agrees. And. . .he's happy. He's happy you are here and accept our whelps as your own."

Philip smiled. "Of course they are, and always will be. Just like the two of you." Xavior nudged Philip playfully, making him laugh. It wasn't until I felt some tension fade that I realized Xavior had been worried about my parents accepting our whelps. Though I don't think it was all him. It was one thing to accept that your boyfriend was a dragon, and quite another to see him in all his dragon glory, along with your son's dragon offspring.

Why I ever thought my parents wouldn't accept us was probably something I should bring up in therapy. I knew, deep down, it had nothing to do with them, but a small part would always worry. Like Xav and I were worried now about our whelps. Would the other half of their family accept them if they never shifted?

FROZEN

Xavior

Our whelps wouldn't shift. Dr. Alexander had never seen or heard anything like it. Then again, she mentioned we were the only mated pair in the family who weren't both shifters.

Jordan offered a hypothesis. "Maybe they are waiting for Greg to shift. Isn't it normal for mated pairs to take turns?" His glamour was firmly in place today, showing a neutral light pink flesh tone. I wasn't sure if it was because of the current situation, or something else. I also couldn't smell any emotions from Jordan, only the subtle citrus and spice notes I usually associated with him.

"How does it work if I can't shift?" The disappointment in Greg's voice hurt. I never should have given him that damn potion.

Catherine frowned. "It's possible they are picking up some underlying change the transfiguration potion caused." Catherine looked around, then turned to me. "Has Greg's smell changed since he took the potion?"

Ah, now I knew what she was getting at. He always smelled like sandalwood and sage, combined with something slightly metallic, and he smelled more like that while under the effects of the potion. I looked at Greg and he answered the best he could for me because an affirmative would only confuse things.

"He's not sure, and he's frustrated." He looked at me and spoke. "Like he has more to say."

Jordan shook his head. "If the potion caused the problem, whatever that may be, then might it be the solution?"

"I won't advise Greg to use another transfiguration potion. It nearly killed him last time," said Catherine.

"True, but what if we use a glamour instead?" Jordan said with a shrug.

"Glamour? How?" Greg's curiosity was fully present. I can't say mine was any different. A glamour that large would take some talent and personal magic to pull off. Not to mention a lot of components. I knew Jordan was capable of it. What it would end up costing Greg and me? That was the real question.

"Well, it would make you look like a dragon, but you wouldn't be able to respond or fly. You'd be able to move around some, but you'd tire out easily under the glamour's weight. You also wouldn't have the same protection dragon scales afford."

"Because they're fake," Greg said.

"Yes." Jordan seemed concerned about it. He glanced at me, then looked at Greg. If he was concerned I'd lash out if something happened to my mate again, he was right.

Catherine sighed. "It's worth the gamble. If the problem is around Greg not being able to shift, an illusion might be enough to do the trick."

Greg looked at me, our connection full of concern. If we didn't try something, the whelps might have more delayed development. If the illusion didn't work, we'd deal with it. Regardless of the outcome, we had to try something. I vocalized my agreement, and Greg smiled at me.

"We're willing to try," he said as he looked at me, then turned to Jordan. "Whatever you need to make it work, we're willing to try it for the sake of our whelps."

Will we ever be able to repay Jordan for everything he's done for us? I only hoped it wasn't some ulterior motive. Jordan was my best friend and business partner. Fae weren't known for their altruistic attitudes, and Jordan was a shrewd executive where our business ventures were concerned. I had to believe that our friendship meant something more to him than being able to collect a favor.

A few days later, Jordan showed us the glamor he made from scratch. We didn't ask how he put it together, but he took a sample of Greg's hair, one of my scales, one of Greg's ties, and a copy of the image I had made of Greg and me as dragons that I kept in my library. When he walked into our den with the green silk tie I'd given Greg, I was skeptical.

"Why did you need to use one of my ties?" Greg looked at the dark green fabric. We were okay with losing the memento. The tie was worth nothing without our whelps.

"First of all, it's not just a tie. It's from the fae tailor, the same one that made your suit for the holo premiere." Jordan came over to Greg and looped the fabric around his neck. "It's enchanted all on its own, making the wearer look their best. You need that for your whelps. The glamor has to be convincing enough to convince them to shift."

Jordan's hands moved swiftly. Greg was only wearing a pair of his basketball shorts. The look was oddly sexy as it drew attention to Greg's abs and muscular arms. My thoughts wandered until Greg looked at me, smiling. He knew where my head was at and he felt the same longing I did. While we were worried about the whelps, being stuck hadn't helped other frustrations either.

In contrast, Jordan dressed in a button up and slacks, though the button up was open at the top, and the collar was stiff so that it framed his neck in a stylish way that pointed like an arrow to his crotch. I blinked to dispel the distraction. Greg looked away as Jordan finished tying the tie and tacked it together with a tie pin that had a symbol I didn't recognize stamped into it.

Ah, so I wasn't the only one affected. Our mutual horniness was definitely a distraction we didn't need right now. I tried to concentrate on our concern for the whelps, and Greg's relief flooded our connection. I'd guess he'd been trying diligently to avoid a hard-on. Which I tried to avoid thinking about to keep us from falling into our self-made trap.

"You rotate the pin," Jordan said as he took Greg's hand and put it on the tie. "Three times clock-wise." Greg nodded. "It gives you five minutes for every turn after that." Jordan stepped back and let go of Greg. "I wouldn't suggest using it for more than ten minutes."

"Is it a onetime thing?"

Jordan shook his head. "I don't make one-offs." He looked up at me. "I'll leave you to it." Then he turned and left. He and Catherine would be waiting outside if they were needed.

Greg looked at the tie, then up at me. "Fuck, we're going to owe him a lot for this, aren't we?"

Jordan had given Greg a way for us to be together as a family, as dragons, and maybe more. Magic was tricky, though. We would definitely owe the fae for this one. This was a large favor, and it wasn't cheap.

I sighed and made an affirmative sound. Greg sighed too.

"Do you want to call them?" I nodded and let out a series of tones that would bring our whelps to the nest. Greg stripped off his shorts. We had asked about him wearing protective gear but Jordan said it would cause problems with the glamor. For this to work, Greg had to be nude of everything but the glamoured item.

Greg turned the tie tack four times. He was human one minute, and a dragon the next. The whelps became excited and climbed him, licking and cooing. Greg settled down into the nest and I made room for them as they roamed over him, exploring his form. They weren't as careful as they usually were. I saw pricks of blood well up where Sweet pea had scrambled up Greg's back.

Hang on, Love. Hang on. I hadn't realized how long five minutes could be while I watched Greg wince as the whelps moved around him.

I decided not to wait any longer and shifted. After so long being a dragon, it felt odd to be in a smaller body with two legs. The whelps took note and trilled in excitement as Sweet pea came toward me first and slowly shifted.

She toddled forward on unsteady legs, and I picked her up. Her tiny fingers immediately went to my whiskers, which had grown rather unruly in the weeks after they had hatched.

Snow pea climbed off of Greg and came around to face him. They waited. Then I realized what was happening. They were waiting for Greg to shift. It made sense since Snow pea always preferred Greg to me. There was an attachment there. And the twins were attached to each other, so what one did, the other did.

Greg looked at me, desperate. We had a minute or two, if that. Timing was crucial. If Snow pea didn't shift, they might not, or it might be a while before they tried again.

"Hey Sweetie, do you want to help me and your papa with your sibling?" Their hands were occupied with touching my face and theirs, then their ears. But when I pointed at Greg and then at their whelp-sibling, they shouted in excitement. I brought her over to the nest and Snow pea moved toward her, their eyes wide with interest.

I touched Greg's snout. "Next time, we'll set a timer." He nodded. I looked him over and saw welts of blood along his body. He was panting. There might not be a next time if he didn't shift. There was no way to know what kind of damage the whelps had done to him until the glamour wore off. I closed my eyes and kissed his snout. Just as I was about to move away, I felt his lips on mine.

The cuts on Greg's body were deep, but not mortal. Snow pea's head swung away from their sister and toward us. Their eyes grew wide as they moved toward Greg and shifted. It was much slower than his sister's, but eventually he crawled into Greg's waiting arms and patted Greg's face as he hugged him.

"I'll get Catherine," I said as Greg nodded, smiling, though clearly in pain.

Jordan and I entertained two very fidgety biped babies while Catherine worked on Greg's wounds.

"You're lucky. They're mostly superficial. They could have pierced something vital," Catherine said. Her hands glowed as she knitted Greg's flesh together.

"But it worked. The whelps shifted and Xavior isn't stuck any longer." Greg winced and grinned in turns.

While our whelps had shifted, Snow pea's new form wasn't completely human. He had webbing between his toes and fingers, and a thin gossamer skin on both sides of his body that was attached from his wrists to his ankles, along with another swath of the same skin between his legs from groin to ankles. His eyes weren't human shaped, but a smaller version of his dragon's with an amber glow to them.

I created a playpen to contain them while they played and explored as bipeds. Jordan glanced between the twins and Catherine as she worked on Greg. Greg and I had grabbed what was at hand before we had called Catherine and Jordan to help him. I had pulled on Greg's shorts and Greg had grabbed a blanket, though it was pointless since he had more than a few wounds along his whole body.

"Maybe they are vestigial, and he'll grow out of them." Jordan whispered as he glanced at Snow pea.

"Maybe. But if they're not, it doesn't matter. He's healthy, and that's all we've ever needed." I reached over to touch Snow pea's black hair. Same as Greg's. Sweet pea's hair was a dark brown, and her eyes were humanoid, but they contained the same dragon coloring as her brothers.

"As you say. I'm happy I still have a knack for glamours. It's been a while since I made such a grandiose one."

"It was rather ingenious, Jordan." I understood what came next. "What do we owe you?"

Jordan turned to me and looked at our twins. I gripped the playpen. Whatever history the fae had with dragons and their whelps, I couldn't believe Jordan would ask that of us. I didn't want to believe it. We had trusted him and not negotiated for his magic before we took it. He was within his rights to ask for a high boon. The stories about pledging your first born for fame and fortune were not exaggerated or myths. Truth was, no fae had asked for such a thing in a very long time.

"Do you think me so callous?" Jordan caught my tension. "We've known each other a long time, Xavior. Do you think I would ask such a thing?"

"Maybe not from me." Because it wasn't me he gave the magic to. If Jordan asked for that, it would go beyond breaking the fragile trust the two had, and it would break Greg, knowing he put either of his whelps in danger of being separated from us.

"I'll forgive you for thinking that, once. If only because new parents scare easily. But you are not far off the mark. I want a family, but not yours. Not exactly anyway." He glanced at Greg as I suppressed a shiver.

BY PROXY

XAVIOR

I waited a few nights until we had our routine down. Baths, meals, shifting once a day. Greg used the glamor to encourage Snow pea when he wouldn't shift. The whelp could fly about in either form with little trouble, much to his sister's frustration and delight sometimes.

Some nights, we slept in the den as our whelps slept in the trees. Other nights, we slept in our suite. Tonight was a den night. I even replaced our nest with a proper bed, which made Greg happy.

He rolled into bed a wounded, tired, grateful parent and I settled there with him, watching the trees around us for movement. All we heard was gentle breathing.

Greg pulled me close and kissed my head. "We'll need to figure out when we can have a night to ourselves. As much as I love our twins, I miss you."

"Same here." I kissed him but was too exhausted to do more, which surprised me. Though Greg was in much the same condition.

He turned on his side and caressed my shoulder. "Something's worrying you. Is it Snow pea? Or has Sweet pea done something sneaky again?"

"No, nothing to do with the twins. Well, not exactly. It's Jordan. He's asked for a favor." I glanced at him, then looked at the twins nestled near each other in the tree limbs above our heads.

"Shit. Well, we knew he probably would. But it's better he's asked now, isn't it? The longer he waits, the more it's worth, right?"

"Yes, supposedly."

"What's he asked for?"

"A proxy."

Greg sat up. "What do you mean by a proxy?" I followed. This wouldn't be easy to explain, and I had a feeling I'd already started the conversation off in the wrong direction.

"Let me say first that if we turn down this request, Jordan is within rights to ask for something more later. Not that this isn't a big deal, because it is, and it involves you."

"Involves me how? What does he want me to be a proxy for?"

"Well, as fae grow older, their ability to produce offspring diminishes like every other species on this planet, except they've figured a way around it."

"You mean fae can't magic themselves into an erection?" Greg smirked, and I smacked him with a pillow.

"That's not the case, and you know it." I tucked the pillow under my arms. "What they lose in being able to reproduce, they gain in magic."

"Okay, that makes sense, but why does he need me?" Greg shrugged.

I fiddled with the pillow and couldn't look him in the eye to explain. I knew he must have felt how conflicted I was about telling him. He confirmed it with the next words out of his mouth.

"Xav, tell me what's going on. What does Jordan want?"

"There's a ritual that can imbue a lesser magical being, or an individual without magic, with fae traits for a short time. During that time, the proxy acts in the fae's place, having sex with their partner or partners, hopefully to produce an offspring."

When I peeked at him, Greg's face was slack. His disbelief hung between us, and I didn't know what to say next.

"He wants to magic himself into me, then have me sleep with Catherine?"

So he understood, sort of. The ritual, as they had described it to me, was more involved than that. "Kind of, but not exactly. It's more like a threesome situation. Someone would be between them."

"I'd what?" His voice was quiet. This wasn't good.

"You have to understand that fae don't see a problem with this. Nor do mages, for that matter. It's the offspring and the magic they value."

"Oh, so I'm what, supposed to be a container? Or how did you put it, a lesser being?" Greg got out of bed and stalked the space between the bed and the banked fire.

"Greg…" I tried to reach for him, and he pulled away. "I didn't agree to anything. Besides, I can't. It's up to you and…"

He turned toward me, anger coming off him in waves. His voice was quiet. However, given the state of his pheromones, it was as good as shouting. "So he told you, knowing I'd feel obligated, knowing I'd agree to damn near anything to protect you and our twins, instead of asking me himself."

Greg wasn't wrong, and part of me was very upset with Jordan for putting a wedge between us like this. They'd worked well together for the last year, and Jordan had helped us several times already.

He paced and talked to himself. "Never mind the fact that somehow I'd be related to a fae and a mage and there might be a child, which I'm just supposed to what? Walk away from? Ignore that I ever contributed and hope for the best?" He looked at me, frustration and anger written across his features.

"Why can't they use medical intervention like everyone else? I would have considered a donation if he had asked me. Besides, how the hell would he expect me to participate? I've never done any of that before, and I'm certainly not interested in Catherine for more than friendship. Not to mention how awkward it would be afterward. Why ask me? Why drag us into this?"

He was understandably upset, but logic was there. He was working out the puzzle, and I knew more than I'd said, so I continued now that I could get a word in edge-wise.

"He's my friend, and they're desperate. They've tried medical intervention. If they can't produce offspring from their union, he'll lose Catherine."

"He doesn't have to be her consort. Couldn't they have a relationship like everyone else?"

"Mages take commitments very seriously. While the Alexanders don't necessarily hold to all the old ways, they hold to their relationship practices for the family matriarch. If they were to see each other outside of the bounds of the consort pact, they'd lose everything. The magic is binding. She'd no longer be head of the family. Jordan would lose his magic. And if they don't have offspring, he loses Catherine. They have one year left."

"So? Isn't she already married? What about that relationship? Doesn't her other partner matter?"

"Primary relationships are protected. She could break that relationship, but she would have to prove that her partner wasn't acting in the family's best interest. And she still loves Howard. And Jordan likes him. A lot. They all pursued this consort pact, thinking they could make it work somehow."

"And how do you know all this?" Greg sat next to me on the bed, his anger cooling.

"Jordan talked with me while you were sleeping off Catherine's healing. He's sad and frustrated. He wants a family again, and he feels like it's slipping through his fingers, all because he's. . ." I couldn't quite say it out loud.

"Too old." Greg glanced at me with a frown on his face.

"And it's not you he wants for the ritual. It's your parents."

"My what?"

In retrospect, I probably should have led with that, but I'm not sure it would have turned out any better. "Apparently, while you and I have been dealing with things in here, Catherine and Jordan have entertained your parents."

"By entertained, you don't mean. . ."

I gave him a pointed look, and he paled even more. "I did not need to know that." He fell back on the bed and stared up at the tree canopy. Our twins were wrapped around opposite branches but within reach of each other. "Why ask you to ask me if they could have asked my parents themselves?"

"Because it's our debt to pay, and Catherine and Jordan have known you longer. It's an old fashion way to do it, but for them, it makes sense. Jordan can say his favor to us was repaid, and if your parents don't agree to help, they don't lose face in front of people they respect." Because that was clear to me that Jordan very much respected the Lyndon's and did not want to make them uncomfortable. But making Greg uncomfortable was a different kind of respect, given how fae work. Jordan trusted Greg, or he never would suggest anything like this to repay the favor.

We laid there for some time, quiet, listening to the embers in the fireplace crackle, and the twins breathing. My heartbeat sounded loud in my ears. Something shifted between us. The pheromones in my proximity changed as Greg's anger settled into frustration, then acceptance. He reached for me, his hand caressing my shoulder, encouraging me into his arms. I went willingly, spooning into him, wanting nothing more than for us to comfort each other.

Jordan's strange request aside, I wondered if Greg would understand why they were pursuing this. After all, his idea of relationships and sex were much more reserved than those around him, myself included. Time and again, he had shown he was willing to respect how others lived their lives, regardless of what standards he had for himself. Not that long ago, I was set against having offspring. He would have accepted that, just as he accepted when I changed my mind. In his previous relationship, he had set boundaries with his partner, only to have those violated repeatedly. His anger was understandable, given his friendship with Jordan. Though I agree with Jordan. If he had approached this topic with Greg, the chance of a favorable agreement was low.

Jordan was desperate. I knew that and even understood it. He really loved Catherine, in only a way a fae can, which means he would do anything to stay near them, to be there for them, to see every wish and desire granted. I knew his love for Catherine was true because he had shown the same to me, and still did, within the boundaries of our current friendship. He would die for her, as much as he would die for me, and nearly did.

Most who didn't interact with the fae regularly considered them a selfish species who were very guarded and insular. It's not because they want to be. They know all too well how easy it is to fall in love and the power it can hold over them when they love something or someone.

As a long-lived species, maybe one of the longest, their love does not fade with time. They love with their complete selves and it stays with them until their dying day. I know this because Jordan told me about Anitha. Had he told Catherine about her? I imagine so. To understand him was to understand his first love.

He wouldn't go to these lengths for just a dalliance and certainly not for a business deal—socio-political or otherwise. To him, Catherine was everything. To risk a fundamental part of his being, his magic, for a union with her that can only continue if it produces offspring when he had no idea if he could still have children, could only have been made of Jordan's love for Catherine. It was the same reason I chose to try to have offspring with Greg, because I loved him and he deserved everything I could give him.

I didn't know if I'll be a good parent. I was worried about it even before I found out I was pregnant. I knew Greg would be, and in many ways, he was already proving that to be true. He sacrificed his health as much as I had for our whelps and did it knowing he likely wouldn't live to see them be adults. It's something we chose, knowing the limitations. In that way, we were a lot like Jordan and Catherine. Hopeful for a future that we might never see.

"Hey," he whispered softly in my ear. "I'll talk with Jordan. We'll figure it out."

"Thank you." The relief I felt nearly caused me to cry. When Greg placed a couple of quick kisses behind my ear, I felt tears slip across my face.

"I know you care about him. I'm sorry for not listening first and letting my anger get in the way."

"Fae will go to great lengths for those they love. He respects you, and cares about you too, Greg. I know it seems manipulative, but he could have kept our favor and asked your parents directly. In his own way, this is like asking for your blessing."

Greg sighed. "Honestly? When I thought it was me they wanted for the ritual, I was horrified and flattered at the same time. I don't know how I feel about my parents being involved."

That made me smile a little. I suspected there were a lot of things Greg didn't know about his parents. It wasn't my place to tell him. Like anyone who struggled with parts of their identity, they would need to choose how to share it with him. Given what I knew about the Lyndon's, and Greg's mother Narissa, it was likely kept from him to protect him. Hopefully, whatever he discovers won't cause him to change his relationship with his parents.

"They're adults too and have a right to their privacy as much as you do. They deserve the chance to decide if they want to be involved or not," I said.

"True." He took another audible breath. "I try to keep that in mind."

That was all I could ask. "I love you, Greg."

"Love you too, Xav," he replied as he pulled me in closer, wrapping an arm around my waist, holding me tight until we drifted off to sleep.

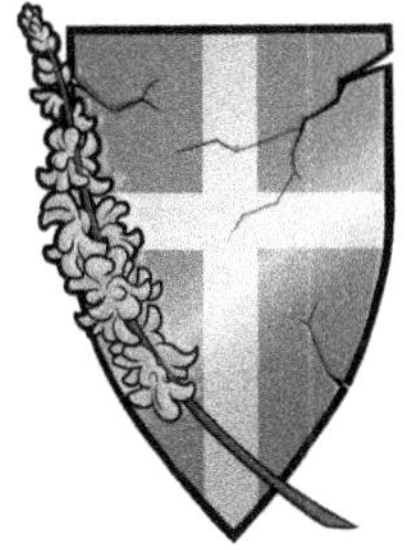

HARD FACTS

GREGOR

The next morning, I found Jordan and asked to speak with him. When the door shut, I felt a mix of emotions that I tried to settle. Though the first question out of my mouth was, "Why?"

"You'll have to be a little more specific, Gregor."

"Xavior explained, but I'm still having a hard time understanding why you want me involved. This seems like a very personal thing and not something I should have a say in, considering I'm not directly involved."

"Ah." Jordan found a seat, and he gestured for me to find one as well. The room was well appointed. It was one of the smaller rooms on the first floor that served as a tearoom or a meeting room. Rooms like this surprised me all the time because even though I've lived at Xavior's estate for a while, I hadn't seen the full extent of the place.

I sat across from Jordan and braced my hands on my knees and waited for him to continue.

"It's not my way to be indirect." He sighed. "I sought to solve several problems at once."

"It was an interesting way to learn that you and Catherine had slept with my parents." I gripped my knees.

"Were you unaware of their preferences?"

"Yes!" I didn't mean to say it so loud, but it still unnerved me. Knowing your parents had sex was one thing, and one I didn't really think about. It was another to know they practiced non-monogamy when you had never seen or heard them talk about any other relationships.

Jordan apparently found that odd and gave me a curious look. "They are aware of your orientation and lifestyle, obviously. Why wouldn't they tell you about theirs?"

I opened my mouth and closed it. Opened it again, and then tilted my head. "I'm not sure." Though I could guess at some things. They had been upset about Keith, but not his lifestyle, but his lack of concern for me and our lack of communication. I had thought that Keith being unable to commit to me as his only partner was part of the problem. Had my parents thought I'd judge them the same way? It was likely, considering how things went with Keith and my absolute need for Xavior and me to be monogamous when we started dating.

They were accepting of me my whole life when my mother wasn't. I'd never asked them what they did with their time away or with friends. They would mention dinner parties and trips. Beyond asking whether they had a good time, I never asked for details. Had I inadvertently made my parents hide part of themselves even though I was an adult that could, in theory, understand?

The fae hadn't said a word. When I looked at him, he seemed concerned. "You thought I knew."

He nodded. "Had I known otherwise, I wouldn't have come to you with this. Xavior didn't feel it was his place to ask since they're your parents, though he was aware and offered to broach the subject with you as my friend."

The quip Xavior made on our first date. Damn his nose. He had known about Keith too, but had said very little because he felt it wasn't his place. Did everyone think I was so fragile? The resounding "yes" in my head made me realize how much progress I had made with therapy and how much more I likely needed.

"So, if I ask them, and they decline, what else would you require?" A favor was a favor, after all. I knew the basics of how the fae worked. Jordan and I were more than acquaintances, but not friends enough to gift something as large as the glamour he had created.

"If they decline, I'll ask nothing else. It puts you in an awkward situation as it is, and that is an indisposition I don't put on you lightly. But I think our best chances are with you asking them."

"Xavior explained the ritual, or well, the basics of it." Jordan looked surprised. "If I can ask anything, it's that my parents won't be harmed if they decide to do this. Also, that whenever it happens, it's without my knowledge." My face felt hot from second-hand embarrassment. If it was beet red too, it wouldn't surprise me.

Jordan smirked. "They won't come to harm, at least not any they don't ask for."

"Oh, for fuck's sake." I whispered, covering my face. Jordan laughed.

"You are way too easy to embarrassed, Gregor. How do you and Xavior even manage?"

"Quite well, actually," I said, taking an indignant tone. Xav never complained, and I knew they talked because Xavior and I talked about how much he could discuss with Jordan. Before that, Xavior had told him very little, much to my surprise.

Jordan grinned. "Given the two whelps down the hall, that's obvious enough." He paused. His eyebrows furrowed for a moment as he leaned forward. "Have you not had a night for yourselves?"

I shook my head, admitting that much heaped on more embarrassment. But I was embarrassed already, so what the hell did it matter?

"Catherine and I could sit for the weekend." He was quick to add, "and it's not a favor. I'd see it as our duty considering how we've been here since the beginning. Plus, I'm rather fond of your offspring."

"The twins do like you and Catherine. It really would be nice to have a weekend together alone." I looked up at Jordan, hopeful. "Are you sure?"

"Of course." Jordan smiled. If this was his way of making up for the epic amount of embarrassment I was about to put myself through, I'd take it. "Let us know when and we'll make arrangements." His smile widened. "Becoming parents is always the easy part."

We shared a laugh, considering everything that had brought Xavior and me to this point.

"May I give some advice?"

"Certainly." One didn't turn down free advice from a fae. It was considered very rude. Whether or not you use it was entirely up to you.

"You have a beautiful system of support. Between your parents and Xavior's, along with his sister and her husband, besides Catherine and I. Don't be afraid to ask. We may not always agree to help, but it never hurts to ask, Gregor."

The way he said my name was reminiscent of the way Grandpa Jack would talk with me sometimes. I swallowed hard and swiped at the corners of my eyes. To hear Jordan's concern and offer of assistance took the pressure off in a way I hadn't expected. I cleared my throat, willing myself to say something.

"Your kindness and generosity are noted. You have my heartfelt gratitude."

He grinned. "Always the clever one with the words." He stood. "Now, if you'll excuse me, I'm meeting Catherine for brunch."

"I thought she had returned to Spain." My confusion amused him because his smile widened in the disturbing way that fae could sometimes do just to unnerve other species in the room.

"Yes. She has."

"Isn't it after noon there?"

"Gregor," his tone had turned into a warning. "I'm happy to continue answering your questions, but eventually you will arrive at information which, as we have previously discussed, embarrasses you."

"Oh." I coughed and covered my mouth, realizing what he might be referring to. "Well then, don't let me keep you."

Jordan laughed. "I hadn't planned on it. Good day, Gregor."

"Good day, Jordan." He left the room, and I sat with my thoughts for a while before I went to find Xav and discuss taking a weekend for ourselves.

MEMORIES AND TIME

XAVIOR

"Fuck, like that. Just like that." I breathed out as Greg thrust into me with abandon.

We hadn't been to my house—just a few blocks from where we used to work—in some time. While we wanted a weekend to ourselves, we didn't want to be too far from our whelps. I could be back at the estate in fifteen minutes. We even brought a flying harness if an emergency came up so Greg could come with me. The trip into town with our pheromones out of control because of the lack of our whelps not being in proximity made the drive seem like an eternity instead of an hour.

It surprised me to find the twins were perfectly happy with Catherine and Jordan as we were leaving. One whelp or the other always wanted our attention, so when they didn't cry, I felt a little betrayed and happy. Being a parent was odd.

We barely made it through the front door before he had me bent over the cloth covered couch, eating my ass and opening me up so I could take him. Greg started off gentle until I pressed him for more, so he'd stop teasing me. I rode the twinge of pain as my insides moved with each thrust and every impact of Greg's hips against my ass while he buried his dick inside me.

"You're so tight." Greg ran his hand up my back and down again, his fingertips caressing my scales before gripping my hips. His thrusts were just fast enough not to tease and slow enough to let us enjoy the moment. Not that there wouldn't be more of this. An entire weekend of it, in fact. That alone made me lightheaded. It had been too long. And yet, there was the smallest seed of guilt.

He leaned over me to whisper in my ear, as if anyone could see or hear us. Maybe someone could. It's not like the windows were completely opaque. Though the most people might see were shadows. Very suggestive shadows. "I remember the last time I made you come on this couch. Your face was perfect. The way you were pinned under me, and how I had my hand in your hair. Do you remember what you said?" Then he moved, leaving me to gasp softly from the loss of his warmth and the press of his flesh to mine, while each thrust reminded me he was still there.

Words failed me. His hand slipped up my back, causing my scales to surface in the wake of his touch, sliding along until it reached my neck. Then his fingers softly plowed into my hair, which was longer now since I hadn't had it cut in a while. I felt the slight sting as they contracted into a fist and punctuated the movement with a gentle pull.

"Do you remember, love?" Greg asked.

Fuck, I was about to explode. I moaned as his thrusts turned slower and more brutal. He used his grip to tilt my head as he pressed himself against me again. His heated body flush with mine.

"Can you tell me?" he asked softly.

"I wanted you inside me."

"And where am I now?" he whispered.

"Inside me." Fuck. "Fuck, I'm going to come." Greg pulled me up by my hair as his free hand sought my dick, squeezing it, as he pushed into me as deep as he could go while he jerked me off. I made a mess and sighed as the euphoria of my orgasm rippled through me. Greg held me tight and kissed my cheek and neck as I shook in his arms.

"I missed you," he whispered.

"Same," I said with a soft chuckle. He was still rock hard inside me. When he moved, it set off another tremor through my body. I clinched around him, driven by the sensations his dick created as it grazed my seminal gland. Greg continued to hold me tight as I begged for more. "Come in me. Fill me."

He let go of my dick as his other hand slipped from my hair to my shoulder. His seed covered hand found the bend of my hip. He pushed me back down over the end of the couch and returned to his rhythmic thrusts. I pushed back against each smack of his hips, eager for his release. He groaned as I felt a warm pressure fill me, then ease, as he dropped his forehead to my shoulder. I touched his head and kissed his brow.

"Can you make it up the stairs?" I asked in a playful tone.

He groaned before he responded. "Thirty seconds more and I'll be able to move. Promise."

Our bags were still near the front door and discarded clothes were flung everywhere. "We need to plan weekends away more often."

"Agreed," Greg replied as he panted, still leaning on me.

"Do you want me to carry you up?" While I was teasing, he responded by stepping back from me, sweeping my legs with an arm and catching me with the other.

"Let me help you, if you're so eager." He kissed me as he walked us toward the stairs. I moved to wrap myself around him, pressing our torsos together. Something we'd not been able to do in a while.

"Fuck, when did you develop all of this muscle?" I ran my hands along his contoured shoulders and arms. He'd never been this well defined when we worked together. I hadn't minded, but I certainly admired it now.

"Training regiments for stunt doubles are pretty arduous. When you couldn't shift, I kept up my training out of the sheer need to keep myself occupied while I couldn't help you." He kissed me as he reached the top of the stairs. "When I couldn't help our whelps and we waited for them to shift, it kept my anxiety at bay."

He held me up with seemingly little effort, my ass balanced on his well-muscled arms. I held onto him a little tighter, emotions flooding our connection as we thought of how difficult things had been. I thought he'd put me down on the bed and go for round two. Instead, he walked us to the bathroom. His face turned serious, and I braced myself for the words that would follow.

"I didn't like feeling helpless, or making you feel you were alone in taking care of our twins. You did so much to get them here and put yourself through a lot. I've been in awe of you through all this, and you've been so patient with me, even through your frustration and pain." He kissed me softly and caressed my face. "I love you Xavior Alonso Brantley."

The smile on my face could have lit up a city. I knew how he had felt through the whole thing and never once had he resented my body when it was distended and warped from the egg, nor had he left my side when I really needed him. He took risk after risk for our whelps, and he never thought what it might cost him in return. We'd been lucky, sure. But this was only the beginning. "I love you too, Gregor Silvanus Lyndon."

We kissed, cleaned up, fondled each other in the shower, then blissfully fell into bed, where we got our first full night's sleep in some time. I woke up the next morning in a panic the moment I couldn't sense or smell the twins.

Greg put his hand on my shoulder and propped himself up on his elbow. "You okay?"

"Not used to being without them." From carrying them, then watching the egg, and finally their first shift, it seemed off to be so far away from them after so long.

Greg sat up and kissed my shoulder. "We can go home if you want."

I put my hand on his and turned toward him. "You'd do that, even though we planned to spend the entire weekend here?"

"I don't care if we planned to spend five minutes here. If you're worried, you'll be miserable. We both will."

It occurred to me I wasn't the only one missing the twins. Our connection was looping through the same emotions, which meant they weren't one sided.

"You're already miserable."

He smiled, then shrugged. "I know we needed time to ourselves, but I miss them." He laid back, propping himself on his elbow, which created a tantalizing line of muscle that led to other things hidden by the covers. The momentary distraction from my worries was welcome.

Greg had taken another direction, worry shifting to admiration for our son. It felt like sunshine after a cloudy day within our pheromone connection. "Snow pea is using his webbing to manipulate all kinds of things. It's absolutely remarkable. I keep wondering why he has it and Sweet pea doesn't."

"It's a good question. Sweet pea has at least one family trait. The tufts of feathers she has are definitely from my mother's side." Greg nodded. I wondered how often my parents talked about us as whelps. It was amusing to think about as I added to Greg's line of thinking. "Catherine suspects that the webbing Snow pea has might be a mid-shift aspect, like my family can do with certain dragon features. Or it could be permanent. Only time will tell."

"If it is permanent, we'll have to figure out clothing that makes sense for him. He won't be able to wear pants with webbing between his legs."

"I know plenty of designers that would love to make him accommodating clothing." Which was true. Jael would jump at the chance, and so would Jordan, for that matter. And in Jordan's case, he has a whole design house he could leverage for the purpose.

Greg grinned. "He's only a few months old. Let's not make him a fashion icon yet."

"Never too early to start, love." I turned toward him, leaning down to press my lips into his. "Never too early." Greg laughed and pulled me back down for more affection that turned into something more heated and satisfying.

Later that day, we rolled ourselves out of bed and ordered lunch. As Greg unpacked the food from the deli down the street, I received a text.

"Jordan says the twins are fine," I said, then read further. "They've been up in the trees most of the morning after they ate breakfast."

"Are they sure of that? Sweet pea likes to sneak around when she thinks no one is looking. She almost made it out of the den by herself not that long ago."

I text Jordan to remind him to ease Greg's concern. He and Catherine had access to the den via charms I made for them a while back. The twins could leave any time they wanted, as they were dragons, but we hadn't introduced them to the wide world outside yet. The fear of losing them was very real, considering how sneaky our whelps were.

Jordan sent me a picture after I had mentioned our budding escape artist. Both whelps had bones they were chewing on. "They're safe." I showed Greg the picture, and he smiled at the goofy photo of the whelps trying to stay in the trees and hang onto their prizes.

"Did he replicate those? They look as big as they are."

"Either that or he glamoured something to look like a bone."

As we ate, Greg had a look on his face. "What is it?" Feeling concern in our connection.

"When should we give them legal names? As fond as I am of their nicknames, we'll have to call them something other than peas, eventually."

I smiled. "I suppose. We'd need to do a formal presentation for our families. It's a dragon tradition."

"Should we make plans to go back to Spain, then? Or will your parents come to your estate?"

"Our estate," I corrected.

"Not legally," he countered. Before I was pregnant, Greg had been fine with making everything legal. After, something made him hesitate, not that I minded. Unless we eloped, it was bound to be a huge affair, given my family and all.

"Is that a proposal?"

Greg smirked, "I'm not half-assing that and you know it."

I smirked back as I finished my second sandwich. "I know, but one could hope."

Greg reached for my hand. We laced our fingers together as we finished our lunch.

For me, it didn't matter. I'd wait as long as he wanted to, even though we were better than married in the eyes of my family, especially given our whelps. Greg held off dealing with the legal part of our relationship. I couldn't blame him for that. Being a dragon with a long history made it complicated enough.

"So, where do you want to hold the naming ceremony?" he asked.

"It makes more sense for my parents to come here. Besides, they haven't been to the estate in a long time. It'll do them some good to have a change of scenery."

Now that we'd decided where, the only thing left to do was come up with names.

THE FAE-VOR

GREGOR

A few weeks after our weekend getaway, Xavior and I invited everyone to stay as our guests for the week of the naming ceremony. So while Xavior had the whelps in the den for dragon time, I met with my parents for breakfast.

"Not that we aren't glad to see you, Greg, but you could have brought one baby with you," Jennifer said.

"I could have, but I also have something to discuss. Something rather embarrassing, and I wouldn't want to have us all upset in front of them."

My parents looked at me. Dad set down his cup of coffee. "Are you and Xavior okay?"

"We're fine. Better than fine, actually." They seemed to take a breath at that revelation.

"That's good to hear. Sometimes children can put a strain on a relationship where you'd least expect it." Mom was smiling, but there was some undercurrent there. Did they know about Jordan and Catherine already?

I took a large gulp of water myself and set the glass down. "Actually, to start off, I want to apologize."

"What for?" Dad said. Both my parents looked perplexed.

I took a breath and let it out slowly before I spoke. "If I've ever made you feel you couldn't be fully yourselves around me, for whatever reason, I'm sorry. You've always been accepting of me and exceptional parents, and I've always been grateful for that, considering my mother's attitude. Your business is certainly your own, and I respect that, but I guess it makes me wonder if some things you've kept from me because you thought I wouldn't have the same respect for you.

"You need to know, I'm absolutely not upset that you didn't tell me. However, I am disappointed in myself that I might have caused you to think I wouldn't have understood or given you the same respect you've always shown me."

They both looked at me with confused expressions. "Are you sure everything is alright between you and Xavior?" Mom asked again.

"Yes. I'm not talking about us, I'm talking about the two of you, being. . . non-monogamous." Not to mention that Jordan was a former lover of Xavior's, and now was involved with my parents. Somewhere in my brain I was quietly screaming about that, but for whatever reason, it didn't weird me out as much as I thought. Or maybe my cognitive dissonance about the whole thing was absolute on the topic. Who knows at this point? Mostly, I wanted my parents to know that it was their choice and wouldn't think of them any differently for it.

"Oh," Mom said. "And how did you? . ."

"Ah, well, that's the interesting thing. Jordan approached me with an offer."

"Wow, that's bold of him. I mean, we had a good time, and I know fae are somewhat lascivious, but he could have waited until you and Xavior were more settled with the whelps." That Philip was indignant on my account for the completely wrong reason, and yet, wasn't surprised that Jordan might have approached me was funny. I literally covered my mouth and laughed. This was all becoming absurd because the fae in question was trying to do too many things, or people in this case, at once.

"Greg?" Jennifer touched my arm. I waved her off.

"Sorry, it's just Xavior and I owe Jordan a favor. He created a large glamour that helped our whelps shift for the first time. Jordan asked me to approach you about something, which he sees as covering the favor regardless of your answer. Plus, if you decline, it would save their dignity from the up front refusal. And possibly their disappointment. From what I understand, Jordan and Catherine like you both very much."

Philip smiled, and Jennifer cleared her throat and finally mentioned the unspoken topic. "Is this about their infertility problem?"

I looked at her. "They mentioned it to you?"

Jennifer tilted her head a little. "Catherine did. She was rather distraught about it. She loves her husband, but she's also fallen very hard for Jordan. And from what I understand, he's rather taken with her as well."

I shrugged. "I don't claim to understand mage relationships, or the possible magical backlash involved, but they are desperate. And while I'd wonder if having a child amid a new relationship is a good idea, I'm not one to talk." Because, well, sometimes timing doesn't work out in one's favor. I took a sip of my water, trying to calm the nerves I had about discussing such delicate things with my parents. Though from what I could tell, they were handling it just fine.

"Jordan explained that because of the mage element, the consort part, they have another year, or they have to separate. I think I'd be more concerned about it if I hadn't seen them with our whelps. Both of them have more experience as parents than either Xavior or I do," I said.

"I didn't know that about Jordan," Philip said.

"Something Xav told me once. It was a long time ago, before they met. His children have long since grown up, and being half-fae, likely aren't alive any longer. Neither of them went into details with me, but I had the impression that Jordan very much liked the idea of him and Catherine having a child."

Philip's eyebrows furrowed slightly. "That doesn't explain everything, does it? What did he ask you to do?" Dad asked, and both he and my mom watched me with a heavy air of tension between us. Or maybe I was the only one that was tense. This was all so awkward.

"Well, given your recent associations with them, they were wondering if you would participate in a fertility rite? They've tried science and other kinds of magic, but Jordan says there's an old rite that lets an older fae convey their attributes onto a non-magical being. . . to act as a proxy." I glanced between the two of them and they looked at each other. Jennifer covered her smile with a sip from her teacup and Philip grinned.

The heat of embarrassment crawled up the back of my neck, and I covered my eyes. "I don't want to know, honestly. I'm good with you being in an open relationship, or non-monogamous, whatever, not that you need my approval, but all I ask is that I don't hear details."

"Xavior's right, you're way too easy to embarrass." Dad laughed. "I'm a little surprised, though. While you never brought anyone home, or talked about who you were with, with the exception of your ex and Xavior, you were obviously seeing people. When we'd visit you while you were in college, it was very apparent you were well liked."

I dropped my hand and glared at my father. "I was on the basketball team. Of course people liked me." An indignant tone crept into my voice. I didn't make a habit of introducing anyone I was dating or seeing because it all seemed so temporary in college. If I was being honest with myself, I still wasn't sure about my parents back then. Mother's rebuke had hurt. Being out with Philip and Jennifer and everyone else was still fairly new. I envied other queers that could express themselves from the start, like my childhood friend, Jake. He knew he was pansexual before I could even admit I was gay.

"What was it, four or five people, Jenn?" Philip teased.

"I remember Henry, and Victor. Oh, and Dwayne. What was the name of the other one?" Mom asked. They rarely embarrassed me like this, but were enjoying themselves way too much.

Before Dad could offer a name, I blurted it out. "Nate. From Senior year."

"Right. Nate." Dad grinned. "They all looked at you like you hung the moon. What happened to Nate, anyway? You two seemed pretty serious."

They knew all of this and let me take my time with it, even if they joked about it now. It hadn't been easy for me to accept that part of myself at first. Even though it wasn't a secret, I didn't talk about it much or hit the clubs like some of my friends did. The guys I dated were very open. Their parents were welcoming. Mine would have been too, but I didn't want to cause problems. I'd already lost one parent. I didn't want to lose more. Though in hindsight, they never would have done that to me. Even when they were icy with Keith, they still tolerated him. They absolutely loved Xav and were happy to show their affection for us. It was one more thing to add to a long list of why I was so grateful they were my parents.

"We graduated, and I went to the academy and he went to grad school. We were too busy to see much of each other. By the time I was doing safety patrols, he had hooked up with a shifter and moved to Oregon, had kids and everything."

"Disappointed?" Mom reached out and patted my hand.

"No, not anymore. Nate was a good guy, but if it was meant to be, it would have worked out, right?"

My parents nodded. The trip down memory lane wasn't as interesting to me as it used to be. When things were tough with Keith, I thought about Nate like the one that got away, and then felt guilty for it. But what I have now was so much better than all the rest. These days, my fantasies were all about Xavior. Sure, I'd appreciate someone from time to time because I'm human, but Xavior was it for me. If there was one hope I had, it was that Xavior might survive well past me and love someone enough to keep him going. For me though, he was it, no matter what our lives would bring.

"You're thinking about Xavior." Jennifer asked.

I smiled. "How did you know?" Breakfast resumed. Loving Xavior never embarrassed me. Something about us being together gave me a kind of bravado I'd never had with anyone else.

"You have more confidence, you sit up more, and you get a warmth to your eyes when you think about him." I'd never looked at myself in a mirror while thinking of Xavior, but it all sounded plausible coming from Mom.

"Thank you. It means a lot to know that." She patted my hand, happy I was happy.

Once we finished breakfast, Philip circled back around to my original topic. "Greg, Tell Jordan and Catherine to give Jennifer and I the day to think about it. If we decide it's not for us, we'll let you tell them to preserve their dignity. Otherwise, we'll speak with them." I nodded. It sounded sensible to me. "Though I have one question for you," he said as they walked me to the door of their suite.

I waited to open the door until he asked whatever he was concerned about. "Would you mind if you had another sibling even if we're only related via this rite or magic, however this might work?"

"What's one more sibling?" I smiled. "I'd always wondered why the two of you never had more children, or adopted, for that matter."

Jennifer's smile faltered a little. "We thought about it," she said as she glanced at Philip. "For us, you were enough. Besides, we would have had to go through either adoption, surrogate, or artificial womb programs, and we didn't want to put you through that."

"Me? I don't understand. Why would that have mattered to me?"

Dad sighed. "Same reason we waited until you were through college to make anything official. Your mother was always a concern for us. If she wanted to make life difficult, she could have."

"Over a sibling? It didn't stop her from having more children and marrying someone else. Why would it have made a difference?"

Jennifer took my hand and walked us to a couch in the suite to sit down.

"Sweetheart," she ran her hand through my hair. I leaned into that touch because something was bothering her and all these odd confessions were confusing. "I'm trans. We were afraid that if your mother found out, she might have tried to take you away from us. We couldn't bear that. Your father and I were determined to give you some place that wasn't so filled with rhetoric and hate."

Tears trickled down my cheeks. Mom and I dashed them away as they fell. They had given up so much for me. I pulled her into a hug and held her tight. "I'm sorry."

"Don't, Greg. This isn't your fault. Your father and I made our decision together and we've never regretted it. We had you, after all. Our little sunshine." She smiled at me and reminded me of all the times she encouraged me and loved me for exactly who I was and never once made me feel unworthy of her love and affection.

Dad came near and leaned over to kiss both my mom and me on the head. "Adults protect their children. You'll understand that now that you have your own. Your childhood was difficult enough." He touched my head as I looked up at him. He had his arm wrapped around Jennifer. We stayed like that for a while until our tears dried up. Under the gratitude and love I felt for them, the venom I carried for my mother, Narissa, became a little more poisonous.

"I won't tell Xavior if you don't want me to."

Jennifer shook her head. "He'll want to know why you're upset, if he's not concerned already." She sighed softly and held my gaze. Hers was filled with love and concern in equal measures.

"I'm sorry we kept this from you for so long. We didn't want you to have to keep something from your mother. Your Dad and I had wished things turned out differently with her when you were older, that maybe she would see reason and tolerance. We both tried to talk with her after she disowned you, but she wouldn't speak to either of us," Mom said.

Dad spoke softly, though there was a small thread of anger in his voice. "Your mother was very adept at learning things and using them against people if it gained her something, regardless of whether it was legal. It would have been a nightmare of proceedings and other stresses we wanted to avoid for you and us." Jennifer patted Philip's hand, still grasping her shoulder.

I knew that all too well. Narissa had monitored the school where Jennifer used to teach when I attended. I knew because Narissa told me, giving me some twisted excuse about safety and parental rights. I wondered how much my parents had endured of my mother's harassment that I wasn't really aware of until now.

As I left my parent's suite, I made sure they planned to come to the den to visit the twins. When I found Xavior, he and the twins were curled up together. Both of them were under his wing, taking a midmorning nap. He opened one eye to look at me and I held out my hand to stop him from moving and interrupting nap time.

Xavior tracked my careful footfalls until I reached his side. I crouched down to kiss his snout and sighed as I pulled up pillows and blankets next to him. I picked up a good deal of concern from him, but I tried to project appreciation and calm.

"I'll explain later, promise." I kissed his snout again, then curled up next to him and our whelps. He gave the softest acknowledgments, and we drifted back to sleep for a few hours more.

WHAT'S IN A NAME

XAVIOR

We decked the estate out in the house colors of a dark forest green and a cream white. The twins had adorable matching outfits, though one was green for Sweet pea and the other was cream white for Snow pea. Not that we couldn't tell them apart, but it was nice to do so at a distance.

The naming of dragons was more or less a small affair within a family, but word had spread, and gifts from all over the planet showed up at the estate. I'd met Edward in the foyer as he directed another large delivery of gifts to a room down the hall.

"I've moved the deliveries to the larger sitting room. The local parcel mages have advised me that there will be more arriving in the next few days."

I shrugged. "I'm sorry for the inconvenience Edward, it's not as if we put out a registry for the twins."

"It might be better if you had, Mr. Brantley. Based on what's arrived already, there are some gifts that might be. . . inappropriate."

"Like?"

"A night light of demi-fae that dance around the room while singing, for instance."

"Oh. I see." Historically, devices like that were used to train dragons to hunt demi-fae. "Who sent it?"

"An older relative of Gavin's partner, Brice, from a red dragon family in Wales." Edward frowned, which I could understand. You didn't want to offend family, but some were very reluctant to be in the present day.

"Let's keep everything together for now unless a package needs special care. Greg and I will wade through it all after everyone leaves. Maybe Jordan will know what to do with it." The likely answer from him would be to throw it on a pyre, but that would depend on how it was made. Burning magical items was generally a bad idea, and even more so given who it came from.

Initially, our plans were to have my parents, Greg's parents, along with Jordan and Catherine for the ceremony, but once Faith heard she asked to be invited and I couldn't say no. I'd been to all of her whelp's namings except Lena's because of how things were between Greg and I, and then my house arrest.

Greg prompted me to message Denis, too, and let him know so he'd be included. The brief message contained the date and time, and what we planned on naming the twins, a polite salutation, and that was it.

Regardless, Denis never replied. Whether he and Emory had planned on having offspring was a mystery. My guess was no, since they'd been together for several centuries. But who knows? Things change. I hadn't planned on it either, and here I was with a partner and twins. Life was strange like that.

"Refreshments are ready in the sitting room off the garden when the ceremony's completed," Edward offered.

"You'll join us for the ceremony, won't you, Edward? It would be my honor to have you there."

Edward gave me a slight smile, then nodded. "Of course." He'd been part of my household for as long as I'd been in the United States. I never asked what he was, and over the years, he's never asked for anything more than to run my household and watch over my affairs while I traveled. I'd taken for granted that he'd been with me all this time and was a constant point of stability for me. He handled my family with more grace and patience than anyone I knew. That alone made him family to me, regardless of if he thought he was or not. Not that I could ever convince him to act like it, or retire. He always maintained his distance until Greg came into my life. It warmed my heart that he allowed himself to be included in this moment, too.

Greg and I had dressed up in cream color button downs with green slacks so dark they were nearly black in some light. I went out to the garden area via the rear access to the front foyer. Edward followed me, and I met Greg, who was standing with our parents watching the twins being passed from one adult to the next.

"Their so big already," Jennifer commented as she held Snow pea and played with his hands. The webbing between his fingers glittered in the light, as did his golden eyes.

"Dragons do a lot of growing in their eggs," my father, Ransford, said. "By this time next year, they'll resemble a human of three to five years."

"It's pretty amazing. We were watching them fly, or I guess glide, around Xavior's den. Even at this age, they're very graceful with their movements." Philip, Greg's father, sounded amazed and delighted at the same time.

Corley, my mother, had Sweet pea. She was making bird noises to my daughter, and Sweet pea was mimicking them.

The entire scene filled my heart in a way I never thought possible. When Faith and Trevor walked into the garden area with Lena in Trevor's arms, Faith looked slightly flustered. "Sorry, Lena needed a potty break."

I walked over to my sister and her family and gave her a hug first, then Trevor. They both gave me odd looks while Lena giggled until I let go of her father and gave her a kiss on the forehead. "You ready to name your cousins?" She nodded. I couldn't believe she was only two years old, but like my father said, dragons grow fast their first few years.

Before I walked away, I took my sister's hand. "I'm glad you and Trevor are here."

"Us too." She glanced at Trevor, then looked at me, giving my hand a squeeze.

As I moved back toward the main group, I gave Greg a look, silently asking if he was ready. He nodded and reached for the nearest whelp, which happened to be Sweet pea. I went to Jennifer and took Snow pea from her.

Jordan and Catherine followed us to the little stand of lavender oil that was set up for the ceremony. Jordan picked it up first and stood next to me, and Catherine stood next to Greg. The crowd made a general semi-circle around us and quieted as soon as Greg spoke.

"Xavior and I want you to know how delighted we are that you have joined us today. While we had talked of having a family, I don't think either of us actually thought it would happen. Then when it did, we certainly hadn't planned for twins." There were a few chuckles. "However, now that we're here, we wouldn't have it any other way." Greg motioned for me to continue.

"Jordan. Catherine. We're humbled that you both agreed to be the whelp's godparents. We couldn't ask for better people or better friends to help us today," I said.

With that, Jordan held out the dish of oil for me to dip my fingers into. Back in the day, they used blood for the ceremony, but that had gone out of mode more than a century ago. Lavender smelled better anyway. I swiped my fingers across Snow pea's forehead.

"As blood of my blood, I give you the name Everett Jackson Brantley Lyndon."

Everett smiled, and everyone clapped. Fun fact, whelps didn't make their own pheromones until they went through puberty in their late teens to early twenties. So there was no way to scent whether a whelp was actually happy. So the smile on his face meant either he was, or he had gas.

Greg and I had tried the names on the twins before the ceremony, and they responded favorably beforehand, so we hoped they'd do the same here.

Jordan handed the lavender oil to Catherine, and she held it up for Greg. He dipped his fingers in the oil and painted Sweet pea's forehead with it.

"As blood of my blood, I give you the name Sasha Laurel Brantley Lyndon."

The twin's first names came from my side of the family. Everett and Sasha were my grandparent's names from my father's family. Jackson and Laurel were Greg's grandparents. He talked about Grandpa Jack sometimes, but all I ever heard from him about Laurel was that she was gone before he was born. He asked his father once and received the same response.

Sasha smiled, and everyone clapped again. "Now, if everyone would like to join us for refreshments, we'll have them in the sitting room off the garden," Greg said.

"Follow me if you would, please," Edward said as he directed the small crowd to the sitting room, where the doors were open for the light breeze and smells of the garden.

We stood there for a moment with the twins and looked at each other. "Hey there, Dad," Greg said with a grin.

"Hey yourself, Papa," I responded, then chuckled.

"That sounds so weird. You should be Papa. I'm the younger parent."

"Oh, age before beauty, huh?"

"Not necessarily." Greg stepped closer. "I'm not the one with stunning emerald eyes."

"You know, the reason our whelps have golden eyes is probably because of your brown ones."

"Is it?" Greg asked, amused.

I nodded, though I wasn't sure if that was true. He leaned over and pressed his lips to mine. The twins giggled as they watched. "Come on, our family is waiting for us," he said. I took his hand, and we walked to the sitting room, where everyone clapped again and then patiently waited for their turn with our whelps.

BROTHER OF MINE

XAVIOR

With several dragons, a mage, and a fae in the house, Greg and I thought it might be time to try letting the whelps outside. We knew they had climbing skills and gliding. The thing we were worried about the most was that they would end up stuck somewhere and we wouldn't be able to get to them. With an estate full of trees and the building itself having nooks and crannies to disappear into, it was enough to keep one up at night. But we couldn't keep them inside forever.

So, in an effort to keep them to one area, we started with the patio near the shallow wading pool and water features on the left side of the estate. We organized a whole cookout with everyone's favorites, and let the whelps play in the small water-falls and splash pads artfully surrounded by a moss garden and shade trees.

Greg and Edward were working with the grill, and I made myself responsible for seeing to everyone's drinks. We had a canopy set up over a long table to keep everyone shaded and cool while we were outside.

The whelps had all shifted and were playing tag in the grass. I'd never been more glad that they were all too small to have any fire breath. The dry season was almost here. An errant fire would get out of control quickly.

"Your place here is pretty nice. We should come visit more often," Faith said as she came up to the drink station and poured herself another lemonade while I was making Jennifer a mojito.

"I'd like that. Plus, Greg and I wouldn't have to be here for you to visit. Or your family." I muddled the mint and sugar, then added some rum and mixed it up some more.

"Already planning my next break?"

I shook my head. "Maybe a stop, not the whole thing. You helped me a lot when I was struggling with things and you had your own problems. I'd like to return the favor."

"You've been hanging out with fae too long." We both laughed. "Seriously, I appreciate the offer. It would be nice to have my family together somewhere other than our little hamlet outside of London." That hamlet was fifty acres of woods, fields and a house build in a similar style to our parent's manor.

"There's enough space here for everyone, and their families, too. Maybe we should do a reunion here? Though I have no idea when Denis plans on coming back. Maybe a reunion would be enough to guilt him into a visit," I said.

Faith chuckled. "Don't count on it. He and Emory have always been private, almost to the point of isolation. The only reason we saw anything of him before he left for the Moon was because Emory was already at Moonbase twenty-three and he was waiting for clearance."

"You have a point. I've never met Emory, I only ever hear about them and how tall they are, and whatnot. Denis never talks about Emory either."

She turned around to look at the whelps playing nearby. "As much as he would give you a hard time about your ex, he didn't enjoy shoving his relationship in your face, either."

"Well, maybe not, but Greg asked me to send him a naming ceremony invite and we've heard nothing from him."

My sister gave me a look, and I knew what she was going to say. "He's your brother, Xavior. I know you're not best friends or anything, but Greg's right. I have never understood the animosity between the two of you. You're twins, but it's like you're from two different planets."

"Maybe he finally returned to his." My tone was barely civil. Denis not responding to our invitation might have upset me more than I realized.

"Xavior!" Faith practically growled at me.

I held up my hands in surrender. I reminded myself that I wouldn't be here if it wasn't for him. Greg's ring had saved me twice. Though every question or inquiry I had made about it went unanswered or, 'I'm busy and I'll get back to you later about it, brother.'

"I'm sorry, I shouldn't have said that. I love him. He's my brother, but he definitely makes it hard to care about him sometimes."

Just as I was finishing Jennifer's mojito when I noticed all the adults' heads turn, and a few stood, as one of the staff escorted two people in uniform toward our group. Greg and I looked at each other and Faith caught our glance, too. Thankfully, Trevor was ahead of all three of us and walked over to the whelps and shifted. He lost the clothing he had on, but that was easily replaceable. No one would even think to bother the whelps while they were being guarded by a large obsidian dragon.

As the staff member and the visitors stopped short of coming any closer to the group because of the very large dragon in the yard, I walked out from behind the drink station, handed Jennifer her drink, then walked around the wading pool to meet Terri, my staff member, and our new arrivals.

"I'm sorry, Xavior. I said you were with family, and they said it concerned your brother, so I thought it best to bring them along."

Their uniforms were from the United Science & Exploration Association, or USEA for short. They organized projects like preserving natural habitats across Earth, deploying medical teams to natural disasters, exploring and protecting the oceans, and they were in charge of the moonbases that were the main staging grounds for operations out to Mars and Jupiter's moons, eventually.

"It's alright Terri." I stepped in front of my staff member. I knew they wouldn't have let them on the grounds, let alone led them to my family if they weren't legit, but my instincts were on high alert with whelps nearby. "Hi, can I help you?"

The two uniforms looked at each other, then one reached out their hand. "Good Afternoon, we're from USEA. I'm Lieutenant Elizabeth Dawson, and this is Captain Tig Harrison," Dawson said. The lieutenant was a Black woman approximately the same age as Greg from Ghana according to her insignia, while the captain was a little older, and from one of the Six Nations along the East Coast based on the insignia he wore, along with other ribbons and metals near his name tag.

"What's this about?" I asked. "Terri said it was something concerning my brother?"

"Xavior Brantley, we're sorry to inform you that there's been an accident at Moonbase twenty-three, and your sibling has suffered what we believe might be a fatal injury," Harrison said.

At that exact moment, I didn't know what to say. I had to swallow a few times to even utter a syllable. Then Greg was next to me, his hand in mine. I looked for the whelps, and noticed Trevor was moving them toward the trees, upwind. Either he knew something was wrong or he was preemptively saving the whelps from being distressed, because I couldn't imagine my pheromones giving off anything happy right then.

"I'm Xavior's partner, Greg Lyndon." Greg shook their hands. "What's happened?"

Harrison repeated himself, and I closed my eyes. The story was the same until Harrison revealed an additional detail. "The reason we've come personally is that Denis Brantley's partner, Emory, indicated that a person named Gregor Lyndon could help. If that's you, sir."

"Help how?" Greg glanced at me and I was just as confused. If Denis was dead, then there was nothing either of us could do.

Dawson spoke up after a nod from Harrison. "I've reviewed footage and have reports from witnesses. We believe Mr. Brantley is slowly executing a phoenix cycle, but because of the Luna's minimal atmosphere, he can't complete it. He's radiating a small amount of heat, which might be enough to keep his cells alive, for now.

"Emory indicated you might posses an ability that could either allow him to complete his cycle or reverse it," Dawson said.

"Oh." Greg's reply was basically what I was thinking. It could work, based on our own experiences, but there were still studies being done about magic performed away from Earth. There was no way to predict what would happen on the moon.

Faith walked up behind us and touched my shoulder. I turned to toward her. "It's about Denis."

"We should tell the family. Trevor is still in protection mode." She nodded in his direction.

Terri stepped up then. "Maybe I could be of some assistance?"

"That would be extremely helpful, Terri. Could you take Trevor a towel? They should shift when he does and then help him move them into my den, please."

Greg fidgeted a little, knowing someone else was taking care of the twins, but Faith nodded to let me know Trevor understood. We walked over to where our parents were waiting and explained what had happened to Denis.

OVERLOAD

GREGOR

After we hashed and rehashed all the details, I excused myself to check on the twins. Xavior stayed while I made a beeline for our den. Once inside, I saw Terri and Trevor entertaining the whelps with a colorful movie on the holo screen.

I reached out and touched Trevor on his shoulder to gain his attention. "Looks like things are quiet here." I gave him a half smile, and he got up and we walked a few steps away.

"It must be bad for you to smell so anxious," Trevor said.

"It's about Denis. There was an accident and they think I might be able to rescue him." That was the short version of the conversation they were having outside.

Trevor crossed his muscular arms and looked at me. "Do you think you can?"

I shrugged. "I don't know that I have a choice. It's Xavior's brother, and apparently he's one of USEA's top scientists. They want to rescue him if it's possible and his partner, Emory, gave them the idea that it might be."

"Rough." He put a hand on my shoulder and gave it a sympathetic squeeze. His amber-gold eyes glowed slightly in the dim light. In his dragon form, they were the same as the three whelps glued to the holo movie. "If you're good here for a few, I'm going to grab some clothes right quick."

"Sure." Trevor headed out of the den with a jog-walk while holding onto his towel, his long locs gracefully swaying across his broad back.

While Trevor went to get dressed, I joined the whelps and thanked Terri for their help with the guests and the whelps. As they left, they promised to send snacks and at that moment, I couldn't be more thankful for everyone Xavior employed. They were quickly becoming invaluable in helping us manage our family and everything that entailed.

When Trevor returned, he and I spent the rest of the afternoon with the whelps, sharing snacks and laughing at cartoon characters. Focusing on keeping our worries about Denis at bay for a little while longer.

Officially, I might have earned the worse parent ever award. I'd fallen asleep until Xavior showed up and tapped my arm. I looked up to see Trevor wave at me with a tired Lena draped over his shoulder, and rotated my head further to see our whelps resting in the trees. The holo was still going, but at a fourth of the original volume.

"You okay?" Xavior asked as I sat up. I sensed conflict or, to be more precise, he was conflicted, but over what I wasn't sure, though I had a good idea.

I rubbed at my face and glanced around, then looked at him. The advantage of our connection was that while I might not say how I felt, he knew. Which meant we could move past all the social niceties of the white lies couples told each other when they didn't want to burden their partner. I shook my head.

Xavior nodded. "We should talk." I nodded at that, agreeing.

"They haven't eaten dinner, though we had a lot of snacks." I pointed up. "Could someone watch them for a bit?"

"I'll ask the group chat." Xavior pulled out his phone and messaged our families. Ransford and Corley showed up ten minutes later.

"We'll take them to dinner with us when it's ready. Don't worry," Corley said. Her fiery complexion looked odd in the den's light. As if she was a source of illumination all on her own. I hadn't spent a lot of time around Xavior's mother, or phoenixes, so it's possible that it was a trait of her species.

As Xavior and I walked out of the den into the backyard, I started our conversation by asking about his mother. "Is it me, or does your mother glow? I don't mean that as a figure of speech, either." I smiled as Xavior chuckled.

"No, your senses aren't tricking you. She glows. The brighter she is, the closer she is to a phoenix cycle. At the end, it's like trying to stare at the sun, but that's only minutes before she dies."

"Shit, that must be terrifying." I was very glad Xavior didn't have that kind of cycle. I couldn't imagine explaining that to our twins. If he even had a phoenix cycle. We didn't know whether the one time he died was it, but neither of us wanted to find out.

"Yeah." He sighed. "It helps to know that she comes back from it. She has another fifty years or so before it happens again." He offered his hand to me and I slipped mine into it, entwining our fingers and giving his hand a squeeze. Before long, we found ourselves on the walking path through the back of the estate.

The light had faded as we walked. Xavior could see fine, which I knew, so I trusted him to guide us. The companionable silence was on purpose. He was waiting for me to talk.

"As much as I want to help Denis, leaving you or the whelps is out of the question. I can't do it. I don't want to do it. Even if I'm one of Denis's best options to survive, the damage it could cause our family is too great. I can't take the risk, Xavior. We can't."

Whelps form parent and family bonds in the first five years of their lives. Those bonds set who they can trust, and who they would rely on later in life. If I left, I'd be putting all of that in jeopardy. Along with possibly killing Xavior and myself from the effects of withdraw via our own connection.

"What if I told you there was a way to save Denis and not kill the rest of us in the process?"

"If the answer isn't the USEA flying us all to the moon, then I'm not sure I want to hear it. Even then, I'd have serious reservations."

Xavior squeezed my hand. "That's one possibility, but the bases don't allow offspring to travel with their parents until they are two years or more to avoid major problems with their development."

"We wait that long, and Denis might not make it."

"Right."

"I take it your process involves something else?"

"Jordan has. . ." I cut Xavior off.

"Are we always going to owe him favors? Will he ride to our rescue every time something goes slightly off? I had to talk to my parents about their private matters because he did something for us. What will he ask for next time? One of our future offspring?"

Xavior had slowed, but with my last quip, he stopped, which made me stop too. "Don't joke about that." His voice was low, and if I didn't know better, it sounded threatening.

"About what?"

"Fae used to take whelps. It was a very long time ago, but they would take them and train them for their own armies, then use our offspring against us. It's one reason there are very tenuous relationships between dragons and fae. Both species have very long memories."

I pulled Xavior toward me and wrapped him in my arms. "I didn't know that, and I don't think Jordan would actually do that to us."

"When the twins shifted, and Catherine was patching you up, I might have accused him of it in a moment of panic."

"Xavior." I pulled away a little. "You really thought he would be capable of that?"

"No, never, not really. But like I said, we have long memories and all the worries about the twins shifting, and you being hurt, and what we owed for the glamour I thought the worst." Xavior made a soft noise that sounded like a sob and clung to me. "I thought the worst of him, Greg. My oldest friend. How could I have wronged him like that?"

"Oh, Xav." I held him tighter and kissed his forehead. "It was stress, that's all."

"Jordan said something similar, but he could have taken it wrong, left, and I wouldn't have been able to fix it."

"This isn't about Jordan, is it?" I made a guess, because really, I couldn't imagine Jordan abandoning his best friend.

"No one wants to ask you to do this except the USEA. But my parents and Faith would be devastated if you didn't try."

"What about you?"

"All I keep thinking is, Denis had his career and his relationship much longer than I have. We literally just met and had twins. Then he gets himself stuck in mid-regeneration on the Moon? It's as if my brother takes a special interest in fucking over the only thing I've ever done right in my life."

"Xavior," I chuckled. "I'm sure that's not true. He might be somewhat calculating, according to you, but I seriously doubt he planned the accident."

"I know, I know. Which makes me a horrible sibling. He doesn't deserve this. And I never had a chance to talk with him about everything else that happened. He never knew the names of our whelps. He won't ever meet them if you don't go, but if you do, I might lose you both, which I don't even want to contemplate."

The sigh slipped from my mouth before I could stop it. In the short time we've known each other, I knew Xavior's relationship with his brother was a tenuous thing. This dilemma, forced to choose between his brother and me, would eat Xavior alive, even if it took fifty years. He might be more concerned about me now, but in fifty years? Who's to say he wouldn't blame me for his brother's death and their unfinished business? I couldn't have that on my soul or condemn someone to a slow death if there was actually a way to make this work. "Tell me Jordan's plan."

LET SLEEPING DRAGONS LIE

XAVIOR

"No. No fucking way. Absolutely not."

In hindsight, I should have predicted that reaction, but it seemed like a plausible solution. Jordan would use magic to put me and the whelps in a dragon's sleep inside my den. It was old magic, but Jordan was confident he could do it with Catherine's help. Greg would revive Denis, then have Denis open his side of the den to wake us up. Dragons could sleep for up to six months without food and water. It was like hibernation, but it would be magically induced.

"What if something happens to me? What then?"

"Jordan could wake us up."

"Not if he can't get into your den because you're asleep and the doorways fade. It's the same reason we can't get through to Denis via his den, because he's in a phoenix cycle, and we don't know how stable it is, or where it's at."

Greg was listing off points I knew, but didn't say out loud. "And if I can't rescue Denis, and we can't get in to your den because the doorways are gone, what about that? Not to mention withdraw. We haven't even tested how long we can go without each other's pheromones. The last time was barely a day." I had made Jordan and Catherine charms to enter my den, which should hopefully work even if I was inside asleep. Jordan trusted his magic. I did too. I could see and sense that Greg had some serious reservations about it.

"It's the option that makes the most sense." Because what it meant was that if I lost both my brother and Greg, I wouldn't have to face it, and our children wouldn't live without their parents.

"It's a fucking horrible idea. I'd rather you resent me in fifty years for not saving your brother. You'd be alive and so would the whelps."

Always count on Greg to drill right down to the root of things. Our connection wasn't always an advantage, like right now. No matter how confident I was about the idea, he could sense the subtext.

He paced along the walkway in our backyard. The stars were out, and the moon was bright even with it only being half full. I reached out and touched his arm to stop him. He turned to look at me. "And so would you."

"Yes. We could be safe and not take a horrible risk," he sighed, reaching for my hand and holding it in his.

It was a horrible risk, because the only other answer was to send both Greg and I to the moon and have our families look after the whelps for several weeks. They wouldn't suffer withdraw exactly, though it was possible they could develop issues from the separation.

"If everyone's here, at the estate, would that be enough? Would that keep them safe and healthy?" Greg wondered out loud.

"We can ask Catherine. She's researching our family medical history and her mage archives. Maybe she can come up with something."

We held each other, upset and overwhelmed. "If she doesn't think it's safe, we're not going. I don't care what the USEA says, or anyone else. I'm not putting the twins at risk for your brother.

Emory can hate me. I can live with that. I can even live with you being upset with me, but I won't risk the whelps," Greg said.

"Okay." There wasn't anything else to say. I agreed with him. In some part of my heart, I was already grieving for my brother. Maybe not the one I currently knew, but the young whelp I grew up with before he changed and we became so distant.

We stood there for a little longer, holding each other, then quietly headed back to the house. We found everyone in the sitting room where we'd had refreshments after the naming ceremony. Only a few days ago, it had been a place of joy and celebration. At the moment, it seemed as if we were all preparing for a funeral service.

Everyone stayed quiet, even though we caused a stir when we entered the room. Lena, Everett, and Sasha were all asleep on the floor together. Bottles of wine were open, and someone had brought snacks. They attempted dinner, but Everett and Sasha weren't having it without us.

"What did you decide?" Jordan asked. Everyone was thinking about it. They all glanced at him, then at us.

"Xavior and I will go if Catherine can figure out how much risk our absence would cause the twins. And if you'll allow us to host you all here at the estate, to help." We hadn't decided who would tell our family and friends what we were planning. After all this time, I still couldn't stand to disappoint my parents. They loved Denis. Of their three whelps, I was the fuck-up. Greg rescued me again. Playing the fairytale knight, though in this instance, it wasn't much of a fairytale any more.

No one spoke, so Greg continued. "We know we're asking you to uproot yourselves for a few months, regardless of whether everything works out." Greg glanced around. "If we can't reduce any risk to Sasha and Everett while we're gone, we won't go. Xavior and I won't risk their future. We hope you understand." He looked at my parents. I looked at the floor. I couldn't watch their one hope hang in the balance based on research from our family physician.

To my surprise, my father stood and approached us. "Xavior." I looked up. "Gregor." He touched the side of our faces, as if he was trying to memorize them for his next art piece. "If it was a choice between the twins and Denis, I would not regret your choice. I don't think Denis would either. He knew the risks when he went there. Life is full of risks. While my whelps might have more chances than most dragons, not one of you is more important than the others."

His hands slipped down our shoulders and took up our hands in his. He squeezed them. "But know that if you go. . ." He looked Greg and me in the eyes, one after the other. "Corley and I will stay here to do everything we can to help your whelps. We give you our word."

He drew us into a hug, and we held onto him. My father was slightly taller than Greg. At times, he seems so imposing to me, but right now, he seemed like a man resolved to do what he could for his family, whatever that might be. When he let go, Greg and I found my mother right behind him, following suit. That brought us to tears and then everyone else came in for a hug, too. The whiff I got from the room was a mixture of hope and fear. Everyone wanted Greg to succeed in rescuing Denis, and we hoped we weren't damaging two very young lives in the process.

THE PLAN

XAVIOR

"USEA says the routine quarantine for travel takes three days, but we also have two weeks of mandatory training that all passengers need to go through before they are cleared for space flight. The only positive thing about that is that if we ever want to go back to Luna someday, we won't have to go through the training again," I said.

"Ha, Ha. That's exactly what I'm going to be thinking about as they spin us in three hundred sixty degree circles, and throw us in a pool to show us how to move around in zero gravity." Greg sighed as he read over the intake instructions we'd had from the USEA.

The agency had agreed for both of us to go, for medical reasons. Based on previous records, they knew that having us apart for too long would cause problems. They needed Greg to be as fit as possible for this, so it was only logical that I kept him from having withdraws. Though it was a near thing. I was still, technically, post oviparous, and they had no data in their agency on dragons that had laid an egg, then went to space shortly after. Catherine came through again and cleared me herself based on pre-pregnancy records and post-oviparous comparisons that showed I hadn't moved much from the baseline, other than trace pregnancy hormones and my weight, which I was happy with, and so was Greg.

She also came up with a clever way to maintain our scent in the den for the twins. A timed pheromone mist will be released in the trees, and pillows with our names on them will carry our pheromones. My worry was that we'd come back and the twins would think their parents were pillows and not individuals. Though Catherine promised that wouldn't be the case.

"It's three weeks then, two for training and quarantine, three days for travel, two days to figure out how to save Denis, then we have two days to revive him so we can access his side of the den to come home to be with the whelps," I offered. Three weeks wasn't so bad.

"Did Denis ever mention whether his den worked on the moon?"

"No, but it's not like we talked, either. If it doesn't, it's five weeks at best and Catherine says she and Jordan can help everyone keep things going for six weeks before the twins might have problems."

Missing developmental milestones was not a good thing for dragons. Instincts, smells, and social queues were developed in the early months and years. Dragons who lose their parents early never really recover from that. Both of us going on this rescue mission was an enormous risk, but it was the only one we could see working to avoid doing something really drastic.

"Did you show Jordan and Catherine where the connection was in your den?"

I nodded. "We should be able to knock from Denis's side of things. Jordan and Catherine can remove the barrier. If not, they can have my family help them."

The twins were sleeping in their cribs. I found it endearing that Everett nearly always slept as a dragon while Sasha slept as a biped. Whelps were interesting like that. I'd have to remember to ask Faith about interesting quirks her whelps had. It reminded me there was one more thing to take care of before we left.

I grabbed a tablet from the desk in our bedroom. It used to be my suite, but it was ours now. Whether we were legally together, I needed to make sure that no one outside of my family could make a claim on my estate ever again. I brought the tablet to Greg, and he set down the one with our instructions. "What's this?"

"I had Uncle Renard draw up legal documents that make you and the whelps the sole heirs to my holdings, properties, and my den. In the event that something happens to all of us, it reverts to your parents, Faith and her family, and my parents." I sat next to him as I continued to hold out the tablet."I'd like you to sign them before we leave."

Greg looked at me. "Are you sure? I'd be alright if everything went to the whelps. The likelihood of me outliving you is. . ."

"I don't care what the statistics are, I want us protected from the Coopers or anyone else. I've also added a provision that if something happens to us, Jordan and Catherine are to act as guardians for the twins until they reach fifty."

"Is your family alright with this?" He took the tablet from me as if it might explode.

"Greg, if you save Denis, my family would give you anything you want. He's their beloved son, after all."

The glare on Greg's face matched his scent. "Would you cut that shit out? Maybe your parents haven't always seen eye-to-eye with you, but they are here, Xav, helping us with all of this. Offering to disrupt their lives to help the twins. Nothing I've seen the whole time I've been around them makes me think they love you any less than Denis."

Was this going to be our first actual fight? His eyes widened as he sensed my anger. I stood and saw a look of surprise and subtle fear on his face. If he wanted to paint me as the asshole here, then fine, I'd give him one.

I kept my voice low, and I got in Greg's face, gesturing at my frustration. "You didn't live with them for half your life or have them disapprove of your first serious relationship, only to prove them right, then hear repeatedly how Denis is achieving this, and Denis has improved that, and Denis is speaking in Geneva and he's nominated for an international award." I paced, trying to cool my anger. It didn't help. I gestured at the tablet Greg had set aside. "For fuck's sake, he's one of the USEA's best scientists and their people are literally willing to tear our family apart to save his fucking ass, so don't you dare tell me he's not the favored one. He's done everything my parents have ever wanted while I struggled just to find my way."

He stood and reached for me, touching my arms. I crossed over my chest and moved away while he followed. I kept moving to get away from him until we were outside the suite and Greg had gently closed the double doors behind us.

"Xavior, I'm sorry." I had my back to him, unwilling to see the look of disappointment on his face. I don't lose my temper that often. The last person I wanted to be upset with was Greg. "I should have asked why you said what you did instead of admonishing you for it."

"Don't." He moved closer and caressed my shoulders.

"Don't?" he said with a curious voice. He smelled like regret and a sour note of insecurity. Greg was rarely either of those things and I knew that was my fault, too.

The question drew some of the venom out of my words. "Don't apologize. And stop trying to de-escalate. I'm fucking sick of constantly being upset or angry and feeling like I should hold it all in because we're around our families or the twins."

"Or me?" I didn't answer. As the silence went on, his left hand went from caressing my shoulder to wrapping itself around the front of my neck. He pulled me back toward him and some of the tension went out of my body, but not the anger I felt. His insecurity was gone, replaced with determination, apparently unwilling to let me continue in my current state.

"What do you need?" he asked.

"I don't know." I dropped my arms and closed my fists, determined to be difficult.

He chuckled. "That lie was so big I felt it in my throat. Let's try this again." His hand tightened, but not enough to make it hard to breathe or talk. "What do you need?"

"I need to let go of this anger I feel toward Denis and my family." Greg kissed my temple, but kept his hand tight.

"That's a good start. What else?" Greg's voice was low, seductive, caressing a part of my brain that enjoyed his dominate side.

"I feel trapped. . . by everything. Like nothing is my own anymore." His thumb caressed the pulse at my neck as his breath ghosted over my right ear. The sound of his voice and his breath across my skin made me shiver. I could easily break his hold, a part of me wanting to fight him. Yet another part wanted to hand over control, if only to rid myself of all the mounting frustrations I felt.

"Close your eyes," he whispered. I did so and waited. Our hearts beat together, the scent of him threatened to soothe me and I wouldn't have it. Anger welled up, and I grit my teeth, prepared to knock his hand away. I must have tried to move at least, because he tightened his hand to the point I gasped. It was a not-so-subtle reminder that Greg had trained for most of his life to encounter and handle dragons. He had been a public safety officer longer than me, too. My brain was swimming with the rush of his pheromones, changing from calm control to something darker and more dominate, eliciting fear and excitement from both of us.

"You have two options. You can come back into our room, and I can fuck your brains out in the bathroom while we take a shower. Or you leave the house right now, fly, then later when you come back and clean up, you can fuck me."

My brain had liked the two options he presented, but I wanted to prove him wrong. "Don't tell—" He pressed his thumb on my pulse, stopping my words and making me feel dizzy, not only from a lack of air, but his absolute control of the situation.

"I love you, but fighting me wasn't an option. You haven't flown in a while and you're angry at nearly everyone. Also, we haven't had a proper fuck in some time." He nipped my ear. I felt myself respond, dick hardening in anticipation. "Now, you ignore your choices, but I think you'd feel better if you didn't. You've been avoiding your dragon nature for some time. It's not good for you, or the twins." Or him either, but he was willing to put himself in the way of my anger and offer another path, or two.

The realization sparked more anger. I reached up and touched his hand. Acknowledging that I had myself mostly under control, he let go of me. I could still feel the imprint of his hand along my neck, along with the soothing pressure and the command in his voice that had me torn between my choices. Given the amount of anger I was holding onto, I needed to clear my head. Only flying did that.

His eyes were on me as I undid my robe and dropped it on the floor in front of him. I walked away with my back to him, naked, down the right side of the dual staircase that led to the foyer entry. Out of the corner of my eye, I caught him bending down to pick up my robe as I reached the bottom of the steps. My feet carried me to the door, then outside, where I shifted and used the driveway to take off.

Fuck, he was right. The minute the wind was in my snout, with the smells of the countryside, it eased something that was wound up tight. While Greg and I had been together during the entire process with the twins, and a few days with each other, I hadn't taken time for myself.

This disaster with Denis possibly meant that I wouldn't be able to shift again for weeks, or fly, or enjoy the one thing that made me what I was. How had I let myself go this long without flying? My family had flown while they were here. My parents had even watched Lena several times so Trevor and Faith could have a morning or an evening flight together.

Somehow I'd grounded myself amid everything and Greg had realized it, but hadn't pushed. He knew he couldn't until I was ready. The regret welled up as I remembered yelling at him and I flew higher to catch another thermal. Our connection was strong, and from high in the clouds, his caring and concern were here with me. None of this was easy, and he understood me better than I gave him credit for sometimes.

It was nearly dawn before I came home. I landed in the backyard, shifted, then walked up the outside steps to the patio that overlooked the garden attached to our suite.

A light coating of dust and muck covered me. It happens while flying, unless you fly in the rain. I took a moment to center myself before I went inside. The sun slid above the horizon as I opened the patio door.

Greg was asleep in our bed with the whelps tucked in with him. They must have woken up while I was gone. One was cuddled to his chest, head resting on Greg's shoulder, and the other was tucked in at the back of his knees with a green scaled head resting on Greg's thigh. At the rate they were growing, they'd both need their own rooms in a few months.

My phone was on the desk where I left it. Quietly, I moved to retrieve it to snap a picture and then share it with our families. The caption was "Daddy and the whelps."

Sasha cracked open one eye and looked at me. I held up my hand, and she relaxed again, clearly not ready to wake up. Everett was the early riser, but if Greg had fed and cleaned them up, they probably wouldn't wake again for a little while longer. We'd have to wait until someone else in the house was up to take the whelps. But as soon as they were, Greg's ass was mine, literally.

THE EXECUTION

GREGOR

My deep sleep became an instant panic. I shot up from the bed, throwing the duvet off when I realized the whelps were gone.

"Sasha? Everett?"

Xavior was alright, that much I knew through our connection. Last night when he was flying, I sensed a riot of emotions from him that kept me awake until cleared his mind. Flying always did that for him, whether he admitted it or not. That was the advantage of our connection. Then the twins woke up, and after feeding and cleaning up messes, we all crashed again, waiting for Xav to come home.

Sleeping with two small whelps quickly gaining mass, teeth, feathers, and claws was no small feat for someone with soft parts to protect. Their head ridges only had nubs at the top when they hatched, but were quickly growing like the rest of them. Being nudged by one wasn't pleasant when they became too excited. They also had padding on their feet that let them move silently. If they had left our suite, they could be anywhere.

No answer meant either they were playing in something they shouldn't or they were gone. How was it that this kept happening to me? I snatched my phone from the nightstand and pulled up the family group chat.

Once open, I saw images of the twins chasing each other outside, running around with Lena, who was twice their size as a dragon. The post was from Faith, and only five minutes old. It went a long way toward letting my heart beat normalize. I gave the post a heart and flopped back on the bed, dropping my phone next to me.

My nose picked up tantalizing hints of pancakes and bacon when the bedroom door opened, and Xavior came through with a tray laden with food. My stomach rumbled in response as he placed the tray on the small dining table.

"Hey," he whispered as I gravitated to his side and leaned in to give him a kiss. He had showered already and dressed in his usual T-shirt and shorts, but his feet were bare.

"Hey," I responded, and kissed him again. "Feel better?"

He nodded, then pointed at a chair, wordlessly inviting me to sit with him. I second I reached for a piece of bacon, he gently slapped my hand. The shock of it sent my heart back into a gallop as I watched him pick up a piece of bacon. He held it between his fingers, silently offering it to me.

We'd never played this game before. I opened my mouth to ask a question, and Xav held up a finger. I closed it. He glanced at the bacon, then at me, and moved it closer to my face. I took the subtle hint and leaned forward, keeping eye contact, while I bit a piece off of what he offered. A jolt of desire and sheer satisfaction sang through our connection. Switching things up wasn't new, but him feeding me like this wasn't something we'd done before.

I chewed, and he offered another bite and wondered how far I could push things as I opened my mouth and took the rest of the piece from his fingers, then licked at the grease. It wasn't exactly elegant, but Xavior's eyes flashed with the deep emerald-green of his dragon.

He gently pulled his fingers from my lips as my tongue swiped one more taste. Then he used his thumb to trace my lips. I held his gaze as he teased. When I tried to talk again, he put a finger over my lips and shook his head. The connection was full of warmth, affection, and a deep longing. Those emotions represented the foundation of what we understood was our love for each other.

Xavior had explained why love never came through our connection as one emotion. Love wasn't a static thing in a connection. It morphed based on the connection or connections, circumstances, and the passing of time. Whatever represented love for Xav and me now wouldn't be the same next week, or maybe even next year.

I chewed as a comfortable silence settled around our breakfast while Xavior fed me bite after bite. Alternating between a fork and his fingers, feeding himself in between the bites he'd offer me. Breakfast was fairly lavish for the two of us, comprising bacon, pancakes, eggs, fruit, and a few pieces of Brie. There were a few berries left on the plate when I waved him off.

As he ate the last few berries, we watched each other, tracking each other's movements, intent on what the other did next as our lust and desire mixed with everything else that flowed through our connection. A wipe of fingers on a napkin, the licking of lips, the subtle flare of nostrils. Each moment we studied the other added to the delicious tension between us.

Xavior offered his hand. The tension ebbed slightly as I took his hand and let him lead me toward the bathroom.

He deposited me on the edge of the bathtub while he stripped down to nothing making my hands itch with anticipation and the need to touch him. Xavior came to me, only wearing a smile on his face as he held out his hands. I took them and stood. He slid his hands up my arms and then down my sides until he reached the top of my boxers. A look of permission was all he need to ease them off my hips, then past my thighs until they hit the floor. He stood, gave me an appreciative once over, then offered his hand again. I teased him by put my fingers in his palm, feigning a daintiness I did not have. He grasped them gently, then led me into the massive shower was recently upgraded with a voice system, like the one from the resort.

"Shower, rain sequence."

The lukewarm water cascaded down. I watched as his hair changed from a red-brown to a deeper red as the water soaked it, then rippled over the muscles in his arms as they flexed while he reached for a bottle of lube we kept on the shelf and slicked himself up. I wiped my hands through my wet hair while I watched him. The habitual motion triggered a shift from admiration to one that sent a small spike of fear through me. An inhuman growl escaped his lips as his eyes shifted from human-irises to a dragon's.

Xavior stepped closer, and I fought my instinct to step back. He was playing with me. Sometimes we played a little game of hunter and hunted. My heart beat ticked up as I stood waiting for him to make a move. My pulse was in my throat before I gave in, glancing away. I lost my breath as he pushed me hard against the shower wall.

The polished marble stones felt cool against my back as his lips crashed against mine. His hands grabbed my hips, then my thighs as he lifted me with little effort, and I bent to his will. This was going to hurt, and I didn't care, because I wanted my dragon just as fiercely as he wanted me.

Each nudge of his cock against my hole pressed it open further. I willed my body to relax, but that only eased the burn somewhat. Once the head of his dick was inside me, he stopped for a moment to look into my eyes. Fear and need were in his gaze, which mirrored what I felt from him. I tried to convey my passion, longing, and most of all, my forgiveness as I wove my fingers into his hair, pulling at it slightly and giving him a nod of approval. He adjusted me and drove in deep. Then pulled out slightly, and pushed himself as far as he could go. He picked up his pace with each thrust, only punctuated by our grunts echoing off the shower walls, mixing with the sound of a gentle rainfall.

Nothing mattered at that point. The world could end and the only thing that existed was the dragon fucking me and our connection to each other. Emotions grew heavy and wove together out of instinct. Pleasure and lust, along with a primal need from Xav dominated our shared understanding. It was moments like these that I wished I could smell pheromones rather than just respond to them.

Between thrusts, Xavior moved my legs, one after the other, so my knees were positioned over his shoulders. I pressed my hands to the marble directly under where my back touched the wall to steady myself against each hard thrust. He stepped back, bringing me with him. I let my arms fall away from my body as I floated in a show of his dragon-born strength.

My mind thrilled at his clear display of power. Reminding me he was so much more, even as a biped. It spoke to how controlled he kept himself around me. How much finesse he usually used to interact with the world around him, even as a dragon. He was always so careful. Even now, he calculated how much he could get away with. If I had been younger, less physically trained, lacking the muscle and tone he admired, he wouldn't have attempted to fuck me like this. In this way, I was made for him, connected with him in a way that he would know the moment I couldn't take any more.

"Fuck, Xav. That's it. Keep going." The rhythm he set and the smack of our flesh set my mind adrift as my balls tightened and my hard dick tapped against my lower abdomen, dripping pre-cum.

Xavior grunted, growled, shoving himself into me while his need built. In our connection, he wasn't single minded about his pleasure. He knew what I could take, and what would cause me to come for him. Maybe it was a little masochistic to let him use my body as a cock sleeve as he drove for the orgasm his body and mind desperately wanted.

Claws pierced my lower back, shooting pinpricks of pain through my body, causing it to throb and mix with the pleasure I already felt.

"Mine, mine, mine. . ." he chanted, over and over with his claws marking my flesh, making punctures and bruises no one would ever see. Later, I would take a great deal of pleasure having him lick each wound, each bruise, as he begged to ride my cock to make up for it while I told how much I loved him and how wonderful he felt while buried in one of his holes. Sometimes we even watched ourselves as dragons, fucking in his backyard. He particularly liked the part where he was on his side while I fucked him and used my paw on his long velvet soft dick, making him come while I roared as my orgasm took me.

We suspected that the magic that was inherent in dragon cum was part of the reason we had spent the next three days fucking non-stop. It wasn't until we grew curious one night and watched the footage that we confirmed it, then realized how incredibly turned on we were watching ourselves. It was still an odd feeling when I recognized myself in the pearl scaled dragon with ruby red eyes. While I knew I couldn't really be that dragon again, I also knew he was there, just under the surface of my skin, waiting.

A pleasurable frustration bloomed in our connection as I felt his cock thicken, opening me wider. Even though he was in control, his mind still wanted permission. Craved it, actually. Our connection flooded with his need as he danced on that delicious edge, holding himself back, riding it like a wave that only desired one voice, one word to give him his long awaited release.

"Xavior." His head snapped up at the sound of my voice, and his dragon eyes met mine. He slowed for a beat before he pushed faster, anticipating what I would say. "Come."

He buried himself deep, holding me tight to him as he filled me. He retracted his claws and worked his hands up my body, pulling me to him, anchoring me against his chest as he slipped to the tile floor with me in his lap.

I held him for a time and kissed his forehead, brushing his hair aside, admiring his rain soaked face as he took large breaths. When his softening cock slipped from me, I unwound my arms from his shoulders and put my hands on them to maneuver myself into a standing position, then slid my hard cock along his cheek. "Did you think we were done?"

Xav looked up at me with his wide-eyed dragon gaze, holding it as he opened his mouth and swallowed down my dick, using his dragon tongue to tease and lick everything from tip to root. I braced myself on his shoulders and gently thrust into his mouth as he wrapped his hands around my thighs. His half growl-moans vibrated along my dick in tandem with his talented tongue. "Fuck, fuck, yes, just like that." He slid his hands up to my ass and gave it a quick double squeeze, which was his version of encouraging me to talk more. "Fuck, that feels amazing." The sound of my voice did things for him, which I was fine with. Turns out my dragon enjoyed being told just how much he pleased me, especially when he was on his knees. "It doesn't matter how many gentiles you've had in your mouth. My dick was the one you've been waiting for, wasn't it, love? It fits so perfectly and you swallow me down so well. No one else compares to how well you suck me off."

His tongue worked me over as he absorbed my words and tried to gag on my dick. Interesting fact, dragons have no gag reflex because they rarely chewed their food. It didn't stop him from trying.

Xav's left hand slipped from my ass cheek into my ass crack to rub at my still gapping hole. He easily slipped int two fingers as I kept my pace. Once he found the right spot, he massaged it while he sealed his lips around my dick and sucked hard. I bucked into his mouth, chasing my impending orgasm.

"Yes, yes, Xav. Your fingers feel so good." I panted hard as he kept at it. "Harder. Make me come." He thrust his fingers into me with abandon as I grunted and grabbed a handful of his hair, pulling his head close and pressing his face into my groin as I emptied into his mouth while he swallowed everything I gave him.

I let go of him and walked, legs still quivering from my orgasm, over to the tiled bench, arranging myself so I had one knee on the bench and one foot on the ground. I glanced at Xavior and noticed he was already hard again and he didn't hesitate to take up position behind me, then push himself back into the mess he left behind.

"Now, you'll fuck me until you come or say red."

"Yes." He started slowly, wanting to hold himself back. In our connection, I could feel his excitement and desire spilling into carnal lust. Xavior's hips met my ass cheeks and stayed there for a moment until he pulled back. He loved watching my body take his length and got off on the connection between us. He enjoyed watching me do the same when he was on his back.

"Do you like how that feels? How it looks?" While parts of me were screaming, my adrenaline was still going, partially fueled by my connection with Xavior, and my unquenched desire for him.

"Yes. Fuck," he said as he pulled himself out again. I could only feel the head of his dick keeping me open. "I love the way your body accepts me. Pulls me in." He slowly pushed himself back in.

I clinched down on him, eliciting a groan from him was beautiful as the low note echoed off the tiles. I was half hard from the sound alone and gently stroking my dick as he continued. "That's because you're mine, my mate. You're supposed to be there. I've always needed you. I love you."

He trembled as his hands passed over my back and gently caressed bruises and claw marks before he pulled me upright, laying against his chest he caressed the rest of my body and wrapped his hand around mine as we stroked my dick all the while keeping his thrusts slow, letting me squeeze around him until he pulled back.

"I love you so much. So much. You're my heart and have no equal." When his hands reached my thighs, I knew his next few thrusts would be demanding and brutal, leaving bruises there as well.

We confessed our love to each other all the time, but this was what I needed. Not to only satisfy a biological need. He gave me things all the time to show his affection. I knew he loved me. We could take care of ourselves. Did we technically need each other outside of our biological connection? No. We were adults capable of taking care of our own needs. A genuine relationship took the connection further. Did I want him to need me as much as I wanted to need him? Yes.

These dominant and submissive moments weren't about one of us constantly having control over the other. They worked because we allowed ourselves to express our needs. Even if sometimes we had to be prodded into it. Today, Xavior needed control, and I wanted to be needed.

His was more brutal at first, claiming me with each thrust, then he bent me over again and pounded into me with pace I tried to with my hand, pumping away while losing myself in our connection of combined desires. "That's it. Fill that needy hole again," I breathed out as he moaned in response, close to coming.

"Oh fuck, by the elements. . ." The wet sounds we made became sloppy ones as he spilled into me and didn't stop. He was still hard. I liked that.

"Shower off." Our pants and grunts echoed as he kept going and we tried to see if I could get another orgasm out of him before I gave in to my own. The sounds of his need rang in my ears and I panted with the edge of my orgasm, squeezing my dick to hold it off a little longer. "Come with me. I need you to come with me," I begged him, chanting it.

Xavior moaned and grasped my thighs even tighter as he rutted into me, then angled slightly to graze my prostate. "That's it, love." He moaned. "I'll fill you up if you come for me. Show me you how much you need it."

"Fucking hell." I couldn't hold out any more. The noise that escaped my throat as I spilled into my hand was echoed by Xavior's as he unloaded into me for the third time. We stayed locked together until the endorphins faded.

Xavior eased out of me, keeping his hands on my hips. Muscles protested as I moved, as I stood and put my other foot down. He steadied me, turning me slightly so we could hold each other. Other things made themselves known by the various pangs of pain and discomfort that were the precursor of much worse if we didn't take care of it soon. Our connection must have told him that much because he maneuvered me so I could lean against the shower wall.

"Can you make it to the bath while I grab a potion?" I nodded. He kissed me before he left the shower to prepare a hot bath with some additional herbs, healing salts, and one of Dr. Alexander's healing potions that would set me to rights. In an hour, most of the pain and aches would vanish and I could go about my day.

When I heard the whirlpool tub come to life, I pushed off the shower wall and slowly walked across the large closet-sized space, out the shower doors, and to the left until I found myself at the tub and gingerly perched on the edge.

Xavior came back from the main suite and handed me a small bottle, which I quickly drank while he prepared the bath. In no time, there was wonderfully warm water caressing all the right spots while the potion worked. Xavior held me in front of him while I relaxed in his arms. The bubbles from the tub's jets soothed sore muscles while he traced invisible images. Each symbol he drew was a reminder of his affection and love. He often used our symbol language while he couldn't speak as a dragon. It was lovely, but it also had the subtext of the nerves he still felt about the whole situation with his brother.

"We'll survive this like we have everything else." He stopped drawing symbols and wrapped his arms around me, pulling me tight against him. "At some point, the universe will stop testing us."

Xavior made a nervous chuckled. "We have twins. You're hoping too much," he said as he pressed his lips into my temple.

I joined his laughter with an ironic one of my own, agreeing with him. "Probably." I caressed his arms as he held me. "But our twins aren't you and Denis. We're different, and so are they." His breath was heavy on my cheek. A stillness crept over us as the water jets shut off while our emotions continued bubbling.

"How much time did you buy us this morning?" Even with relatives willing to babysit, nothing lasted forever.

"We have until lunchtime. So maybe two more hours before the twins become restless."

"Having Lena here has been an unexpected boon. We'll have to find other parents and set up play dates."

"Play dates?"

"Didn't you play with other children when you were a whelp?"

"Sometimes, but it was weird. Dragons grow fast in their first year or two. Take Lena, for example. She looks like she's five, but barely has the verbal skills necessary to communicate with others at that age. After a dragon's fifth year, we physically age like a human or fae until we hit puberty at twenty. Then it slows down even further when our aging cycle starts." He sighed. Concern began replacing the languid brain chemistry we'd spent the better part of the morning creating.

"We'll figure it out. We have time." A smile pulled at my lips, realizing I'll have so many things to look forward to as they grow up. There was a lot to do between now and then, but the time would fly by before we knew it. I tried not to think about the one obstacle in the way of making sure we had that time with our whelps. I closed my eyes, and we continued floating until the water cooled and we had to rejoin the reality outside of our comfortable bubble.

TRAINING STATION

XAVIOR

The first week of training for our space flight was rough on both of us. We cried ourselves to sleep several times. We weren't aware of how much being separated from the twins would affect us.

While our families had stepped up to take care of the whelps, and we had made plans and contingencies, we gave ourselves over to fate and the two-week training that was required to go to Luna. Once we were being pushed to our limits, throwing up from g-force, and acclimating to life inside a closed environment, the reality of our situation became very apparent.

Thankfully, they housed us together in private quarters. Besides the privacy, I had flight plans logged with the training center every two days so that I could get out and stretch my wings while I could. That was Greg's idea, and I thanked him for it profusely after my first flight.

Once we arrived at Moonbase twenty-three, I could definitely forget about flying, but shifting was still possible in a designated contained space that was barely big enough to stretch my wings. Just thinking about it reminded me of the bubble. I hoped we wouldn't be there long enough to undo all my therapy work after I discovered that tight spaces made my dragon anxious. From schematics and drills we did on the ground, material space was at a premium and they used every nook and pocket as storage or to sustain the infrastructure. The moonbases were literally a web of linked tight spaces.

While operations and flights to and from the moon had become standard, it was still a very precarious environment. Everyone that went had to learn about emergency escape drills, fire suppression, decompression protocols, and even general maintenance of things like air filters and toilets. Instructions were available, of course, but making sure you knew how and where to access panels to get to those instructions could mean the difference between life and death, or a very inconvenient mess.

The twins were immersed in family and loving every minute of being spoiled. With each image and video sent, we asked questions and obsessed over the details. Mostly we bothered Catherine about anything we thought might be something for her to check up on. When I had seen Everett drooling and gumming everything from his clothes to a branch, I realized they were teething.

Teething dragons were a little different in that their teeth were already pretty sharp, but as bipeds, they were practically nubs. It also coincided with their egg tooth dropping off. It can add up to miserable whelps and rapid shifting to get away from the pain of either losing their egg tooth or having their biped teeth come in. Catherine's solution was to make teething rings that were durable for either form, which seemed to help.

"Everett's egg tooth is loose. We expect it will probably fall off in the next day or two, and his biped bottom teeth are coming through fine. Sasha's top teeth have erupted, but her egg tooth is still pretty solid," Catherine explained.

I wiped my face with the back of my hand and tried not to sniffle over our holo chat. Greg was stoic, but I could feel some pretty intense emotions from him.

"I know this isn't the most ideal situation and I sympathize with how you must feel missing these milestones, but we'll send updates every day, even if they aren't exciting." Her reassurance felt like a platitude, though I knew better. Catherine was just as concerned as we were. "They've been sleeping with your pillows nearly every night. We can't go to bed without them now, whether we're in your suite or the den. They fuss until they have them. Oh! And Jordan tells me he's caught them swapping places to share the pillows when he's checked on them."

We laughed, happy that they were healthy, but our connection held an unmistakable sadness. "Thank you, Catherine. We needed that," said Greg.

"I'm glad to assist." She smiled. "I'll let you go so you can call your parents, Greg. They've figured out a clever way to help wear off some of the twins' excess energy. But I'll let them explain."

We ended the video call with Catherine and called Greg's parents. They looked tired when they answered.

"Hey guys, how's training going?" Jennifer asked.

"Well, Xavior holds down his food better than me. I think I've vomited four times." I held up my hand and mouthed five to his parents, and they laughed. Greg reached for my hand and held onto it.

"Catherine tells us you've figured out how to manage twin energy." I wanted to know more positive things about our twins. Things that didn't have to do with missing milestones and growth spurts.

"Yes! It's rather exciting. We discovered it somewhat by accident," Philip said. "We were in the den for lunch and one twin, though I still don't know which, though I suspect Everett, glided over the dinner table and snapped up a sandwich like it was nothing."

"So we wondered if we could encourage them into a game of targeting," Jennifer said. "Kind of like falconry, but with dragons."

"Exactly." Philip was excited. "At first we used branches, setting things up so they could land on those. But Faith and Jordan helped with some more protective gear since the twins both have pretty sharp claws. Faith and Trevor are amazing with them and us. They showed us how to handle the accidental grabs and misses since we don't have scales. Both twins have improved a lot since we started playing." His joy and love of the twins came through the holo, perking up our spirits. Letting the sadness fade into something less painful and tangible.

"So now, went we're in the den, we play games. Sometimes with food, sometimes with balls or toys they can grasp easily," said Jennifer.

Greg looked at me and I looked between him and his parents, then shrugged. "I guess if it works, it works. And if Faith and Trevor aren't worried about it, then it should be alright." Though I wasn't sure. That kind of training could get out of hand. Though I suppose it wasn't much different from me playing tag with them.

"Faith and Trevor say they're more advanced than dragons their age. Most whelps can't fly, let alone glide. Even Lena has a hard time keeping up when they take to the trees." Jennifer smiled, observing us. I understood why when she explained further. "Faith said she contacted Gavin to discover if there was anything in the family histories. Catherine said she hadn't seen anything like it either and there wasn't anything in the family's medical histories about advanced flying."

Greg frowned. "Maybe it's some residual effect from the potion I took?"

I didn't think so and Philip shook his head, too. "Catherine thinks if that was the case, once they came in contact with water, it would have reverted. She mentioned something about the possibility of a mutation. From her perspective, it doesn't matter as long as they're healthy. She'd rather not risk their health performing any potentially stressful exams to find out."

We nodded, agreeing as Greg squeezed my hand. We talked a little longer and then signed off. I could feel Greg's worry mixed with mine. As we crawled into bed, Greg offered his shoulder and I settled into his waiting arms, happy for the comfort.

"If anything serious happens with the twins, we are calling this off and going home."

"I won't argue with that." My hand wandered down Greg's arm until it could touch his. Then I moved it until it rested on my cheek. I had shaved my beard down to the style I normally wore. He caressed my cheek and as our gazes met. "Denis made a choice, and as much as it would hurt to choose between the whelps and my brother. . ."

Greg kissed me and held me tighter. I wanted to curse my brother for doing this to us, but it was hard to hate a man who might already be dead. In another week and a few days, we'd find out for sure.

ZERO HOUR

XAVIOR

The rest of our training went well. Greg and I were both cleared for flight. Everett lost his egg tooth, and Sasha was set to follow her brother. There was a fight over a toy between the whelps where the twins bombarded Lena with whatever they could grab. Trevor stepped up to stop it, but not before all three whelps were covered in shit. Some things never change.

Greg had just returned from working out when we had received the news via holo messages. The incident appalled Greg while it made me laugh. Greg wasn't amused by my response.

"It's not funny," he grumbled. "What if it made them sick?"

"Catherine's there." My mentioning our family doctor did not placate Greg. "What is it you're really upset about?"

"It's too fast." His tone indicating he was more upset with himself than anyone else. "It's been two weeks. They're losing teeth. Having a fight. Gliding between trees and gaining weight." He paused. "And we're not there."

I moved up behind him and rested my head on his shoulder. He'd taken off his workout shirt and tossed it into the laundry bin. "Are you having second thoughts?"

As he shook his head, I wrapped my arms around his waist. He had maintained the definition he'd gained from stunt work and even modified his workouts to accommodate our impending shift to a lower gravity. The feel of his abs under my fingers was nice.

When we first met, he was fit, though his tone and muscle definition were more pronounced now. It was a sharp contrast the rounded stomach, puffy cheeks, and extra weight pregnancy gave me. Greg treated my stretch marks like battle scars. We'd discovered the skin was weirdly sensitive when he used his tongue. The thought made me shiver, and Greg chuckled.

"You didn't hear me, did you?"

I did. "You were talking about us, the whelps, and Emory."

He laughed. "Close. I wondered if they knew about the whelps at all. You only messaged Denis for the naming ceremony. Did he know you were pregnant?"

"Um, maybe? Faith talked to him a lot. Maybe she mentioned it."

"You didn't tell him yourself?"

I shrugged and held him closer. "We aren't really that close. When we were younger, we used to be, but he changed after I left home. More and more these days, we only talked to each other if it was necessary."

"Like the ring?"

"Yeah, like that." Normally, after he worked out, he'd head to the bathroom and shower, but he knew his sweat and pheromones were comforting to me, so he waited. "When we were younger, we did everything together. One time we thought it would be hilarious to dive bomb each other with cow shit. I think we were six, maybe? I remember my father being livid about having to clean shit out of our feathers." Greg laughed, and the vibrations of it hit my chest and slid down to my dick.

"Well, no denying the twins are related, then." My hands moved of their own volition as I cupped Greg's tits and caressed his nipples. The moan that floated out delighted my senses and made me hard.

He reached back to pat my leg. "Wanna shower with me?"

"After." I unwound myself from his body and grasped his arm, urging him to turn toward me. Once our eyes connected, I couldn't stop myself from finding his lips and pulling him against me. Ever the active participant, Greg reached for my shirt, removing it as I pulled at his sweat pants, while he toed off his shoes.

Greg backed me up to our bed and sat me on the edge. He was being gentle, with light touches and kisses. Until he went that direction, I wasn't sure what I wanted other than to have him near me.

He worked his way down my torso, licking at stretch marks and kissing his favorite spots. I hadn't realized I was on my back with my legs open and my feet propped up on the bed until my heels almost touched my ass and Greg's mouth engulfed my dick.

"Fuck, fuck. Oh, fuck, yes, just like that." Greg had a technique that was all his own. His tongue would tease as he sucked, then plunged me all the way to the back of his throat while he tickled and licked sensitive veins. What seemed exceptional was his willingness to not become bored or even stop with my first orgasm. Sometimes we'd play a game of denial with it, seeing how long I'd last until I actually said red, our safe color, instead of begging him to stop. Today, he had other plans.

My dick slipped from his mouth and as his hand wrapped around it, his lips and tongue touched down on my balls, which he licked, alternating between the tip and the flat of his tongue. Then, continued further to my seminal canal, which was still sensitive because it hadn't closed over yet. Then, just as I was easing into the wild sensations from Greg's tongue playing with that hole, he moved further down and began rimming me.

"Oh. Oh fuck. You're gonna make me scream."

Each lash of his tongue was a pleasurable torture of hot, wet sensation. He took me to an unbelievable high as he used his tongue with talented efficiency in combination with his hand. I grasped at the bedclothes and fought to keep my legs open even as my feet clenched the mattress. When all his work brought me to the edge of an orgasm, he slipped a finger into me and massaged my seminal gland.

"AH, sh. . . blessed elements, fuck. Fuck!" I came all over his hand while he made a pleased groan across my sensitive areas, making me twitch even more from over-stimulation. While I watched, he put his mouth back on my dick as he inserted another finger. I gasped and writhed as pleasure and pain shot up my spine. Through our connection, Greg knew he had me close again.

"Just one more for me, Xav. You wanna give it to me, don't you?" He panted out before he shoved my dick back in his mouth.

"So, fucking, demanding," I said, laughing until he quickly ramped up his efforts, making me gasp before I unloaded into his mouth again.

Greg rested his head on my inside thigh while I caught my breath. Greg toyed with my dick the whole time while I groaned with aftershocks. I could feel our heartbeats creating a steady rhythm, echoing the pleasurable feedback loop we'd created through our connection.

When I reached out and tapped his head, he left off and moved up the bed and laid next to me. Still rock hard. I trailed my hands through the hair on his chest, tempted by what his sweat pants were restraining. "Not that long ago that you were worried about whether or not I would like your blow jobs. Now I can't get enough of them."

He grinned. "Just wait until I have false teeth in forty years."

It shocked me he would say something like that. First, I have a good imagination, and second, it was a fairly simple procedure to repair or regrow teeth. Very few people had false teeth unless they were allergic to the enhanced growth medium or avoided a dentist. I narrowed my eyes at him.

"You're not allowed to grow old, Gregor. I forbid it."

He laughed. "What about you? It's not like you're immortal. Maybe we'll end up with false teeth together. Do dragons lose their teeth with age? Maybe I should give yours a once over just to be sure." He reached for my face and I playfully swatted his hand away.

"I know where that's been, and no way you are sticking them in my mouth."

"You sure about that?" He moved toward me again and grabbed his hands, then rolled on top of him. He chuckled as he looked up at me and laced our fingers together. When I shifted my weight slightly, he groaned as I trapped his hard-on between us.

"That feels uncomfortable for you. Would you like me to do something about it?" I teased by moving slightly while I still had him penned down. We were pretty evenly matched in strength unless I used my dragon for more. The image of having Greg on my dick and me holding him up while the shower rained down on us flashed through my mind.

Greg must have caught the erotic nature of my thoughts through our connection, as he groaned again. "I'll take anything you're willing to give, though we should try to keep bruises to a minimum. We have pre-flight physicals tomorrow morning."

A pang of concern flashed through me, and Greg caught that too. "Hey, Xav, look at me." I hadn't realized I'd closed my eyes. "I'm teasing."

I knew that, and yet I pulled away. He caught me before I could let go and rolled us again until he was on top. "I'm not afraid of you. You've done nothing to me without my consent. It's only that we've been really aggressive with sex lately and I bruise easier."

He did, and we have. "You're right." Greg pressed his lips to my cheek, then my neck, and I gave him a very satisfied noise for his efforts.

His voice was soft as he continued to worship me body. "We've had to steal what time we could since before you laid our egg. It's a wonder we're both still in one piece," he said with his lips pressed to my clavicle.

Blow jobs during nap times, quick fucks in the shower, silent hand jobs to ease the day's tension after the whelps went into their cribs. The one weekend break and the morning I had arranged for my sister to watch the whelps were the longest we'd been intimate together without the possibility or the actuality of being interrupted.

"Once they're in their rooms, it will be easier," I offered. "We can take our time."

"True," Greg said. "But we're alone now with a room to ourselves and a bottle of lube somewhere in here."

I magicked the bottle to my hand and opened it. Greg grinned as he lifted himself and I reached between us to apply a generous amount on his dick. His moaning amused me, and I didn't let go of him until he was fully hard. Greg moved to his knees and reached for my legs, lifting me slightly and settling my ass on his lap. It didn't take long for him to slide into me because of his previous efforts.

"Fuck, you feel amazing, Xav." Each thrust ripped away thoughts and worries. Greg bent forward and angled himself to get a response out of me. "That's it. There's my dragon." He didn't stop driving into me as he grabbed the lube, poured some into his hand, then wrapped it around my growing dick.

"You got one more for me, Xav?"

I groaned and panted as he picked up the pace a little. The slap of skin and the smell of sweat in the air, along with his pheromones, made me hard again. The rawness I felt and the winces of pain added to it. I wouldn't last long with the pace he set.

When Greg's steady pace faltered because of the pleasure building up in our connection and my body, he grinned at me and redoubled his efforts, squeezing my cock as I felt my balls tighten. I returned the favor by squeezing his dick with my through every thrust into me he made.

"That's it, love. Grip my dick. Fuck yes, fuck. Xav."

He throbbed inside me and that's what pushed me into my pleasure-filled state as I felt his cum coat my insides and slip out of my loose hole. Greg was still milking me for each shiver until I couldn't take it anymore.

"Red. Red. Fuck. Oh elements, I want more, but I need a break."

"You sure?" Greg's hand hovered over me.

"No. Yes." I made a noise, and Greg chuckled. He liked that way too much, and I liked it too or he wouldn't do it. So he changed tactics.

"Think you can stand long enough for us to clean up?" He laughed when I shrugged.

"I'm of a mind to just leave it until morning. The bed's already a mess."

Greg frowned. "I'm not sure I can sleep in my own funk, and I was pretty funky before we started."

"I like your funk." I reached out for his hand. When he took mine, I prompted him to lie next to me again. "Your funk is comforting."

"Maybe for you." He laughed. "Seriously though, I need a shower."

His self-consciousness amused me. I kissed him to prove a point. His eyes widen with surprise until he relaxed into it. After a breathless pause, he whispered. "You've never kissed me after I've eaten you out."

"It's because you've never stayed in bed long enough. Same for when I've done that to you. I'll have you know it's adorable and frustrating," I whispered back as our noses touched.

"You honestly don't mind?"

"Greg, you literally swam through my shit after I pushed out our egg, then kissed me before I cleaned up. I think we're past being grossed out by each other."

"Fair point." He kissed me again, and I chuckled. We didn't leave the bed until the alarm went off the next morning.

FLIGHT OF THE DRAGON

XAVIOR

Magic, while in flight, whether it was an airplane or a space shuttle, was prohibited. They drilled this absolute into our heads during training. To drive the point home, we heard stories of individuals using magic or shifting with minor to major consequences. If it wasn't for the techno-magic often working on aircraft and shuttles, it would have made sense to have onboard inhibitors. Instead, there was a lot of work with the public to remind everyone not to use magic and remind us of the fines it carried if caught, and that was for the simple stuff.

USEA put us through several scenarios during training, some especially designed for magic users, to teach us to stop instinctively reaching for magic. I only failed once when someone puked and I tried to avoid being splattered. Instead of containing the mess, it blew up. I'm fairly certain it was outside interference since we were still doing Zero-G training within Earth's influence. Everyone was a mildly upset with me after that session, except Greg. He thought it was hilarious. Given he'd worked in public safety as long as I had, vomit, while disgusting, seemed pretty minor.

As we packed up what we would take with us on the shuttle, we were quiet, only communicating through nods and soft touches. At the appointed time, everyone leaving on our shuttle moved toward the pre-flight area where we'd do our final checks, get into our flight suits, and make our last call before we got ready to board the shuttle.

The shuttle was equipped with a communications package, but passengers were often limited to one call during the flight. They had text messaging available, but even that mode of communication was hampered by distance. It was also partly tradition to make a call before you left Earth. They were recorded too, in case something happened to the shuttle. It was comforting and part macabre at the same time.

Greg started the call. Once we connected, everyone at the estate was waving at us, saying hello all at the same time. When they quieted, my father spoke first.

"Edward was kind enough to set up the large holo conference device in one of your larger rooms so everyone could participate," Ransford said. It also indicated how seriously they were taking this. My father rarely did something he considered part of Faith's role, respecting her position in the family.

The image of everyone standing together, willing supporting us in this wild endeavor to save another family member was all at once one of the most beautiful things I witnessed and gut wrenching. I glanced at Greg and sensed we were feeling the same things. He dashed tears from his eyes and then gave all of us a huge smile.

"Hello, family," he said through his happy tears. I followed his lead as we all shared a light, nervous laugh.

"As most of you know, our two weeks of rest and relaxation are up. It's not Firebaugh Resort, and the food could have been better, but I can't complain too much," I said, as everyone responded with amusement and soft laughter.

The twins seemed happy, but also picked up on the undercurrent in the room, visibly becoming more anxious as they pointed at us and glanced around, wondering why they could see us but couldn't touch us.

Philip was standing next to Ransford with a grim smile on his face. "We know you're both doing this for family. Know that we love you both and we'll do everything in our power to keep the little ones safe and healthy. Our hearts go with you. All we ask is that you come back to us no matter what happens."

"That's the plan," I said, trying to lighten the mood. Everyone shared a soft laughter as the tension eased somewhat.

Faith came forward, holding Lena in her arms. "We wish you both a safe journey, the favor of the elements, and a swift return."

We hadn't thought about what we'd say to everyone in our final message before departure. Some folks had written speeches just for the occasion. Greg and I reached for each other's hand. Standing in front of our combined family for what might be the last time. Space travel was fairly safe, but things happened sometimes.

"Whatever happens, please know that Xavior and I love you all. You make us feel very fortunate and privileged beyond measure to be part of this family. We'll do our best to bring Denis back." Greg rolled his shoulders, standing taller as the weight of his words settled between us and the room full of people that carried the same hopes we did.

When the children became more distressed, Lena included, Catherine stepped in to end the call. "Both of you, stay safe. Our love and hope go with you." Everyone waved and then Catherine made the hand-swiping motion to end the call.

The last thing we heard before the holo stopped was Everett's frustrated cries. I lost it. Greg cried too, and he held me while I dealt with the emotional turmoil of leaving our family behind.

I wiped my face as Greg kissed my temple. "I'm over it. Let's get up there, save Denis's ass, and come home. If I ever leave the house again, it will be when Everett and Sasha are ready to learn how to fly."

Greg grinned. "Well, that should be sooner rather than later. Good to know." I gently slapped his chest. In response, he touched my face and gave me a kiss, before looking into my eyes, as serious as ever. "We got this. We'll figure out the Denis situation and then we'll come home." His words were just short of a promise. The uncertainties were so many, and the lessons we learned in such a short time tempered our optimism. The truth was, Denis's situation was the most dire we'd ever faced, including me being accused of murder.

I took a deep breath, working through my emotions to better center myself. Greg followed my lead, and we pulled out our pre-flight checklist and started the long process of getting ready.

Our flight suits were custom designed to fit our bodies precisely. To the point, they made sure we maintained our current body weight and muscle mass throughout the training program. Even a few pounds could throw off the fuel calculations. Not that one person adding or losing a pound or two was the problem. It was all the passengers and crew together. Adding up the changes could cause a significant impact.

I had initially worried that my pregnancy weight would be an issue. The USEA reassured me it wasn't, and in fact took the approach that forcing anyone to shed body weight before a flight was unhealthy and detrimental to the safety of the individual flying.

At this point, the routine of getting ready was nearly rote. We still checked each other as we went, per our instructions. Someone else would double check us and our gear before we boarded the shuttle, as a matter of protocol. While flying in space was mostly routine now, it still put a lot more gravitational force on an individual than an atmospheric flight. Our flight suits, along with the ergonomic seating, would minimize the G-forces and kept blood from pooling where it shouldn't.

Our ground flight coordinator walked into our prep room as we finished up. "Lyndon, Brantley, you're up next," she said.

Greg reached out and touched my face. "Ready?"

"I'm already there… kicking Denis's ass."

Greg laughed as we grabbed the rest of our gear, walked out of our prep room and down the hallway that would take us to the boarding area for our last check. After that, we were escorted onto the shuttle and strapped in. The whole boarding process took about two hours. Then clearance to lift off took another two hours as they readied the accelerator and did all the technical pre-flight checks for the shuttle, engines, and rockets that would carry us into space.

The Accelerator was a large curved runway with a booster system on a track. It allowed the shuttle to start in a horizontal position and use its momentum and the attached rockets to lift it into a vertical so that it could reach a fuel efficient escape velocity. To me, it looked like a gigantic slingshot.

When the thirty-second countdown to liftoff started, Greg reached out to hold my gloved hand. He was excited, scared, but mostly in good spirits. It squeezed at my heart how much I loved him. I was proud of Greg and pissed at Denis in turns for making us risk so much. Most days, I forgot how little time I'd have with Greg. My only consolation was that I knew his end would be mine as well. That thought led me to Emory, and I wondered if they were thinking the same thing and what they would do if we couldn't rescue Denis.

A dragon's mate could go quickly or languish. If Emory was still fighting for Denis's recovery, then it was likely they hadn't suffered pheromone withdrawal yet. Greg and I both knew first-hand how bad it could get. The longer mated partners were together, the more distance and time they could handle. Trevor and Faith had routinely taken five to six years apart between their whelps. Greg and I would never have that kind of time or luxury. I worried about it sometimes, but it didn't seem to bother Greg much.

The engines fired up to full power, and Greg squeezed my hand. It brought me back to earth as I looked over at him and he mouthed "I love you." as the thrust of take off pushed us back into our seats.

The launch was textbook, and we were cruising to the Moon in no time. Because of limited space and safety measures, only five individuals could move about in the small cabin space at a time, so they assigned us shifts. If someone need a bathroom break before their designated time, they switched with someone that was currently on their shift rotation.

They assigned Greg and me to alpha shift, which meant we helped pass meals to beta shift, checked various equipment and monitors, used the bathroom, then strapped back in. During the next four-hour shift, beta would feed gamma, while epsilon and zeta slept or use the entertainment system.

The next upgrades would introduce gravity once the shuttle was at cruising speed. They had worked out a fairly good system with the moonbases and thought they could integrate it into the shuttles. There was also a midpoint station beyond the moon's orbit being built via robots for the trip to Mars. I wouldn't be surprised if Denis headed there at some point. That was if we could save him. If he got himself into an accident out there, we weren't going to Mars. I didn't care what the USEA thought of him. That was too fucking far.

The landing was less eventful than the takeoff. A horizontal touch down via gas propulsion made for a pretty soft landing, especially since we were outside of any moonbase's artificial gravity field. It took another two hours to shut everything down, grab our gear, and off-load. We'd be living in mag-boots while walking around the station. The boots, like everything else, were a precaution. The last thing you wanted during an emergency was to lose your footing.

Greg was looking at his comm device to find directions to our quarters when a very tall person with an ethereal voice stopped us.

"Hello, Xavior?" They were taller than Greg by almost half a meter, had milk white skin, a mane of bright white hair with various braids interwoven with different beads and trinkets. Their eyes were dark brown and wide, with a patch of brown skin that mostly covered the left side of their face. They were definitely a shifter, and one with a lot of magic. Being near them made my skin tingle as if they barely had control of their magic. Though I could sense the magic, I smelled nothing from them. Were they using magic to block their scent? Or maybe it was being on the moon that affected my abilities. I wasn't sure.

"That's me. You must be Emory." I held out my hand, and they took it. A small pulse of energy shot through my palm. They gave me one quick shake and let go. I don't think I'd ever met anyone as powerful as them, except possibly Jordan. Though Jordan's magic never tried to test mine like Emory's did.

"Yes. Good to meet you, finally." They turned toward Greg. "You're the Knight, then? The one Denis mentioned?" They held out their hand.

Greg's eyes went wide as he returned the greeting. "Uh, yes. Though that's not exactly something I share." Greg glanced around as others moved past us further into the station.

"Ah. It's in your personnel file. I didn't realize it wasn't public knowledge," Emory said.

Greg gave them a slight shrug. "Like I said, I don't mention it, but it's not a secret either."

Emory took that information, blinked once, then moved on. Brushing off the topic as if Greg's unease around the subject was no concern of theirs. "Very well. If you'll follow me. I'll show you to your quarters." They turned and walked down the hall. Greg and I followed. "When I knew you were en route, I secured quarters a few doors down from the one Denis and I occupy. As it is evening on the station, you'll want to stow your belongings, then follow me to the commissary for a meal interval. We can discuss tomorrow's schedule and how we can proceed with rescuing my mate."

Greg and I shared a glance. Neither one of us had factored Emory's involvement in the rescue operation. We had a small briefing by USEA earth-side with the explanation that there would be more information available once we reached the station.

"Will you be our coordinator for the rescue mission?" Greg asked.

Emory didn't look over their shoulder. "No, I'm not allowed, as I'm deemed to be too close to the situation. However, Denis shared his research with me about the ring you wear. I'd like to offer my expertise before the mission briefing tomorrow."

"We would be honored to share a meal with you and discuss the situation," I replied, trying for politeness, hoping that we could learn more from Emory about Denis and his situation. Plus, if they knew things about the ring, it couldn't hurt to learn more.

"I am most gratified to have your assistance, honored siblings."

"Siblings?" Greg mouthed to me. I shrugged. Maybe it was some custom we weren't aware of. Hopefully, Emory would enlighten us over dinner.

We walked for another ten minutes before we arrived at our quarters. Once we secured our gear, we followed Emory to the dining area. The variety of food was much better than on the shuttle. More solid and unprocessed foods were available. While we knew there was very little meat, synthetic or replicated, brought to Luna there was an abundance of plant-based protein options to choose from.

"We grow the majority of the food we have here, though we have seeds and other seasonal options delivered via the shuttles. There are a variety of seafood options available on the weekends as a primary protein if you grow bored with the plant-based varieties offered."

Emory made a large salad with a variety of choices available. Greg opted for hydroponic celery and peanut butter. I followed Emory's lead and loaded up on enough greens to hold me over until breakfast.

They led us to a table in a corner of the dining hall. Emory sat on one side while Greg and I sat across from them. As we ate, neither of us was prepared for the next words out of Emory's mouth.

"I'll need a demonstration of the ring's capabilities to make sure it works," Emory stated before putting another bite into their mouth. Greg and I shared a glance and surprise through our connection. I responded to their request.

"It works," I said in an even tone.

"While I would like to take your word for it, I'd like to see the results with my own eyes."

"No," I said.

"Absolutely not," Greg bit out at the same time.

"I see." Emory sat quietly for a moment. "Very well. I can rely on observational data. Would it be possible for you to give me your account?"

We hadn't talked a lot about what happened at the resort after the mess with Bianca and Mark's deaths. My pregnancy, then the twins, had become our priority.

"Is that strictly necessary?" Greg asked.

Emory tilted their head. "I need to understand if the magic connected to you is yours, or pulled from an outside source. If it's your magic, then you should be able to use the ring here without issue. However, those with Earth-centric magic tend to have difficulty."

Greg looked at me. I shrugged. "From what Denis told me, it's based on Greg's ability. Whether that ability is Earth bound, we don't know."

"Hmm. Denis's research indicated that as well. As he never expected the ring to be used away from Earth, his research did not have data to cover the scenario we now face." Emory took a long drink from their water flask. When they set it down, they continued. "Greg, were you ever tested for magical abilities?"

"Yes, actually. I was told my magic was elemental related, but it wasn't strong enough to narrow it down to which element." Greg frowned. "Is that good or bad?"

Emory frowned. "I'm not sure. If you'll both excuse me, I need to perform supplementary research. We've performed a good deal of experiments on the base with elemental magic. I can correlate the information you've provided and come up with probable outcomes."

"It was nice to meet you," Greg said. We stood with Emory, shook hands again, then sat back down to finish our meal as they took their tray and left.

"Now I understand why Denis and Emory are mates," I said, and shook my head.

Greg glanced in the direction Emory went. "Why's that?"

"They both live for the science, and to the elements with anything else. The rest of us are just a nuisance or an obstacle, depending on the day."

"Harsh, but I think I see what you mean."

I should be happy that Denis had found someone that suited him so well. Though when I thought about it, a slight resentment bubbled up. Before the whelps, and mating with Greg, I might have been excited about a trip to the moon regardless of the circumstances. All I wanted now was the home and family we'd left behind.

RESCUE MISSION

GREGOR

We tried to sleep, then have sex, then tried taking a shower, which was a novelty all on its own. It wasn't until late in the night, local time, that we finally slept, exhausted. Xavior was tucked close with my arm wrapped around his waist, and his head on my shoulder, while his nose was practically in my armpit. The longer we spent away from the whelps, the more he needed my scent and pheromones. The stronger, the better, for maximum comfort.

My response to it seemed different. I felt—possessive. Old fears tried to assert themselves while we were at breakfast. Xavior went to get us coffee while I found us a table. I watched as he stopped to talk with another person in line. I kept my eyes on them as I put our trays down and sat, absently picking up my spoon with every intention of eating my yogurt while I waited for Xavior. Their conversation went on a little longer, and then as the person went to their own seat and Xavior came toward me, I realized I was gripping my spoon so hard it was leaving indentions in my hand. The thudding in my chest eased as Xavior arrived at our table and I dropped my bent spoon.

"Greg?" I only caught his movements out of the corner of my eye as he slowly set down the coffees and sat next to me.

"Hmm." The individual was about Xavior's height, had dark hair and a soft smile with curves. They reminded me of a little of Agent Ives.

"Gregor, stop looking at her and look at me."

I did what he asked out of sheer force of will. My gaze met his narrowed emerald eyes. "What's wrong?" I asked, determined to chase his frustration away. I could feel it like a living thing worming its way into my chest.

"You're being territorial. Which is understandable, but un-necessary." He put his hand on my chest and I took a breath, then another, relaxing under his touch.

"I'm being what?" There was a ringing in my ears that faded as he rubbed my chest. "Why?"

Xavior chuckled. "Because you're in a strange place, without your offspring, with plenty of competition. Not that they are, but the part of you that responses to my pheromones doesn't quite know that."

"But I'm not a dragon."

"Apparently our pheromones don't care."

"Shit." It wasn't something we expected. Though, come to think of it, the only ones around after the whelps were born were family and very trusted friends and staff. "I can't lose my head every time you step away from me. How the hell am I supposed to do this mission if some deep-seated part of my brain goes haywire?"

He kissed my cheek and rested his head against mine. "We'll figure out something. Eat your breakfast," he said as he pulled his tray from the other side of the table. I enjoyed looking at him from across the table, but having him right next to me was even better. Easier to protect.

"You're assessing threats." Xavior's voice pierced my focus, causing me to glance down at my tray to keep myself from scanning the room again.

Old training, old habits in possible dangerous situations. It was ridiculous, considering where we were. Other than the atmosphere outside, the moonbase had to be the least threat-ening place I'd ever been. "Why am I having more instinctual responses than you are?"

"Oh, I'm having them," he said as he took a bite of egg protein. "They're more along the lines of wanting to search frantically for my whelps, or crawl into my den and not come out." The pain in his voice was heavy, followed by a strong pang of sadness through our connection.

"What's the longest you've been away from your den?"

"Never," he said with a sigh. "I've had long periods where I couldn't access it properly, like when we were in the bubble, but I've always had it nearby or on me."

"Our briefing is in a few hours. How can we get control of this?" I didn't like what was happening.

Xavior shoveled his food, eating faster. "Running," he said between mouthfuls.

"Okay." I cleaned up my plate and finished my coffee. Once we cleared our dishes, we went to the hallways with a designated jogging path and started a brisk pace.

"What if this doesn't work?" I asked.

"Then we try sex, and if that doesn't work, I'm open to other solutions. They might have something in the infirmary."

"Drugs? Like pheromone blockers?"

"Or mild anxiety medications. Though I'd rather not go that route if we don't have to. It might delay the mission and make us spend more time here, which will only make it worse."

"Agreed." I pushed harder. Xavior did the same. In less than thirty minutes, we were nearly sprinting. I was panting, but Xavior had barely broken a sweat. The hallways were empty.

"Xav, go, run. Don't wait for me." I knew I was slowing him down. He gave me a pained look, and I narrowed my eyes and growled at him. Xavior had said the other option was sex. Maybe if he thought I would chase him, he would run. We'd played like this before, taking a predator or prey role as it suited us. At the moment, I wanted very much for him to run, and for me to chase.

He hesitated, glanced at me, then ran a little faster. I picked up my pace to match him until we were in an all-out run. He was still faster, but I could feel his worry shift to excitement and desire. I still felt possessive, but also proud. That was my mate running ahead of me. Fast, strong, and intelligent. I pushed harder to catch him, my endorphins willing me to go faster if only to tackle him and claim him for myself.

Further down the hall, Xavior disappeared and the sound of a door opening barely registered. I caught sight of him ducking into an open door and followed. The moment I passed the threshold, the door slid shut, and he was on me. It reminded me of when we used to spar during training at headquarters. We grappled, spinning away from the door until I got my shoulder in the right position and tossed him to the floor, grabbing his arm and locking it in place to keep him there. I quickly dropped myself onto his back, preparing to trap his arms with my knees. The moment I let go to reposition myself, he rolled his body, grabbing my arm, taking me with him

I hit the floor, catching myself with the flat of my free arm, just in time to keep the wind from being knocked out of me. Back and forth, move after move, until we became slow and giddy, either with exhaustion or the low oxygen environment in the mostly empty storage room.

The comm device on my sleeve beeped, letting me know the briefing was in fifteen minutes. "Shit."

"What?"

"We don't have time to clean up."

"Probably better if we don't. If we're the predominate smells in the room, it will keep us calm."

"Sure, unless there are other shifters in there." Xavior brought up his comms device and went through the list of requested attendees.

"Mage, human, witch, human, ah damn. . ."

"What?"

"The attending physician is a shifter."

"What kind?"

"Rabbit."

"That's bad, right?" While humans were predators, Xavior would technically be the biggest one in the room.

"For them, maybe? It would depend on how badly our smell would bother them."

Turns out, it didn't bother Dr. Deacon Wells at all. The were-rabbit was easily a hundred-thirty-five kilos or more, with muscles stacked on muscles. Either the low gravity had helped, or he was naturally that way and half a head taller than me. Xavior looked tiny by comparison.

Commander Susan Timothy gave us a displeased look as she took in our appearance. We stank and we knew it, but we weren't reacting to anyone in the room, which was a win in our book. Timothy wrinkled her nose before speaking. "This meeting will be brief. Information is need-to-know. If you need to share it with anyone else, I need to be notified first."

"What about Emory?" I asked.

Timothy gave me a thoughtful look. "We're keeping them in the loop to an extent, and as much as it helps them adjust to the situation. They know the protocols about these things."

"You don't expect us to be successful?" Xavior asked.

"Based on data, the probabilities are low." Timothy punched up a holo view showing where Denis was located outside of the base, and then what he looked like on the surface. He wasn't recognizable. The dust was slowly settling around him, sometimes sparking when it touched him. He very much resembled a dying ember in a fire.

"We think his exposure to the sun is keeping him alive, regenerating the magic that fuels his phoenix cycle. Our best guess is that he's stuck in a loop and that's why he hasn't burnt out completely. We don't know how much longer he'll last. We've placed exterior UV lighting around the patient to supplement what he gets from the sun while our location is in its night phase." Every location on Luna, whether nearside or far side, had a two weeks of daylight and two weeks of night. We were nearing the end of the two-week night cycle.

Dr. Wells spoke, taking over for Commander Timothy. "We have established a temperature baseline for the patient. Given what we know about phoenix cycles, based on research provided by Emory, we've monitored his temperature closely since we've set up supportive UV lighting. Our team has maintained his temperature between 700 and 1200 degrees Celsius or higher over the last few weeks. The best possible chance for us to approach the patient and attempt a rescue will be tomorrow, during the last day of the night cycle. We predict it will be the patient's the lowest temperature point based on previous data. It presents us with the best opportunity of rescue, with minimal risk to the patient and the rescue team." The rescue team comprising Xavior and myself.

"Thank you, Dr. Wells." She looked around the room. "This will be our best shot at reviving the patient. Given that he's been on the surface for nearly a month, we're not sure that a second attempt will be possible. The end of each night cycle has brought his average temperature down to the lower threshold. We're not confident that he'll survive another night cycle and remain viable for rescue."

Xavior and I looked at each other. The information was cruelly stark. We had one shot. Phoenix cycles usually happened quickly, and we realized Emory clearly hadn't told us everything they knew. The only reason Denis, or Xav and I, might survive was through the efforts of the base's staff and Emory's phoenix research. A month was a long time to languish on an inhospitable surface.

Timothy continued, "If the mission is successful, we'll need to limit Denis's access until we can assess his mental health."

Xavior frowned. "Phoenix transitions can cause some memory loss. Are you worried about more than his memory?"

She swallowed and pressed a few more buttons to bring up a video. It was a security camera showing an airlock. Denis walked into the frame wearing only his station uniform, calmly opened the airlock, closed it behind him, then started the sequence to open the door to the surface. Once the air pressure had dropped to nearly the same as the moon's atmosphere, he entered an override and opened the outer door.

A bright flash illuminated the screen as a small depressurization event blew him out through the open doors with enough velocity that he skipped like a stone across the surface. It took him beyond the external shields, where he eventually stopped. The light Denis had emitted from his phoenix cycle promptly dimmed as his body gathered dust from the surface.

I glanced at Xavior, swallowing my anger. This was the first we'd seen this video. Xavior was in disbelief. "Why didn't anyone show us this on Earth?" I asked. "If he committed suicide, wouldn't bringing him back pose more risk?"

"Yes, Mr. Lyndon. It's why we are taking the assessment seriously."

"Denis wouldn't commit suicide. It's not who he is. There's no way he did this without a reasonable explanation." Xavior was trembling. I reached for his hand. They were twins, after all. If it was true, there were a lot of implications. If what happened to Denis had something to do with his genetic makeup or environment, we needed to know. We already had problems with pheromones causing instinctual reactions. Had Denis stayed away from Earth too long and succumbed to some kind of mental health crisis because of it? Had he actually planned his death? Regret was an undercurrent in our connection. I could guess at what Xav was thinking. They hadn't been close, but could Xav have prevented this? Personally, I don't think he could have if Emory wasn't able to. Though I understood. The desire to help, especially family, was something both of us shared. It was a hard to deny that instinct.

"If you're successful, we'll find out," Commander Timothy said. After that less than reassuring comment, our group went through the mission brief and verified the details, which were set before we even left Earth.

Xavior and I would take a mobile unit with a trailer specifically designed to house Denis in a controlled environment, without oxygen. Our target area was positioned far enough from the base to be outside of the base's shields for safety. The vehicle would deploy its own shields as an additional safety measure once we reached the designated coordinates. From there, we either succeeded or not.

Once everyone acknowledged they understood the mission, we were dismissed. While the USEA wanted to save Xavior's brother; they were not taking any chances beyond the three of us. As we walked back to our quarters, we didn't talk. Once inside, we showered and left to see if there was anything else to eat in the commissary.

We picked over the mid-day meal offerings as our shared mood did nothing for our appetite. The somber air we had deterred anyone that might have wanted to start a conversation, except Emory.

"May I sit?" they asked. We both looked at Emory as they stood patiently, waiting.

"Sure," I said. They placed their blended vegetable drink on the table and sat next to me.

Xavior spoke as they sat down. "We're not supposed to talk about the briefing." I could tell he was still upset about the video and wanted to say something, but wasn't sure if he should.

Emory glanced between us, reading our mood and possibly our thoughts about Denis. "He wasn't mentally unstable. He had a reason."

Whether it was intuition on their part or something else, I decided to go with it. If someone wanted to reprimand me for discussing things with Emory, they could. It wouldn't matter as we were still Denis's best chance of surviving whatever he'd done to himself. "Did he say something to you before the accident?" I asked.

They shook their head. "Not in so many words. We waited too long to return to Earth. We both knew there were risks, but we hoped to have more time."

"More time for what?" Xavior asked. When they didn't answer Xavior's question, he clinched his fists in frustration. "All he ever cared about was his research. It's the only thing that would have pushed him to the brink of doing something this drastic. He's lucky he had our mother's gift, or he'd be dead."

"Denis wouldn't consider it luck. Given what we were working on."

"What is it you were working on?" I asked. Emory clearly knew more than they were letting on.

Emory shook their head. "Without him, it doesn't matter. If you bring him back, he can explain."

Xavior's hands relaxed. The empathy I felt hit me square in the chest as he watched Emory. They had lost their mate, their partner, and Emory's life possibly hung in the balance. It was a familiar situation for both of us.

Xavior reached out and touched Emory's hand. They looked up. "We'll do our best."

Emory nodded. "I know you weren't close. He regretted that. He had hoped he could reconcile with you. Explain his distance. There's much he wanted to tell you."

"Hopefully, he'll get the chance. If he remembers."

"He will," Emory said with confidence. Whether it was from something they knew or stubborn optimism, I couldn't tell. They finished their drink and stood. "Good day to you both."

We wished them a good day, and they left us to our food. I picked at mine until couldn't stay silent. "They know something, but aren't saying anything. Could it be out of loyalty to Denis?"

"It could be. They weren't being subtle about it. They knew about your ring, so them knowing about my obsession is extremely likely. I think they aren't telling us because they want to motivate me to get answers from Denis."

"Do you think he and Emory were doing something illegal?"

"No one has indicated that. Though putting Denis through a long psychological eval might be pretense. And Command probably wouldn't tell us about an active investigation."

"Makes sense." I sighed. "Best we can do now is try to review the plan and make sure we're ready for tomorrow." Xavior agreed with a nod and continued eating.

We finished our meal, then went for another jog. This time it was at a more sane pace. We showered, studied, had sex, showered, had our evening meal, studied, had more sex, until we both felt exhausted enough to sleep.

Panting with our foreheads touching, I kissed him before I pulled out. He groaned a little and reached for me.

"Whatever happens tomorrow, we did our best. That's all we can do," Xavior said.

I kissed him again in agreement and encouraged him to press closer. He put his leg over mine as I caressed his back, assured by the scales that surfaced for brief moments. Worry and stress were the themes of the day, with an underlying hint of curiosity, too.

The mystery of his brother's accident wasn't something he would let go of easily, no matter how Denis came out of this.

If I knew anything about Xavior at all, he would make sure he found out exactly what happened. What worried me was if what happened to Denis could happen to Xavior. I tried not to think about it as I held onto him.

PROVING GROUNDS

XAVIOR

Greg woke before me. I could feel him caressing my back as my scales rippled from his touch. It was soothing, though there were times I wish I could do the same for him. Given the danger we were heading toward, I didn't like the fact that Greg didn't have scales. The surface wasn't forgiving, even for dragons, as Denis had proven.

Once we dressed and had breakfast, we spent the early morning shift prepping the all-terrain vehicle in the large ground transportation bay. The bays were used to ship supplies between the different moonbases, along with staging scientific studies on the surface. From what I learned during training, there were over two dozen bases on the nearside of the lunar surface, and four on the far side. The far side bases were underground and handled most of the operations for the radio telescope stationed at Daedalus crater.

The rover was equipped with two seats in the front cab and had a small mobile unit attached to the back for us to work in.

The whole rig was automated and would follow a planned route. It was possible to override the automation and take control of the vehicle in case of an emergency, like most things involved with living without an atmosphere. While we would be on our own, there were backups the control center could initiate and a second vehicle ready to scramble if necessary. Though if a second vehicle was required, it would likely be to retrieve our corpses.

The pitch black of the night phase was not welcoming. While the base operated on a twenty-four-hour cycle to help the inhabitants, you couldn't ignore the view out the windows that told your eyes it was 'night'. The rover was equipped with wrap-around lights and a flood light if we needed it. Though the UV lights at the site would be enough to work with.

Most things on the moon were made, printed, or grown to keep the expense of shipping supplies down. The exception was our surface suits. Like the jumpsuits we wore during our flight, these suits were specifically made for our rescue mission. While regular surface suits could handle drastic temperature changes, our suits needed to handle heat well beyond the normal surface temperature shifts. While Denis would be at his coldest temperature, it would still be more than twice the normal surface heat at the equator of Luna.

Once we suited up, we climbed inside the rover and went through our systems checks, then waited for the clearance to start the mission. There was a stretch of time where we could only hear ourselves breathing, which was calming until Timothy interrupted it from the command center with the comms in our helmets, making Greg flinch.

"Rescue One, you're cleared to proceed. Confirm unlock and disconnect."

I brought up the rear and side view imagers that would show us if the rover's clamps released correctly and the umbilical that charged the vehicle disconnected. "Unlock and disconnect confirmed. We are five by five, command."

"Copy that. Drive program initiated," Commander Timothy replied.

The rover lurched forward, then picked up speed as it moved through the garage and then out onto the packed dust around the base. I switched to personal comms to check on Greg. "You alright?"

"Thinking about what you said yesterday. If Denis didn't commit suicide, then why did he put himself out an airlock?"

"I don't know. If your ring brings him out of his cycle, I plan on asking that question. Though I suppose I'll have to get in line."

"I still think Emory knows something. Maybe that's why Command is keeping them out of the loop."

"Emory lost their mate. Command is handling a delicate situation. Most shifters bond in some manner. The lack of pheromones has to be bothering them by now."

"It didn't seem like it, from what I could tell. They were sad, reserved, but I didn't notice any signs of withdrawal, did you? I would have expected them to at least be nervous around you since you're a dragon. Something isn't adding up."

Greg's observation was interesting, because I hadn't picked up on anything that indicated distress, either. Not even from their smell, not that I could smell anything from them, anyway. "You're right. It's interesting. Maybe medical has them on the protocol already."

"Possibly." Greg's curiosity was peaked. I'd been circling the facts around Denis's accident, trying to understand why it happened as we learned each new piece of information. As much as I would like to save his ass and go home, I needed to know why. What was worth risking Emory and his career? And Emory didn't need to bait me into finding things out. I planned to the moment we had decided to go on this little trip.

I toggled back to the mission channel. "Five hundred meters to target location."

The trip to Denis's location was two kilometers out from the base and took eight minutes. Without Earth's gravity, Denis had skipped across the surface, tumbling to his current resting place. Once we picked him up, we would drive another kilometer to a safe zone. The idea being that if there was an explosion, the distance would help and the shields could absorb most of the impact.

"Target location reached," the commander said. The vehicle stopped. I checked the board and looked to my left and saw the large cinder that was Denis smoldering under the layer of dust.

"Location confirmed," I replied.

Greg unstrapped himself from his chair, checked the cabin pressure to make sure it equalized, then opened his door. "Lyndon, exiting the vehicle."

"Confirmed Rescue One," Command replied.

"Don't take too long, honey." The chuckle from Greg over the comms was worth the small affection. If we were too serious, we'd be too tense, and we'd screw up. Too lax, same problem. Before we left Earth, we practiced this at least fifty times. We could do this with our eyes closed if we had to, working as a team, just like our public safety training taught us to. I think that's the only reason they allowed us to attempt this in the first place, though no one ever said as much.

"Opening rear compartment." There was an acknowledging beep as the rear door opened. The rover wobbled slightly as Greg got in the back and retrieved the hover gurney he would transfer Denis to, secure him and return to the back. For the second leg of the trip, we'd drive slower to reach the safe zone so we wouldn't jostle Denis too much.

I watched, and so did Command through the imagers, as Greg approached Denis and pushed the gurney close to the ground. The next step was to lift him in three stages. First his legs, then his hips, and then his head. While our suits were made to handle being near Denis, touching him was another matter. Greg unpacked the special gloves from the side of the gurney and put them on. They were designed to handle the equivalent of the heat from flowing lava and the gurney was made of the same material.

Over several agonizing minutes, I watched Greg move Denis hoping he would stay in one piece, and the specialized equipment would be able to handle the temperatures Denis was putting out.

"So far, so good, Command. We're on schedule."

"Copy that, Rescue One."

Once Denis was on the gurney, Greg pressed a few buttons to secure him in a shield that kept Denis stable and contained him and his phoenix fire. A small flash caught my eye as the shield slid into place. We waited a few minutes to see if anything would change. Once Greg verified that Denis's heat signature remained steady, he brought the gurney back to waist height, and pulled it toward the rear compartment.

"Subject retrieved, nearing the rear compartment now," Greg said, confirming to Command what they were seeing via their imager feed.

"Copy that, Lyndon. Making good progress."

I checked the instruments. "Command, we are nominal across the board."

"Copy that, Brantley."

Greg loaded Denis and secured the hover gurney. We waited another minute to see if his status would change once he was inside. The imager in the compartment came on to show Greg taking readings from Denis to make sure he was still stable enough to move.

"Readings nominal," Greg said as he stowed the diagnostic tool and left the rear compartment. It sealed with barely a sound. Only a slight vibration went through the cab of the rover. A light flipped to green on my indicator dash as Greg got in the cab. "We're ready to go, Command."

"Acknowledged, Rescue One. Initiating second phase."

The cab eased forward, and we started our snail's pace to reach the designated safe zone. I switched to private comms again. Greg looked pale as we steadily moved across the surface. It could have been a trick of the artificial light as well, but I was feeling an extreme uneasiness in our connection, which wasn't normal for him at all. "You alright?" I asked.

"Yeah. I will be. Memories, you know. From when you. . ." His uneasiness grew, and so did his nausea. I purposely ignored it so I wouldn't affect me. Not being able to smell his pheromones right now made not focusing on him easier than it should have been and distressing at the same time.

I hadn't thought about Greg remembering my phoenix event. I was mostly dead, so I didn't remember burning the house down around me. Greg would have seen some of it. I never thought to ask. It seemed so long ago, given everything we've been through together.

Our instructors warned us about puking in our suits. If he puked, no amount of concentration would stop me from having a sympathetic response. When we were training, I kept it together better pretty well. Free falling, and the weightlessness it brings, was something I had an intimate experience with while flying. The only times I nearly lost the contents of my stomach was when Greg did.

"I'm here. We'll get through this." It sucked that I couldn't give more than platitudes. I reached for his arm and gave it a firm squeeze. "Are you good?" I asked.

Greg pressed a few buttons on his control unit attached to the suit and his nausea subsided. It was a medical hack they showed us. We had plenty of reserves, so upping the intake of oxygen didn't hurt and it usually prevented a mess. He took a few deep breaths and gave me a thumbs up. "I'm good."

When the rover came to a stop, we did our required checks, powered down the drive and deployed the shield. This time, we both left the cab to enter the small rear compartment.

Once inside, we closed the door to better control the environment. When I glanced at Denis, I couldn't imagine there was anything left inside the body shaped slag. I looked across the hover gurney at Greg before I pressed a few buttons on the side of the gurney, which adjusted the shield around Denis adding hand ports Greg could reach through. "Command, we're ready to go out here. Do you copy?"

"Acknowledged, Rescue One. We're receiving video now. You can proceed," Command responded.

"You ready for the talent show?" I teased, trying to lighten the mood again.

Greg gave me a weak smile. "Ready as I'll ever be."

We looked at each other and Greg mouthed 'I love you' before he reached out, put his hand through the shield, touching Denis. He had his ring on inside his double gloved left hand. We waited for thirty seconds, a minute, and nothing happened.

"Rescue One, any sign of activity?"

"Negative, Command," I said. "No change to the patient. No sign of external magic."

Greg shook his head. "I need to touch him. The glove is blocking my ability."

"How do you know?" I could feel his frustration, but I didn't feel any kind of resonance that would indicate something magical was happening. A sharp zing or sudden tension sometimes heralded when magic was being used, like when I touched Emory's hand.

"Instinct?" Greg offered.

I frowned and switched to our personal comms. "Greg, we can't go on instinct out here."

"I know. All I have is my experience and the last time this worked, my hand was touching you. The contact mattered. Like how Dad talks to his wood."

If he could see my smirk, I wasn't sure, but he felt my mood through our connection.

"Not that kind of wood." He laughed a little, which was nice to hear. "Like the wood in my father's shop. How he speaks to it. Whatever my ability is, it's like connecting with the spirit of the wood. Letting it speak to you. Touching it to understand what it wants to be."

"Philip must part ent or maybe fae. Some of them have an affinity for forests and such."

"That would explain Jordan's interest in him," Greg said, as he huffed out a sad chuckle.

I laughed. "You are either really, really nervous or so past nervous that everything seems humorous." I could feel both, but they churned just like his nausea.

Command cut into our conversation. "Rescue One, what's your status?"

I switched back to the main comms, "We're discussing alternative approaches. Stand by." Flipping back to our personal comms, "Do you have an idea then?" I asked.

Greg sighed. "We bring up the temp enough so that I can take off my glove and touch him."

Fuck, I didn't like that plan at all. "No, absolutely not. You touch him without your gloves and it's not just the extreme cold you're dealing with, but a barely contained phoenix fire. You set that off, and it might only take your hand if we're lucky."

"That's what the shield is for, right?"

"Phoenix fire is magic, Greg. It can burn you from the inside out. That's what it's supposed to do."

"Oh."

"Besides, Command wouldn't ever approve that."

He looked me in the eye, his gaze as serious as anything I've ever seen. "Ask."

"No."

"Then I'll ask."

"The fuck you will. Greg. Gregor!" He was back on the main comms already. Fuck. Shit. Fuck. I flipped back to the main comm.

". . . I need to physically touch the patient. That's the way the ring worked before."

"Isn't that what you tried?"

"Without my suit, Command. The gloves are interfering."

"Stand by, Rescue One."

No surprise there. Would they come to the same conclusion I had?

Minutes later, "Rescue One, we're calling the mission. If that's the only option left, we're not willing to risk it. Remove the body to the lunar surface, then return to base. Copy?"

My gut churned. After this and a debrief we would head home to be with our whelps, though accepting that meant Emory's life was at risk, and I would have to tell my family that we couldn't bring Denis back. It was the right thing to do. I couldn't risk Greg for Denis. That was unacceptable. "Copy, Command," I said, relieved that they hadn't agreed to Greg's plan.

I moved toward the rear compartment hatch to equalize the mobile unit so we could remove Denis, but before I could begin the process, Greg's shaky voice came over the private comm.

"I'm sorry, Xav. I love you."

Space suits were weird in that you can only see so much. You have to rotate your body to see to the side or what's behind you rather than turning your head. When I turned around, I realized what Greg had done.

Both his gloves were off his left hand. It was turning blue even as he reached through the shield. The ring on his finger glinted in the artificial light. Once he touched Denis, he yelled, and the pain he felt lanced through me. I watched as Greg's hand burned up as it sank through the dust and outer shell into the living fire beneath. Sparks flared and caught in the shield around Denis, and Greg screamed. I couldn't see his hand any longer.

"Greg! Gregor stop!" I moved toward him to pull on his arm, but he knocked me away. My astonishment froze me in place for a moment. Greg never had that kind of strength before. Then a glow, separate from the fire, formed. A white light stretched out from the point of contact across Denis's body and surrounded him. Greg screamed again.

Command had been trying to contact us the whole time, likely watching everything from the imager feed. "Rescue One, report! What's happening? Brantley, Lyndon, report!"

"Stand by, Command!" I watched as Denis slowly reformed and his phoenix fire reverted, reforming his organs, then finally his skin. As the light receded, Denis lay on the gurney perfectly formed, with dust particles floating down onto his body. Denis gasped, taking a breath that wasn't there, and Greg removed his hand from the shield portal, his hand print a tattoo on Denis's stomach. While Greg's ring was intact, his hand looked a lot like Denis had before he touched him. The gurney, detecting life, immediately snapped level one containment shield around Denis to give him a breathable environment.

I checked Denis's vitals, then turned to Greg. "You did it, you asshole." I had a grin on my face for all of a millisecond before Greg pitched forward into my arms, cradling his burn hand. "Fuck, Greg. Stay with me." I dropped him to the floor and picked up his glove. "This is going to hurt." I shoved it back on and locked it in place. He screamed, then passed out from the pain. I nearly vomited from the feeling alone, so I knew it had to hurt.

"Command, we have a medical emergency. Bring us back to base. One patient is in a coma, and another is in shock."

"Acknowledged, Rescue One."

The rover turned around, then picked up speed while I tried to keep Greg from moving too much. I watched as his suit cycled through medications to control his shock and manage his vitals. When they both woke up from this, I planned to berate them to make up for every moment of my near panic-stricken ride back to the base.

SICKBAY

Whatever I thought would happen, I hadn't expected the sheer amount of blinding pain it caused. At the time, the only thing I could think of was Xavior. I couldn't bear to watch him leave his brother behind, return to base, and tell Emory we failed. Then tell his parents and family Denis was gone. He wasn't. I could feel his life force through my hand, through the ring, so I thought. He was there, but stuck.

Only problem was that my glove was in the way. I knew if I could physically touch him, I could save him, though I still don't know how. Sacrificing my hand seemed a small price to pay for Xavior and Denis. If only I'd been a dragon. The phoenix fire likely wouldn't have damaged me much. The last thing I remembered was Xavior shoving my mangled hand into my discarded glove.

Unfamiliar sounds brought me back to the waking world. I listened to identify what I heard before I opened my eyes. Beeps of a monitor, doors closing and opening. Then a touch of warmth next to me, with the soft press of Xavior's hand on my chest, his body protectively curled around right side. I tried to lift my left arm to touch his face and found that it wouldn't move. Fear shot through me. Had they not been able to heal my hand?

"Greg?" Xavior's voice was rough to my ear, but it calmed me. "It's okay. I'm right here, love." His hand moved from my chest to my left shoulder. I hadn't realized I was still trying to move.

"Are you. . ." I tried to ask. My voice was raspy, and my throat was dry. How long had I been out?

"I'm okay." He kissed my lips. "You've been through surgery and asleep for a while."

"Denis?"

Xavior moved a little, and it prompted me to open my eyes. His face was a wonderful sight and the soft smile he had for me warmed me inside-out. "His vitals are normal, but he's not awake yet."

So he was better, but not out of the woods. Would he even remember anything after being stuck in a phoenix cycle for so long?

"Are you thirsty? Hungry? I can get you something."

"I want to see." And understand what happened to my arm. Silent tears slid down Xav's cheeks as he gave me a nod and moved off the bed to ask for help. When he returned with a med tech, the two of them talked over me about pillows and support. I didn't interject into the conversation, feeling the sedative pull of pain medication. The bed moved and suddenly my arm was loose. I looked down at my lap and tried to make sense of what I saw.

My elbow looked fine, but half way below that, there was only a gel plaster that appeared to cover healing skin and stitches. I gingerly touched it with my right hand to check if it was real.

Xavior's voice was quiet as he explained. "The phoenix fire destroyed your hand. It was slowly moving up your arm by the time Command brought us back to base. The only way to stop it was to amputate." He paused, emotions clearly choking him. "I'm sorry, Greg," he whispered.

I squeezed my eyes shut as I felt tears pool, feeling Xavior's sadness. There wasn't anything he could have fixed. Besides, it had been my choice. I had disobeyed an order to save Denis. What was a limb against another's life?

"It's okay, Xav. It's okay." I reached for him with my right arm and pulled him into a hug. "It was worth it. We'll figure it out. We always do." I don't know if the words were for me or him. It didn't matter. Denis was alive, and we could go home soon. That was the important part.

Once we calmed down, we held each other for a while. "Do our families know yet?"

Xavior shook his head. "I didn't want to give them false hope. If he doesn't wake up, it's better to tell them all the bad news at once."

"He better wake up." I sighed, then looked at Xavior. "Not like I didn't give him a hand or anything."

Xavior's eyes widened. "Was that a joke? Did you. . ."

"Why, need a hand figuring it out?" His mouth gaped open. "I've only got the one now, so if that's not enough, I'm not sure I can help you."

"Gregor!" Xavior said, unsure if he was going to laugh or be upset with me. He sounded like Jennifer, which amused me. Did his mom talk to him like that, too?

"What?" I smiled, thought that might have been more from the pain medicine than anything else.

He laughed, softly at first, then it turned into a belly laugh and I joined him. It was a good feeling to laugh amidst everything we were dealing with.

A day or so later, they discharged me with my arm in a sling and instructions to return at least once a day to have my sutures and skin checked.

The following day, Xavior and I were walking around the exercise track to stretch our legs. We were told my injury would delay us returning home. They wouldn't let me on the shuttle until they were sure I wouldn't pop a suture and bleed out. The healing gel was working, so it would only be a few more days, or until Denis woke up and we could use his den to get to Xavior's and go home.

"How's Denis doing?" I asked.

"Vitals are the same. Emory was with him the last time I checked. His doctor did a brain scan and there's a lot of activity. From all appearances, it seems like he's dreaming."

"If he's the same age as you, maybe that's what's taking so long. He's trying to remember nearly four hundred years of his own existence. That's a lot of data to parse through for anyone."

Xavior cocked his head slightly and looked at me. "When did you get a degree in neurology?" He smirked, but I could feel his curiosity and amusement.

"It's a wild guess, I know. But half the reason I took the risk of saving him was because I knew he was alive. Stuck, somehow, but still Denis."

He stopped me, hand on my right arm, eyes meeting mine. "What do you mean you knew he was still Denis? You never met him."

"I don't know, I just did." I sighed. "Look, I know you didn't want me to do what I did." I felt a spike of anger from Xavior. His anger was valid, so I let it go. "I did it because I couldn't live with myself knowing he was still alive and we were going to leave him there. If I had told you what I knew, you still would have tried to stop me. You wouldn't risk me over your brother." A dull hurt and disappointment from Xavior made me gasp. I knew I made a mistake not saying something to him then. I had decided for us and risked everything. He should have been part of that, and I had taken that from him.

"Do you trust me so little that we couldn't talk about it?" He walked away, then came back. His voice, quiet as he spoke. "I had this whole diatribe in my head. About not being the hero, not putting someone else's life above yours, about our family and how I can't lose you." He took a breath, and we wiped at the tears that welled up from our combined frustration, pain, and worry. The hall was quiet, like we were the only two people left on the station. "I decided not to say anything because you lost your hand. It was too much hurt all at once. Greg. It. Was. Too. Much."

I reached out, and he slowly walked into my arms. I held him as best I could as we cried. My lips touched his forehead, asking forgiveness, hoping, with time, we'd be alright. "We promised each other. I'm sorry I did a bonehead thing. You're right, I should have told you what I knew. You should have had a say in the decision." I sighed. "But he's your brother, Xav. You shouldn't have to choose between us."

"Ugh, fuck. Stop being so fucking noble." He laughed a little and stepped back to look at me. "You lost your hand, for fuck's sake."

"Worth it." I made an awkward shrug and Xavior scoffed. "Of course, if your brother ends up being a total asshole, I'll make sure he owes me. Besides, he has to make me a new ring."

Xavior sniffed and ran a hand over his face. "Actually, that's the only thing that survived intact." He reached into his pocket and pulled out the ring. Not even a scorch mark blemished it. He took my right hand and slid the ring on my finger.

"You should be on one knee, you know." I smiled at him and held onto his hand.

"What?" He scrunched his face, trying to figure out what I meant.

"If you're going to put a ring on it, you should be on one knee to ask the question."

Xavior grinned as he held my hand and dropped to his knees. His fingers caressed the bright silver ring. Even the glamour he had put on it hadn't burned away. "Gregor, will you marry me?"

"We're thousands of kilometers from home and a long way from being out of danger. It's as good a reason as any to say yes."

"I love you, you asshole." He stood and planned a kiss on me.

"Back at you, asshole." I kissed him again and wrapped my arm around his waist. "Now, let's go back to our room and see how long we can fool around until the next round of pain meds makes me pass out." I glanced at my comms unit, which had a convenient connection to the small med pack on my shoulder. We had about two hours until my next dose.

Xav put his arm around me and we walked back to our section when his comms unit beeped. Xavior stopped and answered. "This is Brantley, go ahead."

"Your brother is awake. He's asking for you and Lyndon."

Xavior glanced at me. All the emotions we felt hit me in my chest, forcing me to take a deep breath. "Tell him we'll be there shortly."

I offered my hand. He took it, and we walked back to sickbay to meet Denis.

REVELATIONS

XAVIOR

We didn't run, but we walked at a quick enough pace that Greg was a little winded by the time we reached the sickbay. The med tech in charge waved us through. "He's in the fourth room on the right."

I nodded and kept going, knowing Greg would follow. Once the door opened, I took a deep breath as I took in the situation. My brother was sitting in bed, reading from a tablet, with Emory at his bedside. It was remarkable, considering that only a few days ago, he looked like a charred log. Greg's hand pressed between my shoulders, giving me a gentle nudge. We walked in and let the door slide shut behind us.

Denis looked up and set down his tablet. "Xavior. Gregor. I'm happy to see you. Emory tells me I have the two of you to thank for my rescue."

"You do." I held my silence for all of thirty seconds before I demanded an explanation. "Why the fuck did you throw yourself out of an airlock?"

"Xav, not now." Greg squeezed my shoulder.

I turned to look at Greg. "Yes, now. We deserve to know. His employers are definitely going to ask." I shifted my gaze back to my brother. "I think we should have the privilege of knowing why."

Denis sighed. "I ran out of time."

"You what?" This was typical Denis, always cryptic and confusing. Why couldn't I get a simple answer for once?

Emory spoke, their tone polite, but it held a note of warning. "He's not like you. His cycle is less predictable away from Earth. We didn't account for that. He's telling the truth."

"What does his aging cycle have to do with anything?" My frustrations were bleeding into my voice. Greg squeezed my shoulder again, trying to relay calm. "I want an explanation as to why we risked our lives to save you. It doesn't have to be some riddle."

Emory stood, and Denis grabbed their hand. "Darling, he doesn't know." Their head swiveled to meet Denis's gaze.

"Your family?" Emory asked. Denis shook his head.

"Doesn't know what?" My patience was thin, even as the statement piqued my curiosity. We used to tell each other everything. But that changed after our first aging cycle. Slowly, Denis had grown distant and buried himself in his work. When I left to find my path, he hadn't stopped me, only told me goodbye and to write to our parents.

"Every twenty-five years, I have my cycle, like any other dragon. Except, when I have my cycle, it's a phoenix regeneration instead."

"So you're saying that every twenty-five years you go through a phoenix cycle instead of an aging cycle?" Greg asked.

"That's correct." Denis responded. "My appear as a dragon when I shift, however, I am not one, internally. I'm fully male, and always have been."

"What? How?" How, by the elements, had I never known this? "We're twins!"

Denis shook his head. "Our family had a young mage physician at the time. I begged her not to tell our parents when we discovered the truth. I think the only reason she kept it between us was because we were in love and hoped to marry. If our parents knew, it would have risked our engagement."

"Wait." I had to think. Why hadn't Denis said anything before now? "Are you talking about Consuela Alexander?" Denis nodded and glanced away. "Didn't she die from the plague?"

"She did." Denis sighed.

"How are you not dead?" I had to know. If they had a connection, if they were in love, then how had Denis survived?

"I'm not a dragon, I'm a phoenix, and as such, I don't have the same pheromone connection dragons have with their mates." He squeezed Emory's hand, and they sat. "After you left, Consuela and I were planning our engagement. Everyone was happy. A month before we were to marry, she took ill. Her family tried everything to save her. I researched day and night, going through texts, sending correspondence to others that practiced any form of healing or medicine that might help. Eventually, her body gave up. I left the manor after her funeral and planned to never return. Mother and Father were concerned that I had bonded with her, but I could only reassure them I hadn't, that we were waiting. When she died, I wished it had been possible. She was my best friend, lover, and at the time, the love of my life."

Greg had moved at some point to put a chair behind me. When he sat, I followed. How had I never asked? I had an invitation to the wedding. It was before I met Bianca, while I was still chasing Jordan across Europe. We had been meeting in secret when it was still frowned upon for fae and dragons to have relations or keep the same company. Communications home were few and far between, and the ones I had received were about how Denis had wooed an Alexander. I felt very much like a failure and receded from contact. When Consuela had passed, I had written home to find out that the family was in a time of mourning and Denis had left to find solace in traveling, as it was what the couple had planned to do for their honeymoon. He was the perfect son, honoring his fiancé, even in death.

So much time had passed. I had been too much in my head to even stop and reach out to him. He had tried, but I had resented the contact. As I was mulling over yet another failure in my life, as Greg put the pieces together.

"So, your first aging cycle was while you were in a relationship with Consuela. How were you able to keep it a secret? I've seen a phoenix cycle up close. It does a lot of damage rather quickly," Greg said.

"There was a cabin once where Xavior's villa stands. Consuela and I met there often. We hoped to form a connection as soon as my cycle started, to keep it short so we could try for children soon after."

Emory had been stoic through all this, but at the mention of family, they straightened and took a deep breath. I noted that, but didn't stop Denis from telling his story.

"We had ventured to the lake to enjoy the day, picnic, and fornicate. We had barely begun when the phoenix took me. I saved Consuela by swimming to the center of the lake. When I landed on the shore again, we realized something wasn't right. She examined me and discovered other physiological differences. Consuela took my secret to her grave."

"But Emory knows." I pointed out. No one knew how Denis had met Emory. My parents lauded their relationship. A shining example of what I too should have. It never occurred to me to ask how often they visited, or how many times they had seen my parents in all this time.

"Yes, I know. Not because Denis told me. My home village discovered it. The magical signature of our group attracted Denis, and he stumbled into our pocket realm. They thought he was a dragon come to expose us, take our magic, and leave poisoned apples. There are many unkind stories told about dragons among us."

"Your village had been out of the world for so long, it's not surprising that they would be unaware of how it had changed," Denis said, soothing Emory with his thumb tracing circles on the back of their hand.

"It was a horrible reason to torture you," Emory said.

"Christ," Greg whispered. He glanced at me. "They killed him."

"Multiple times," Denis said with a smile. It was odd to see him smile. He so rarely did it was almost unnerving. "I endured it, assuming it was my fate. I did not want to harm them. There are so few purely magical beings in the world. It wasn't their fault."

"How did you survive?" Greg asked.

Denis looked at Emory. "They rescued me. Ostracized themselves from their village to save me. We left and vowed to protect them from being discovered again. We became friends, and eventually lovers. I let our family think we were mated. It was easy enough to fool their noses when we had to."

"By the elements, Denis, why didn't you ever say anything? Even if I wouldn't listen, Faith would have." How had I never known? Or asked? Or conceived of anything he might have experienced.

He shrugged. "It was easier to let people believe what they wanted. It protected both of us."

What Denis had described sounded very familiar. As if a fairytale had come to life. I looked at Emory. "You're a unicorn." No horse shifter I knew had the magic potential Emory had, nor could they make pocket realms. Unicorns had disappeared from the Earth, or so everyone thought.

Emory nodded. "Now you both know our secrets."

"Shit. The imagers," Greg said, glancing up to the corner of the room.

He was right. While Denis's secret might not be great for the moonbase, having anyone know Emory was a unicorn was a risk. They were fountains of raw magic. There would be many that would risk their lives to control or possess raw magic. Based on stories, it was one reason unicorns disappeared.

Emory shook their head. "Do not worry, Gregor. I have protected us. The imagers will see what they want to see and hear what they want to hear, nothing more. We're safe." I'm glad Emory could protect themselves and Denis too.

"So if you knew you were approaching a phoenix cycle, why didn't you leave? Return to Earth for a few weeks, then come back?"

"Ever the curiosity with you. I've always admired that about you, Xavior. I've tried to mimic it."

"You don't have an obsession?" I heard the surprise in my voice and clapped a hand over my mouth.

"No. Because I'm technically not a dragon." Denis smiled again. Emory smirked.

I rubbed my hand over my head, trying to take in everything Denis was telling me. "You didn't answer my question. Why didn't you go back?"

He picked up the tablet next to him, turned it on, and offered it to me. "Emory and I desired offspring. There are laws on Earth prohibiting the engineering necessary for us to produce a viable embryo."

"So you weren't doing anything illegal here? Technically," Greg offered.

"Correct," said Denis, as I looked at the output and measurements on the screen.

"These are vitals." Not only current ones, but histories as well. Growth charts. I pressed a button and an image of an egg structure came up. It looked like an elaborate crystal carving. However, the small pulse of light in the center indicated it was something more.

I looked up from the screen. "So congratulations are in order?" Denis shrugged, but stayed quiet. "It still doesn't explain why you threw yourself out of an airlock," I said.

His calm smile shifted to a slight frown, pheromones telling me he was afraid, as he explained. "The egg is in a very delicate period. If we left, it might not be viable when we returned. We had hoped it would reach a more stable period before my cycle, which would have allowed us to return home and ask if you would be our surrogate." Denis said. He looked at me and I flinched. He wanted me as a surrogate?

Greg and I exchanged looks. While I was processing what my brother had just asked me, Greg took a more tactical approach. "How were you going to return to Earth with an experiment that is literally illegal there?" Greg said. "They outlawed extreme genetic manipulation for a reason. Too many have tried to make things that shouldn't exist or destroy a species with that kind of science."

"We know," Emory said. "It's why we came to work here instead. Our experiments and study center on magic and how it works on Luna's surface. Since the embryo is mostly magic, we were able to pursue our research and develop it at the same time. Past a certain point, it would be considered a viable embryo, not just an experiment."

"What in the all the elements were you thinking, Denis? I understand wanting offspring, I do. But to put yourself in danger for the possibility that it might be viable? Why?" Would I have made the same choice in his place? I'm not sure. Greg and I had discussed our options when we first knew I was pregnant. If we had lacked access to a very talented mage doctor, our decision might have been different.

"It's too precious not too. It's not just a dragon or a unicorn, it's a pegasus, Xavior. The first one in thousands of years, since before the dragon wars." Denis looked at Greg. "And your Knight was the key."

KEY EVIDENCE

GREGOR

To suddenly learn you were apparently the key to a whole species returning from extinction was definitely overwhelming. "What does a Saint George Knight have to do with a pegasus?" When Denis said I was the key, the only plausible reason had to be my Knight ability. Though how you get from Knights to a Pegasus was beyond me. Our twins weren't pegasuses or pegasi, though they had an uncanny knack for gliding.

"Ah, such a brilliant question." Denis looked at Xavior. "I understand why you were attracted to him." I couldn't tell if that was honest admiration or sarcasm. Given Xavior's family, it was possibly both.

"Denis, stop stalling." Xavior's patience was growing thin.

If we were still officers, we'd be obligated to report it, if we were on Earth. But we weren't and with that realization, I had a very sudden empathy for Denis and Emory and their desire to have a child. It reminded me of Jordan and Catherine's situation. It also occurred to me that might not need to worry about peers for our twins.

That momentary, joyful thought was instantly replaced with disbelief as Denis explained, "Not only are you a Saint George Knight, Gregor, you're part dragon. It's where your ability comes from. Extremely powerful magic froze the specific genetics for your ability, which went unchanged for thousands of years. Originally, it was a healing ability, but that ability was used to create another. The means to kill a dragon. We traced your healing ability to a particular group of wind dragons." Denis was more animated as he explained the magical science.

Emory took up where he left off. "There was a time before the wars that unicorns and dragons coexisted. Dragons didn't shift, and unicorns could take any form to protect themselves and only show our true selves to those we trusted. When pre-shifter dragons mated with unicorns, they often produced a pegasus."

Xavior hadn't said a word, and I knew my mouth was hanging open. "I'm a dragon?"

"Yes, and no. Your ancestors were dragons, and in exchange for the ability you have, someone very powerful made your ancestors look human. From what I can tell, there are two branches of the original family. Those that became the Knights, and those that kept or gained their shifting abilities. We've postulated that it might be the first instance of dragon shifters, if not in fact the origin."

I couldn't help but wonder what Narissa would say, considering this information would destroy mother's precious ethos concerning the Knights. The flash of revenge I felt from the sudden desire to make my mother eat her own bigoted doctrine threatened to lead me off into a daydream, but I refocused. "Where's the other branch of the family?"

"I believe there are small bands of wind dragons that are related to you living in Portugal and Brazil. At least they were in Portugal last I had met any according to my notes. The shared lineage between the two is ability. It was how I was able to make the ring. I suspect your ancestors had more control over it before they learned to shift. While the ability was originally designed to encompass protection and healing, it's as if learning this duality caused the ability to split, only allowing very specific access. Then, at some point, those with the destructive part of the ability could no longer shift. While the first event is written into your DNA, the second event is still a mystery. It wasn't evolution either, it was something very abrupt. I don't think I've ever encountered anything quite like it."

"You met wind dragons?" Xavior sounded jealous. I was still stuck on the fact that I was related to them.

"Emory remembered our encounter when they studied my notes. They noticed the properties of Gregor's ability held similarities to the wind dragons we met. Their other unique qualities gave us even more evidence. They are deaf as bipeds, though as dragons, they have perfect hearing. Some of their own legends say that an encounter with a Saint George Knight caused them to lose hearing. And the Knight in question was likely one of their own family members. The correlation between their unique physiology and abilities, and your experiences with the transfiguration potion, makes quite compelling evidence for our hypothesis that your family line, and the Vento family of wind dragons we encountered, are distantly related."

"Is that why the potion tried to kill me?" With every ounce of information Denis and Emory gave us, there were so many more questions. "Wait, how did you know about the potion?" I asked.

"Gavin contacted me when he first started his research into the physical markers of your dragon. Which means it's entirely possible the potion conflicted with your genetics and that's what caused the reaction you experienced," Denis said.

"Or the phoenix DNA the Brantley's carry might have been the issue. We'd have to run tests to know for sure," Emory added.

"That's a problem for a different day." Not that I didn't want to understand and maybe fix it, but right now, we had a pressing issue regarding an egg. "So, how were you able to create the embryo?"

"Technically, the embryo has three parents. I used your dragon DNA and graphed it onto my own and removed the phoenix traits that might be detrimental. Then combined it with Emory's DNA." Denis looked proud of himself. "It's the first viable embryo we've had in all the time we've tried."

"Huh." I sat dumbfounded. When we embarked on this trip, I thought going into space and living on a moonbase were going to be the most exciting things I'd ever do with my life. Now

I've saved a phoenix dragon from an endless loop, contributed genetic material to Denis's embryo, and brought a species back from extinction. I needed a beer or more meds. "While I appreciate all this information, I'm suddenly feeling pretty tired." I touched Xavior's shoulder. "Why don't you stay and visit? I'm going to go back to our room."

Xavior read my face, then picked up on my emotions. "No, I'll come with you. We should let Denis rest, too. It's been a long few days for everyone."

Denis nodded. "Sensible. We can talk again when I'm discharged."

When I got up and turned to leave, Denis spoke as Xavior opened the door. "Thank you, Gregor, for everything. I'm in your debt." I turned and acknowledged his statement with a nod, then followed Xavior out of the room. From there, I was on autopilot until we were safely inside our quarters.

FAMILY VALUES

XAVIOR

"You didn't know about any of that, did you?" Greg looked lost, and I felt it. If I was being honest with myself, I was a little lost, too.

"No! I swear. But it explains some things about Denis."

"That he has vague moral boundaries and lacks anything resembling ethical acumen?" Greg's anger mixed with his disbelief. I couldn't help but think this was my fault.

"I knew when I gave Denis your blood that he would study it. I never dreamed he would use it beyond helping you. He never mentioned it."

"But he hinted at it, in the note with the ring. About talking to you in person. He knew something then and still left Earth to continue his experiments." I watched him pace the small room, his left arm tucked close to his chest. "I understand why you stole my blood. You were scared, and that was before we really knew each other. I forgave you. But he could have asked you or me if he could use my genetic material to create an embryo. Your family has some serious trust issues!"

The comment wasn't said with a lot of venom behind it, but the truth still hurt. "Hey! It's not like you can talk. When I met you, all you had were trust issues."

He stopped, looked at me, narrowed his eyes, then took a breath. Then another. I watched him use the calming technique he learned from therapy. The anger was still there, but he harnessed it instead of letting it control him. "We can't do anything about it now. The decisions we made regarding the ring kept you alive. Let us have a family. Saved your brother and now contributed to bringing back an extinct species. The ends don't justify the means, though since I was used as the means, maybe it's the universe's way of getting back at me for denying who I am for so long."

Greg sat on the bed, and after a moment, I sat next to him on his right side, touching his shoulder. His anger had shifted to remorse and guilt. It was a common pattern. "Why would you think that?"

"I never told Keith who I was. Or Gina, while we were working together. I wouldn't have told you if you'd been anything other than a dragon. My training was the only thing I held on to after my mother threw me out. She rejected me, so I rejected them. It didn't make a difference because the truth came out anyway and I'm better for it, though it's still hard to deal with sometimes."

"Look, you don't have to keep paying for your family issues. We've learned that. My parents were distant. I trusted the wrong people and got into trouble. That almost cost us everything, and you weren't even alive when I made those decisions. You can't blame yourself for Denis. He did what he did regardless of what you would think about it. It's a huge violation and you have every right to be angry at him. And at me for causing it, even if we benefited from it in the end."

I touched Greg's hand, and he took mine and held it. We'd worked so hard on our relationship the last two years, I never thought my brother of all people would do something to drive a wedge between us. Though I knew Denis, and should have predicted he wouldn't stop once he had Greg's blood.

"What Denis and Emory might not realize is that by identifying you as a parent, it gives you rights. You have a say in what happens to the embryo," I offered.

"Or it was their way of making sure we'd help them. They need a surrogate and they were going to ask you to incubate their egg. I'd have less of an objection if the embryo is partially mine, wouldn't I?"

Greg was right, and I wouldn't put it past Denis to think that far ahead. "Fuck." I sighed. "What do you want to do?"

He shook his head. "I want to take my pain medicine and pass out for a little while. It's too much to think about right now." He pulled off his sling, and I helped with his clothes until he was only wearing boxer briefs. His comms unit had been modified by adding a glove that read Greg's hand movements to interact with the screen. He tapped the palm of his hand, which signaled the med pod to administer a dose of meds. I watched his face relax as the pain med entered his system.

"Do you want me to leave?" I looked away. It hurt to ask, though I knew that was one way Greg dealt with things. Maybe giving us space would help both of us.

I snuck a glance at him as he got into bed and made himself comfortable. He eased my internal worries as he patted the space next to him. "No, Xav. I sleep better when you're here." He made space for me, and I quickly stripped and moved to lie beside him.

"I love you," I said. "I know we're confused and hurt right now, but if we can hold on to anything, it's that we love each other."

He smiled. "I have no doubt of that. Besides, you're my fiancé now." He kissed my head, and I buried my nose in his armpit. "I love you, too. Your brother can't take that from us. However, we move forward with this, we'll do it together."

"Yeah," I mumbled into his chest.

His soft laugh helped ease the tension between us. "Besides, you'll have to figure out if you're going to help with the egg."

After one egg, I did not want to have another. "Fucking asshole."

Greg chuckled. "That might be true, but there's very little we can do about it right now."

I knew that, too. We held each other until Greg passed out and then I kept close to keep him warm. At least it meant we could go home through his den and not wait for the shuttle.

PORTAL

Xavior

"What do you mean you don't have a den?" He did, because he used to delight in breaking the wall I put up between our dens to keep him out. "Did you leave your key at home?" I paced the small area that was designated as a living space inside of Emory and Denis's quarters.

"Of course not. I wouldn't want it to fall into the wrong hands."

I took a deep breath and let it out. "Stop being cryptic then. We'd like to go home, and the fastest way is through your den." Greg's patience was waning as well as my own, though he remained silent on the subject. As much as we'd given to save my brother, for him to be obstinate now was bordering on ridiculous.

Denis shook his head and set aside the tablet he'd been reading. Sickbay had discharged him following a full mental health evaluation. According to them, he was fine. He hadn't even suffered from a memory loss like our mum had. It was one more mystery to add to the ever-growing pile.

Denis was on mandatory leave for the next two weeks, which was why we were visiting him in the quarters he shared with Emory. They had reported to their lab this morning, and subsequently were missing out on our squabbling. Our plan was to go home first, see our whelps, and think about Denis's request. We'd given enough at this point. Greg especially.

"You can't use my den, because it's not a den. It's a caustic portal that only non-living things can pass through. Let me show you."

He picked up an ancient looking magnifying glass and walked to a closed storage compartment. We followed as Denis set the glass against the door. It stuck as if magnetized to it, rotated, then sunk into the door's frame and disappeared. When Denis pressed a button to open the door, it slid open as normal, but it replaced the storage shelves with a gelatinous, green sheen. I could see the wall to my den behind it.

"Why didn't you ever develop your den?" I moved closer and Greg grabbed my hand as Denis put out an arm in front of me.

"Because, brother, it's not a den. It's a vestigial part of my dragon nature. It never fully developed, much to my disappointment."

He left us to stare at the odd portal and walked over to pick up a potted plant that was one of many around the quarters he and Emory shared. He picked off a sprig and set the plant back down. "Emory likes plants."

"What are you going to do with the clipping?" I watched, completely curious. Denis, as always, could capture my attention in ways I could never completely understand.

"Watch," was all Denis said before he lobbed the small sprig at the portal. We watched as it sank into the green ooze, floated for a moment, then disintegrated. That would have been alarming enough, but it appeared the disintegration of living matter caused a chain reaction inside the portal that resulted in a contained explosion which blew open the wall attached to my den.

"Holy shit! The twins!" Greg yelled.

"Denis! Our whelps might have been in there!" The smoke cleared to show us wood fragments on the ground in my den.

Based on the bed, the trees, and other furniture in the space, the partition had been next to the fireplace. It looked quiet. Maybe everyone was outside or sleeping somewhere else. It didn't reduce my anger at the stunt.

"Local time is around six in the evening," Greg said, anxiously glancing at his comms device on his right arm. "Hopefully, they're having dinner or are out for a walk."

I turned toward Denis. "Call Faith. They need to know you're alive, and we need to warn everyone to keep the whelps away from the den until they can put a barrier in front of the portal."

He shrugged and walked to a wall and made a sweeping hand gesture that turned on the holo. "Call Faith."

We waited patiently for the call to connect. Once it did, we could see Faith with her phone. "Denis?"

"Hello, Faith. How are you?" Denis replied as if nothing had happened to him.

Sound seemed to stop and then we could hear questions from my parents, Greg's parents, Trevor, even Lena was shouting "Uncle Denis!" in the background.

"Denis, give us a minute to move rooms so everyone can see you and we'll call you back." The call disconnected, and Denis smiled.

I noted the smile and was mildly concerned. "Why are you smiling? You never smile."

"I don't smile around you." Denis sighed. "It's always an argument with you or some kind of conflict. We've never agreed on anything."

"That's not true. We were best friends as whelps. We used to tell each other everything. When did that change?"

"Oh." Denis glanced around, then sighed. "Faith mentioned that sometimes, but I didn't believe her. I knew I should have asked for more stories from her. Maybe kept better notes of our conversations."

"Notes?" Greg asked.

"On Earth, because of the Magical Species Pact, my memories are fragmented. I remember people and places, but unless I write things down, or record myself somehow, I forget a lot of things." He ran his hand through his hair. The gesture was very familiar to me since I did it often myself.

"When it first happened with Consuela, I lost nearly everything of our time together. The only thing I remembered was her face, her name, and the names and faces of our family. I recovered other memories because she shared her memories with me via her magic.

"In Emory's village, I realized time moved differently inside of the pocket dimension they inhabited. The geas didn't apply. I remembered everything they did to me. After Emory rescued me, we started traveling, and before we knew it, I was approaching another cycle. They tried to help me contain it by creating another pocket realm, to make sure we didn't harm anyone. But we weren't powerful enough on our own. The Magical Species Pact still affected me."

After hundreds of years, I could do things with very little energy inside of my pocket dimension, but that's because my dimension was stable. The phrase: The older the dragon, the bigger the horde, was not an exaggeration. Magic collected in one place like that grew and changed with time. Having an entire village of unicorns in a pocket dimension would have warped space-time itself. I could only imagine the struggle Denis and Emory had with trying to contain him and protect his memories. It made me wonder why I hadn't lost my memories after my phoenix episode.

"While creating the small pocket dimension helped, they had no way to sustain it. Their power, while great, couldn't contain the phoenix completely. What they created helped with my memory loss. It's not perfect, but it worked." He caught my gaze, and the sadness there, and in his smell, hit me hard. "It's unfortunate that I remember so little of our first fifty years, Xavior. I'm sorry. Maybe some day you can tell me."

My brother had never apologized to me before. I didn't know what to do with that. I hadn't known any of this and could only wonder why he had kept this a secret from everyone. Would he think we would love him any less? Or think that we would treat him differently? Our mum had similar issues. Why did Denis feel like he couldn't tell us? As if he read my mind, he answered my question.

"It was better to keep you at a distance. You were obsessed with solving problems. I didn't want to be the problem you couldn't solve. Mummy would only lose recent memories, fifteen or twenty years at most, because her cycle was every hundred years. When you live twenty-five years at a time, you lose nearly everything."

"If Emory could make a pocket dimension, why not make one here?" Greg asked. It was a very logical question. Behind it was a hint of anger, probably at what he perceived was a deception. I didn't blame him for being skeptical.

"They couldn't. While they have a lot of magic, it's not predictable here. Their magic is very much tied to Earth. They can still do things, but nothing as powerful as that. Before my cycle, Emory was working on a way to power a containment unit fueled by their magic that could withstand the kinetic energy of a phoenix. We hoped would be enough to protect my mind, too. We ran out of time to test it properly and I was unwilling to risk the base.

"That Emory remembered what I told them about the ring was coincidence. I expected to die on the surface. Better that then kill everyone here, and the one being I care about most."

"But you didn't." I realized. "And you remembered."

"Yes, much to my surprise." He smiled. "It seems the MSP holds no power over Luna. To remember without difficulty is something I've wanted my whole life."

I reached over and pulled him into a hug. "Denis."

Denis hugged me back. "I'm sorry, Xavior. Truly."

I grinned through tears as I looked him in the face and held onto him. For the first time seeing how complex of a life Denis lived. How much he tried to live up to the image of the brother I expected him to be instead of himself. I should have known, but I was too busy being upset or annoyed to wonder why he pushed me away.

"You never forgot about Bianca, though." I pointed a finger at him. "You kept bringing her up!"

"Your time with her was the only notes I had from you. Letters you wrote me asking for advice, your concerns, Faith's mistrust. I don't remember what I told you. I only know that it took you a long time to get away from her, and I wanted to make sure you never put yourself in that situation again."

"Denis." I wasn't sure what else to say. The holo saved me as it beeped to let us know Faith was waiting for us to answer. As my brother reached to answer, I stopped him. "If you don't want to tell our family about your phoenix cycle, I'll stay quiet."

He shook his head. "It's time. I've lived with my secret for too long, afraid of what our parents would think. Wondering about the life they would have made me live if they knew. Even when that stopped being a concern, it seemed easier to keep the secret. Now, it doesn't matter."

I nodded at Denis and wiped my face off as Denis smiled at us and answered the holo. Greg reached out and took my hand. We had a lot of explaining to do to our family, and it would likely take more than one conversation to answer everyone's questions.

For the first time in a while, I felt like I understood my brother. It was a gift I wanted the rest of our family to have. It made me realize that all the planning and forethought Denis had around everything was likely because of the way he lived. When I looked at it from that perspective, while I didn't excuse what he did with Greg's genetic material, I can see why he did it.

Once I knew that, helping Denis and Emory with their embryo was a simple decision. Greg acknowledged my resolve with a squeeze of my hand. He'd been silent through most of the conversation with Denis, but I couldn't think of another person I wanted at my side through all this.

The holo lit up with our whole family present. They cheered when they saw the three of us standing together.

Faith smiled. "Okay, tell us everything!"

If there was one thing all dragons liked, it was a good story, and they were in for a long one.

OF THE ESSENCE

GREGOR

We only had a few more days before we were scheduled to return to Earth. Thankfully, we were still within the safety window Catherine had set, so as long as we were on that shuttle, we'd make it home in time.

My arm was healing nicely. The next step was deciding if I wanted to go through the very painful process of attaching an artificially grown limb made with my own cells or a very realistic bionic one. The first option required a lot of surgeries and a lot of time waiting for the limb to grow. However, bionic arm and hand combination had a shorter recovery time, and had added benefits for stunt work, too.

Xavior didn't care as long as I was happy. Though at the moment, he was anxious about what we had decided to do next.

"It is a procedure that is not without its risks. If something happens while you're in transit to Earth, there will be very little anyone can do to help you. There are medications which we'll program into your monitor. It should help, but the hardest part will be reentry. The egg is designed to handle the stress. We've run many simulations and experiments, but it has never been field tested," Emory said.

Xavior looked at me and took a deep breath, then sighed. "The egg needs someone to incubate it until it's the correct size. Right?" he asked.

Denis shrugged, and Emory glanced between the two brothers. "If there was another way to do this, we would. Emory has poured a fair amount of their magic into the egg to help the embryo along, but it's not enough. Eventually, we would have asked you to come to us, or we would have come to you for help. That was always the plan. My cycle accelerated our timeline."

"How do we explain that Xavior's pregnant and approximately three months along to the flight crew examiners? We still have preflight checks and the ones after landing."

"You don't," Denis said. "The egg is shielded. It won't come across any of the medical tech, and Xavior's body chemistry will still have the trace amounts of indicators from the previous egg. Those won't start changing until two or three weeks after you're home."

"Speaking of which, when do the two of you plan to visit?" Greg asked.

Emory and Denis shared a look. "We plan to follow pending our request for leave." Emory explained.

"If you would permit us, we'd like to stay with you at your estate for a time," Denis added.

"Of course. You want to keep an eye on your embryo," Xavior said with no small amount of sarcasm.

"We want to visit our family and meet our niece and nephew. And we want you to know you have our support, no matter how long this takes," Denis said. "I trust Dr. Alexander. However, our foal is a species that even her family doesn't have experience with. If I can bring her up-to-speed, we'll have more hands that can help you while you're going through this."

"Okay, okay, fine." Xavior looked at Denis and sighed. "Sorry. I'm still adjusting to all this."

"I understand. I don't expect us to resolve our differences in a few days. It will take time and patience," said Denis.

"And therapy," I said, quietly, just as much for myself as everyone else. We all glanced at each other but didn't say anything else about it.

"So, what do we do next?" Xavior asked.

Denis turned and handed me a sample cup. "We'll need more of your DNA."

I took the cup and looked at it. When it dawned on me what Denis meant, I stared at him and tried to think of anything else. Denis confirmed where he expected the DNA to come from as he glanced down and then met my gaze.

"You can't be serious?"

"It will keep the egg from being rejected. It only has a third of your genetics. We aren't sure if that's enough for Xavior's body to recognize it. We need to make sure the egg is coated so that it has the best chance for implantation," Emory said in their happy clinical voice.

"The sample needs to be as uncontaminated as possible," Denis said. I stared at him. I could only imagine what he meant and didn't ask for a clarification.

Xavior looked at me and smirked. "Well then, we should get started on that if we're going to have enough for the proce-dure."

He took me by the shoulders and pushed me in front of him. I was still holding the sample cup, looking at it in disbelief, when Xavior plucked it out of my hand as we walked back to our quarters, which wasn't far since Denis and Emory were only down the hall.

"Don't worry. We'll get you all comfy and I'll do most of the work," Xav said with a fair amount of playfulness. I had noted the shift in his mood, but went with it. Everything had become surreal to a point, and I decided some time ago that it was pointless to fight whatever new reality we were living in. I think at some point Xavior had done the same.

"Well, that doesn't seem fair." Xavior hooked his arm through my undamaged one. "I still have one hand that works." We grinned at each other as we walked into our quarters.

"Let me propose a different scenario." Xavior walked over to the environmental controls and flipped off a safety, then turned a knob. The gravity immediately lessened to Lunar standard.

There had to be a huge smirk on my face because Xavior laughed and stripped. "Can that drop the gravity to zero?"

"Sure." Xavior changed the gravity again and with one push of my boot, I was floating. Xavior grinned.

Before long, we'd shed our jump suits and were experimenting with positions in only our mag-boots and boxer briefs. The gel casting mostly protected my arm and the mild pain meds kept it from bothering me. Xavior took the lead, as he was better at moving in Zero-G than me.

He mag-locked his boots to the floor and looked up at me. I locked my feet to the ceiling, amused at the view. Another half meter and I'd be able to wrap my lips around his dick, but first, I pressed my lips to his mouth. It was awkward kissing upside down, but interesting.

As I unlocked my boots to move again, Xavior grabbed me and pulled me down across his body. I laughed, "You're not really going to do that in Zero-G, are you?"

He didn't answer my question, only pulled my underwear enough to expose my dick and shove it as far into his mouth as he could. "Oh, fuck." I grabbed his legs to have something to hang on to, wrapping my arms around his thighs. It wasn't a perfect hold, but it didn't need to be as long as Xavior had me.

Xavior sucked and licked, which was pleasant enough all on its own, until he shifted his tongue and continued, holding me still, his mouth still, only moving his tongue as if it were his fingers jacking me off. I didn't last long, and the sensation of fluids moving through my body heightened my pleasure, though I have to admit it felt strange at the same time.

As I was enjoying my fading orgasm, Xavior let go of me to deposit what he collected in the sample cup. Watching him wrap his lips around the transparent bio-plastic and push the sample into it was weirdly mesmerizing, even from my stationary, up-side-down position. When he was done, he carefully removed the cup from his mouth and recapped it so that the liquid wouldn't escape.

"How did you manage not to swallow? The consistency has to be pretty weird, all gobbed up like that."

Xavior grinned and set the cup down out of my line of sight, likely near our bed. "I swallowed. You've never produced a small about, Greg. At least not as long as I've known you."

"Oh." I felt my body flush with embarrassment.

"Nothing to be embarrassed about. However, after all this is over and you still want to have a vasectomy, I'm all for it. I don't want to be pregnant ever again. Twice in a row is enough."

He brought me down from the ceiling and slowly rotated me so I could stand on the floor. I clicked my boots back on and once they magnetized; I kissed him until I felt his hard-on press into my leg. When I reached for it, he pulled away. "Where are you going?"

"I'm turning the gravity back to one G."

"Why?" I thought we were having fun, and I sensed that from him too.

Xavior turned the knob slowly, and the gravity reasserted itself back to Earth standard. "Because I need your ass, and I'm not trying to figure out how to fuck you in Zero-G. At least not tonight."

"Oh. Oh!" I chuckled. "I'm sure we could figure something out with straps and harnesses, maybe? Like the ones used to pull the anti-grav sleds around the station?"

"I like where your mind is at, but right now, I need you. Take off your boots and get on the bed."

I gave him a grin as sat on the end of the bed and reached down to unstrap the mag-boots. After that, I took off my briefs too. Xavior had already grabbed our bottle of lube, tossing it onto the bed. He didn't follow me, but stood off to the side, stroking himself. Watching him was enough to wake my dick up for another round, and I copied his steady pace, stroking myself while we watched each other.

We continued watching each other as if it was a contest. The only sounds in our quarters were our heavy breathing and the friction of skin on skin. I blinked once, closing my eyes in self gratification until I sensed him next to me. With a few steps, he stood between my legs, dick tantalizingly close to my mouth as he continued to work himself over. I leaned forward and he let me lavish his cock with attention while I stroked mine. The awkwardness of my left arm, missing a hand, made it hard to keep the same position. He realized it and put one hand on my shoulder while his other went to the back of my neck to help steady me as I continued to suck him off.

The moment I felt him throb in my mouth, he pulled away. The tiniest disappointment threatened to set in until he glanced down at me. "Put yourself on all fours," he said.

I complied, moving up the bed so that he could kneel behind me. The moment I felt him caress lube against my hole, I clinched on nothing, anticipating the stretch and feel of Xavior's dick in my ass. He started with a finger to test the waters. "How does that feel?" he asked.

"Like magic, especially since you keep dragging your finger over my prostate."

One finger moved on to two, with more lube, until I begged. "That's enough, I'm ready."

"Are you? How about my pinkie, too? You ready for that?" Before I could answer, he pushed his pinkie finger into me along with his two middle fingers. My dick was leaking all over the bed and I wanted nothing more than to grab myself and finish what he'd started.

"How close are you, love?" Xavior asked.

"Close, so close." My moans were increasing in volume, and turned into a blatant yell when Xavior grabbed my dick and jerked me off while his fingers were buried in my ass. Coherent words escaped me.

Xavior leaned into me, his hands alternating in rhythms that played along my body, curling my toes. "One of these days, I'm going to tie you down, with your permission, of course," I laughed and moaned as he teased my prostate while his hand rubbed the tip of my cock. "And stuff so much cum into you, you'll think I'm trying to get you pregnant."

I moaned, thinking about the image he painted. The sheer mess we'd make of each other and how much cum that would actually be. Xavior didn't exactly produce small quantities, either.

"Then maybe I'll shift and douse you with my dragon load. Rub it all over you and bring you repeatedly while you're drowning in pleasure."

"Fuck, fuck, Xav."

"You like that?"

"Yes, fuck," I moaned.

He leaned in, lips next to my ear as he was still working me over. "Then, while magic is still riding you, I'll let you fuck me. I'll shove enough of my dragon spunk into your ass and plug it up so your dick will stay hard for me while you come up with new ways to wreck my ass."

"Holy shit, fuck, oh fuck," I mumbled as he kept going, suggesting even more lewd and absolutely fucking filthy shit we could do to each other. I hadn't realized how pent up with need he was, though it shouldn't have surprised me after the amount of time we'd barely been able to touch each other. He was talking about having me strap him to a wall or a cross. I wasn't sure which, when my dick unloaded into his hand and he pressed on my prostate. I lost my voice as my orgasm took me.

Somehow, Xavior captured more of my cum and added it to the cup. I slid to my stomach and panted as Xavior lined himself up with my hole. "You ready for me?"

I gave him an enthusiastic thumbs up. Then he pressed his very solid dick into me, making me groan into our pillows.

How I was still tight after what he did? I didn't know, but he felt huge as he pressed into me and eventually bottomed out. He laid on top of me and every time his dick twitched or throbbed; it caught my orgasm and made me shiver.

"You keep clinching like that. I'm going to come," Xavior said as he hissed slightly while I flexed again.

"That's the point, isn't it?" I laughed. "I want you to, Xav. Don't you?"

"Fuck, yes. By the elements, Greg." He panted. "I was trying to let you catch your breath first."

"Fuck that. Get your ass up and fuck me. I want to feel every bit of you. Leave marks."

Xavior kissed the side of my face and sat up, his cock dragging out of me slowly, making us both groan in pleasure.

"Can you put your arms behind your back?" It was awkward trying to get into position. Eventually, I ended up with my right hand gripping at the stub of my left forearm. He put his hands on my elbows and gently, but firmly, held them in place as he adjusted and thrust himself all the way back inside of me. Once he got a rhythm going, he let go of my left arm and held onto my right hand as his other hand landed on my hips to hold them in place.

I moved my left arm so that I could rest my head on the crook of my elbow. It let me shift where my knees were, which changed the angle, causing his dick to slide over my prostate even more.

Each and every thrust was a meaty slap of his hips to my ass. Eventually, he let go of my hand and focused on my hips as he upped his pace. It shocked me he was still holding out.

"You think you can come one more time for me?" he asked between his heavy breathing and thrusts.

"Hell, maybe. Yes? Fuck!" He moved his hips, grinding in circles that perked my dick up. When I got the barest hint of nails down my back, I clinched around him hard and he gasped, dick throbbing, as his hands landed on my back and he used his hips to drive his point home. Just as he was shooting his load, my dick throbbed and spurt out all over the bed.

Xavior turned it into a game. When I thought I couldn't take any more, he would ask me my color, and I always answered green. While I was sore, we were both so needy we didn't want to stop touching each other. We wanted to squeeze every last moment of the time we had left into enjoying ourselves.

By the time we called it quits, we were a sweaty mess, covered in lube and fluids. The container was nearly full, as was I. Xavior's spunk was leaking out of me and I had the oddest notion to wonder what it would be like to carry Xavior's child. I shook my head at the stray thought.

"What?" Xavior asked, curled up next to me. Our limbs tangled together, mindful of my left arm draped over his hip.

"I was thinking about being pregnant. Then wondered how that became one of our kinks."

"Interesting. Though it makes sense. I've been pregnant half the time we've been a couple."

"That's true."

"Lucky for me you like fat dragons," Xavior chuckled.

"It's not luck." I turned my head to catch his gaze. "I think you're perfect. No matter whether you have abs or a round belly, I'd love you because it's you. All of it." When I thought about tracing his stretch marks with my hand, I realized I didn't have one on that side and sighed and pulled away. He grabbed my arm to stop me.

"Real, prosthetic, or a plain stump, you're it for me. Just try to be less heroic and not lose any important parts, hmm?" he said.

My laughter echoed in the room. I was still learning how to eat and do things with my right and since I was left-handed. Xavior was there, with patience, even when I was frustrated.

"No promises." I kissed him. "Besides, you'll have to deal with me when I'm old and gray, with all that entails."

"Yes. And I don't want to miss a single minute of it."

"Neither do I." From that point on, I was determined to make every minute count.

PROCEDURALLY SPEAKING

XAVIOR

We met Emory and Denis in their lab the next day with more of Greg's DNA.

"This is excellent. I'll add it to the gel mixture." Emory took it from me and went to a container full of clear gel and dumped the contents of our sample into it. They set a mixer-like device into the container and let it slowly swirl the two together.

"The gel will coat the surface of the egg, and act as a lubricant for the insertion process."

Well, that was a bit of a relief. I don't know what I was imaging, but assuming that there would be something to make me more comfortable during the procedure was not one of them.

"Your lab is . . ." Greg was looking around. I hadn't thought about how they would do the insertion, but apparently Greg had.

"We booked a cargo room usually reserved for shifters. It has enough space for Xavior to shift and enough room for us to perform the procedure," Denis added.

Right. It would make sense that I would need to shift. Easier to get to all the right places that way. Which meant either Denis or Emory would perform the procedure.

"Uh. . ." was all I could get out of my mouth. Nudity was one thing. I had no problem with that, but having my sibling or his mate be that close to places I'd rather they were not was mildly alarming.

"I'll be there too. You don't have to worry," Greg said.

"Is that wise? You're territorial. They mess with me, and I'll respond if you respond in a way that sets me off. We've been through this, remember?"

Greg nodded. "I know, but we'll have an advantage. I'll be high on meds."

"We can also erect a privacy field over the procedure area to manage your responses, if that would help," Emory offered.

"Probably." I sighed. "I don't exactly want to think about what you're doing to me, even though I'll know, technically."

Denis nodded. "It's understandable. I'd offer to sedate you. However, we need to be sure the egg is the correct position. If you're in too much pain, or can't feel the egg, then that could become a complication."

I took a deep breath. "So do I get to see this embryo before you shove it into an uncomfortable place?"

"Xav." Greg laughed.

Denis and Emory smiled. "It's just over here," Denis said as we moved to a storage unit. He turned on a light that illuminated an egg. It was definitely egg-shaped, but the shell wasn't smooth. It reminded me more of a cut jewel with facets. The yellow-gold color added to that notion. "Do you want to hold it?"

"Can we?" Greg asked, surprised and delighted that Denis would let us touch it. I felt the same.

"You're one of the parents. Of course you can." Denis unlocked the storage case with his thumb-print and removed the jewel slowly. "Emory and I often take turns holding and talking to them after Emory bathes them in magic. They like it when you sing or hum. The crystal structure vibrates as if they are trying to match the tone."

Denis carefully put the egg in my waiting hands. It felt warm, which was a surprise. Whether it was Emory's magic or the egg's life-force, I wasn't sure. Greg touched it, his finger tracing one of the facets.

"Its so small," he said, as he touched my hands. It was small. Most eggs started out even smaller without the hard shell. "How will it grow?"

"The crystalline structure is designed to expand with the embryo. Shifting to accommodate their growth," Emory said.

"That's amazing." Denis always amazed me, though I rarely admitted it. That he had found a partner in Emory that was his equal and brilliant in their own right was a good thing. What they had created together, even if it would have technically been illegal on Earth, was nothing short of a magical miracle.

"Do you want to see inside?" Denis asked. Emory was already moving. They grabbed something off a shelf that looked like a wand and tapped the egg with it. The egg shifted slightly and became transparent. Inside, the small embryo floated. We could see its tiny wings and body. Its head was already very horse-like in shape. I held the egg out to Greg and he took it with the same care and consideration as he did one of our whelps. After gazing at the embryo for a while, the egg slowly went opaque again, and he held it out to Denis. He took it and returned the embryo to its storage unit, which was probably an incubator now that I was looking at it more closely.

"The wand causes the crystals to realign to make the egg transparent. The crystals also act as the shielding we talked about before." Denis locked the cabinet. "It should also be enough to protect the embryo from radiation while you travel back to Earth."

"Wow." Greg said. "That's very impressive."

"We've been working on this for a while." Emory smiled.

"Why can't you use the incubator you have here—assuming that's what this fancy box is—to finish growing the egg?" I asked.

"This," Denis put his hand on the incubator, "was a stop-gap solution. Enough to keep the embryo viable during their first development phase. The egg needs a constant source of nutrients and magic to thrive. That would take a substantial amount of resources to replicate, which would be very hard to come by without a lot of questions from our employers. Having a surrogate would eliminate the need for those resources."

"And no one else knows about the egg?" Greg asked.

"The USEA benefited from our findings. Because of that, we're allowed some latitude with personal projects as long as our other research progresses. Until recently, everything we've been working on had practical applications elsewhere. The shielding, the magic reservoirs, biological and practical research to understand what kinds of magic would work on Luna. We never really expected to succeed. We've been working on this for decades," said Emory, with a small frown on their face. Worry was what I would have named it, but oddly enough, I still smelled nothing from Emory. It was Denis's worry, and Greg's, and of the two, Greg's was much more potent.

Greg and I glanced at each other. This literally wasn't our jurisdiction, and we weren't detectives or public safety officers any longer. Could we really judge them? "Just . . . be careful." I don't know if Faith could have done better. Maybe she would have better advice when Denis and Emory came to visit.

Denis moved closer to us, and Greg took my hand. "We know what we're asking. We can never repay what you've given us. Nothing in existence would be enough. We are in your debt." He glanced at Emory. "If you ever need us, you can count on us coming to your aid."

I was overwhelmed and thankful when Greg spoke for both of us. "We hope that will never be the case. All we want is for our whelps and your foal to grow up and live their own lives. As long as we can accomplish that as parents, nothing else matters."

"Do you plan on doing this again?" I pointed at the egg. "Making another embryo?"

Denis and Emory exchanged a look. "We hadn't thought about another. It took us so long to get to this point, we hadn't thought about a sibling."

"Well, if and when you consider it, talk with us first, please. I'm really not keen on having another pregnancy. And Greg wasn't too happy with how you used his DNA without his permission." That had to be said. I couldn't leave the room without pointing out that while they may not have technically violated any law on Luna, they had certainly crossed personal boundaries.

Emory nodded. "We understand. Secrecy was important for so long that we forgot ourselves. Now that you know, you deserve to have a choice in the matter. Besides, we'd need your help again if we wanted to have another foal."

I took that answer at face value, unable to sense or smell their intention otherwise. After going over the details for the procedure and prep, we left the lab and went to the commissary for a meal. It was a small celebration of sorts, the sweetest thing on base currently was beets. So we celebrated with beet juice and hoped for an uncomplicated procedure the next day.

"To family and new life," Denis said. We all repeated the toast and tapped our glasses together. The mood wasn't exactly cheerful, hopeful was probably a better description for it.

It was quiet for a while until Denis became animated. "In all the commotion, I didn't ask if you had pictures of the twins. The last message I have from you is about their naming ceremony. I'm sorry I missed it."

I smiled and nodded to Greg, who was hording our collection of recent photos from home. Greg turned on the small holo projector on the table, then pushed the images from his comms unit to the viewing surface. The photos, some of them showing motion, were arrayed in front of us, floating, displaying both the whelps as dragons, and small bipeds. Denis reached up to touch one, and it activated the underlying video capture, complete with sound. It was one of me rocking Everett to sleep, singing to him as Greg caught the moment. Denis touched another one, this one from my den, where the whelps were tucked up next to me, asleep. The next one he picked was the one I took of the whelps tucked in bed with Greg.

"They're beautiful," Denis said as he closed down the holo. "I look forward to meeting them."

"As do I." Emory put a hand on Denis's arm. The open affection between them lightened the mood somewhat. I know Greg and I were proud of the whelps, but we missed them terribly.

"We know you've risked a lot by coming here and taking more risks for us when you go home. We were very serious about our offer. If you ever need anything from us, you only have to ask. We'll do everything in our power to help." The honesty I smelled from Denis was surprising and helped begin to mend some of the open wound we likely shared where our relationship was concerned.

Greg and I glanced at each other, then he spoke. "Honestly, the ring has helped us more than you might have realized." Greg and I took turns explaining what happened at Firebaugh Resort. While Denis knew some of what happened, it was the first he had heard the whole story.

"So, your father has a practice of speaking with dead wood?" Denis asked, clearly curious.

"My Grandfather did too. Grandpa Jack taught my dad and me most of what we know about woodworking."

"And your grandmother?" Emory leaned in, and between the curiosity that Denis showed and Emory's clinical tone, I wondered if they were curious about more than stories.

"She was gone before I was born. Grandpa Jack would talk about her sometimes. Grandma Laurel was a beautiful. Dark hair and eyes, liked to garden and be in nature a lot. The whole time we lived with him, he never had another partner. Every time I asked about her, it would make him sad, so I stopped. I'm sure Dad has pictures of her somewhere."

"How unfortunate," Emory replied.

"Well, maybe. Until Jennifer joined our family, I assumed it was somewhat of a family curse. Not literally, but in the way generations repeat relationship patterns. One I'm happy to say will not be the case with us."

I grinned at him. "Yeah, we have this whole ride-or-die thing going." Denis glanced at Emory, then the two of us, frowning for a moment before the joke dawned on him.

"Pheromones! Yes. yes, your crude analogy makes sense. Ride-or-die, indeed." He chuckled, and I wasn't sure if it was funny to him or the laugh you'd hear in a holo vid when the evil scientist character is amused by the hero's antics. While I was happy we were talking more naturally again, I noted it would still be prudent to have a healthy concern about him.

Later, back in our room, I had a hard time sleeping, though I was tired. The med pod stuck just to the side of my groin, in preparation for the procedure, itched. My fingers traced the hard plastic shell that was already slowly ramping up my hormones so I could carry the artificial egg.

"You're nervous about tomorrow," said Greg. If my body language didn't give it away, I'm sure our connection was flooded with my anxiety and worry. "It's valid, but I'll be there. The procedure seems uncomplicated enough."

"It's not your seminal canal being dilated so an object roughly the size of a grapefruit can be inserted, then shoved into your uterus."

Greg turned so he could touch my face. He was careful of his left arm, bracing the stump against his chest. "I know. You've been through so much, Xav. We both have. If you don't want to do this, say so. You have a choice."

"Do I?"

His eyes searched mine. "Do you think I would choose an embryo over you?"

"No." Logically, I knew that. We'd talked about children. Greg had wanted a large family. I hadn't been sure about one, and now we were on the verge of a third. Hadn't even realized I had cried until he wiped a tear away with his thumb.

"Even if you do this, and we go home, and you don't want to continue, we'll explain why to Denis and Emory. We'll find them another surrogate, or help them develop another embryo so they can find another surrogate. It's just cells, Xav. You don't have to do this for me, or for them."

"Decades, Greg. They've been trying to have offspring for decades. What kind of monster would I be if I didn't help my brother and his mate?"

"They knew the risks and knew you could tell them no. You're not a monster to want to be with me, or your own whelps. We saved Denis's life. We don't owe him anything, and we barely owed him that." Frustration and anger were slipping into his voice and his scent. It was oddly comforting. I kissed his hand and held it to my face.

"Your smell is so tantalizing when you're protective. It makes me want to bury my nose in your armpit and huff it like vapor." He laughed as I put my nose in the crease of his arm. He lifted it to let me have more access and wrapped it around my back.

"Who needs drugs when we have each other?" We chuckled. It was only because of our bio-chemical addiction to each other that I was allowed to accompany Greg, which the USEA used to their advantage as well. Sometimes you had to joke about the complications in life or they'd be too much to deal with.

I pulled away for a moment. "I've never been able to smell anything from Emory." I wondered why I hadn't said anything before now. Maybe because something else more important always came up.

"Are they the only one you can't smell?"

I nodded. "They might use a magical scent blocker. Being a unicorn in an enclosed space would have consequences for them. If I trusted Denis more, I'd feel better trusting Emory, but I don't. Denis and Emory's faith and trust in us to follow through scares me, too. What if we go home and have to terminate the embryo for some medical reason? Would Denis ever want to come home again?" I took a breath. "It all feels like too much. These thoughts are overwhelming and all I want is for us to go home."

Greg kissed my forehead while his hand slipped from my face and rubbed the back of my neck, listening to every word. He didn't stop me or comment until I was finished.

"In the morning, when we go to the cargo bay, we'll test your theory. If you don't get the answers you want, walk away from the procedure. I'll be right there with you."

I moved my head so I could kiss his lips. He kissed me back and held me close. "Whatever you decide, I'll support you. Like always." Elements. How did I get so lucky?

SENSORY INPUT

GREGOR

Xavior asked a lot of questions the next morning. I supported him, even though some of his questions were outlandish.
Like, 'What if the foal became some mythical nightmare and
terrorized everyone? Would they blame him?' The answer was
'no, of course not.' Denis and Emory were very understanding
and tolerant of all his questions, serious and not so serious.
After fifteen minutes of Xavior running down any possibility that
came into his head, Denis stopped him.

"Xavior, you don't have to do this. We can find another way.
While it would mean we would have to wait, we'd rather do that
than continue to cause you hardship you don't wish to bear."

Denis had said the same thing earlier, but this time, Xavior
listened. "I know I don't. I'm anxious. My pregnancy was difficult. I didn't imagine myself doing this again." He paused,
thinking. "The end result was worth it. All the times I groaned
and huffed about it, having our whelps has been the best thing
we could have ever imagined. I want you to have that. You
should have that chance." He rubbed at his eyes, the medications likely having more of an effect on him than he realized.

Emory and Denis exchanged a look while I reached for Xavior's hand. "It's now or never, love." He squeezed my hand, then let it go.

"Okay, okay. I'm ready." Xavior gave me a kiss as he unzipped his jumper, gaze meeting mine. The resolve I felt from him matched. This was it. Whatever happened next, I'd be with him every step of the way.

The privacy screen was up already. He stepped behind it and took off the rest of his clothes, handed them to me, then shifted. The screen adjusted and then it gave him directions about how he should position himself. He laid down, then rolled to his side. I folded his clothes, which was a minor feat one-handed, and left them on another table nearby, then joined him, positioning myself so he could see me.

In some ways, this was worse than when he pushed out our egg. For whatever reason, that had short-circuited our connection, and I hadn't felt much other than his determination and stress. While my pain meds dampened some of it, his anxiety and worry bled through. I put my hand on his snout to reassure him. When I glanced back at his lower half, I could see nothing but the faintest shadows moving behind the screen.

Xavior whined, eyes going wide, then panted. "Xavior?"

"We're almost done. Just a few more moments," Denis said. I hoped so. My imagination was getting the best of me. I swore I felt the pressure in my abdomen as if a ball of gas was trapped and there was nothing I could do to get rid of it.

Emory stepped around the screen and held up a scanner. She focused it on Xavior's midsection. "The position's good. You can complete the procedure," Emory said.

I glanced at Xavior's middle. It didn't appear distended. Last time, it took a while before I could physically tell anything had changed while he was a dragon. "That went much quicker than we thought it would."

Emory smiled. "The medications Xavior took helped. His tissues still had a good deal of elasticity from his previous pregnancy. Denis is placing a plug to assure that the gestational fluids remain in the uterus."

I couldn't imagine how that might feel. My neck felt hot just from the slight embarrassment I felt for Xavior.

"After he shifts, You'll need to help him check it periodically to make sure the plug remains in place."

"Okay." I could feel heat creep across my face.

Emory shook their head and smirked. "We'll follow up with directions. You'll want to check it before you leave on the shuttle tomorrow."

"What about . . ."

"Intercourse?" Emory asked.

My hand covered my mouth as I nodded. Why we hadn't thought to ask about that until this moment, I don't know. It didn't seem important in the grand scheme of things, but yet, it was.

"Should be perfectly normal until such time as Xavior needs to shift to pass the egg." It was a clinical, non-judgmental response to my half-assed question. "We'll give the two of you some privacy."

Emory stepped around the screen and I rubbed Xavior's snout. "Almost done."

"Xavior," Denis called out. "Feel free to shift when you're ready."

He rolled to his feet and looked at me. We held eye contact while he shifted. The hard curve of the shell wasn't visible from what I could see as I moved to grab his clothes. He took his clothes, then put my hand on the lower part of his stomach.

"Wow, that feels different from the last time."

Xavior nodded. "There's more discomfort because of the shell, but I'll manage." I wrapped him in my arms as he pressed his naked form into me while we dealt with a wave of emotions and tried to comfort each other.

Once Xavior was dressed, the privacy screen came down. Denis and Emory were cleaning up their tools and the procedure table. "If you'd like to take a nap, it's understandable. Emory and I can join you for the evening meal interval."

We nodded to them, then hand-in-hand, we left. One shower later, we were both in bed, nude, trying not to think about the embryo we were technically smuggling back to Earth.

"Five days, and we get to see our whelps again."

"Everyone is going to flip when they find out you're pregnant."

"I hope Sasha and Everett will understand. I couldn't stand it if we did all this, only to make things worse with them."

"They are pretty remarkable, Xav. Whatever happens, we'll figure it out."

We sent a brief message to our families about our timetable, what the schedule would be like and when they could pick us up from the transit terminal in San Francisco. The responses came back with pictures of the whelps and our families celebrating Denis's recovery.

"We'll show Denis and Emory. They'll enjoy that, I think," Xavior said as I packed our things. The closure was giving me a hard time with only one hand. Xavior came to my rescue, holding it so I could clip the clasp closed.

Our meal with the other couple was subdued. We wondered how soon Denis and Emory could put in for leave. They were trusting us with their future. It was a lot to take in since Denis had been mostly dead not that long ago.

"We'll do everything we can to make sure the embryo thrives. As soon as you can make arrangements, let us know. We'll make sure the estate is ready," Xavor said.

"Thank you. Both of you." Emory glanced at Denis, then Xavior, then me. "It's custom to give a gift before someone embarks on a journey. While it's usually meant for the beginning of one, it's not unheard of to mark the end of one with a token or reminder."

Emory pulled two small objects, the size of a piece of chocolate, from their pocket and gave each of us one. It resembled the egg Xavior now carried inside of him.

"They are magic reservoirs. I've charged them with my magic. To use it, you only need to swallow it. The magic releases on contact with stomach acid, and the shell will pass through your system easily, to be cleaned and reused."

"Fairly clever, yes?" Denis said, clearly enamored with his mate's ingenuity.

"Yeah," Xavior said with a grin as he looked it over, then pocketed his.

I couldn't help myself. "Wonder if that would make dragon shit more potent for a while?" Unable to avoid thinking of the Christmas gifts Xavior's family gave their village every year.

Emory tilted their head and nodded. "It could at that. As long as it wasn't diluted, it might have three or four times the magical potency of normal dragon feces."

Xavior's lips twisted in an attempt not to laugh. Emory seemed very serious about their assessment. I couldn't help it, as a chuckle escaped. Denis smiled and Emory looked at all of us, their face mildly perplexed.

"Did I say something funny?"

"Not exactly, Emory. We apologize." I glanced at Xavior and he nodded, still trying not to laugh. "It's a lovely gift. Thank you." I put mine away as Emory nodded. "Denis should bring you to Christmas festivities in Spain this year. Have you ever heard of a caganer?"

When Emory replied that they hadn't, Xavior and I told stories about last Christmas and what happened. That led to other stories about Xavior and Denis growing up. We stayed well beyond the dinner hour talking and drinking beet juice.

HOMEWARD BOUND

XAVIOR

While my body seemed to adjust to having a small grapefruit inside it again, I found it hard to find a position comfortable enough to sleep as a biped. It was then that I remembered I would shift sometimes to deal with my frustration.

"Once we pass quarantine, they'll let you fly. They have to," Greg said, obviously sensing my emotions.

I was staring up at the ceiling. "That'll be nice."

The med pod on my thigh was listed as anti-nausea medication, which was true. It also had several other meds packed with it to keep the egg from being rejected. Denis and Emory thought of everything they could. At this point, whatever happened was going to happen.

Greg touched my face. "We're going home, Xav. The whelps are doing well. We'll be home in time, and after that, we'll settle down, build a routine, and take care of us and our family."

"Yes." I gave him a sad smile. "Did you ever think you'd have a foal for an offspring?"

"I didn't think I'd have whelps. Then again, just a few years ago, I wasn't even sure I'd have a family. Now I have more than I ever dreamed."

"Good, I'm glad. Because you'll need to help me figure out how we keep a foal happy. We don't even know if it will be a shifter yet."

"Hopefully Denis and Emory will be here for that part. We'll have our hands full with the twins."

He rubbed my face, and I turned slightly to kiss his palm. "I miss them."

"Me too," he said. "I love you."

"I love you, too." I kissed him on the lips and closed my eyes, opting to at least try to rest even if I didn't sleep.

With our bags and gear dropped off to be stored in cargo, we walked down the hall toward the vehicle that would take us out to the launch platform and our ride home. Denis and Emory walked with us. It would be the last time we saw them until they could take a leave of absence. Given Denis's incident, it was very likely the USEA would grant it sooner rather than later.

Thankfully, our passage was guaranteed, having confirmed our departure three days ago. The final flight readiness check was our last hurdle. I could only hope that whatever magic Emory came up with to conceal the egg worked. My desire to go home was making me anxious, which was never a good thing when you're about to have a medical exam. Once we reached the entrance to the pre-flight area, we all stopped and gave each other somewhat awkward hugs.

Hugging Emory was fine, though it felt stiff. They rarely showed affection to anyone but Denis, but they were trying. Giving Denis a hug was like hugging Xavior, except Denis had a full beard, and the familiarity was uncanny, yet off. Like looking at the same painting in a different art gallery. It was familiar, but not the same.

"Safe journey," Emory said. Denis reached out for Emory's hand and they took it.

"We'll call as soon as we're home," Greg said. They had given us a means to encrypt our communications once we were home. Until then, we'd have to be careful about anything we said regarding the egg without Emory around to do whatever they did to hide what we were talking about.

We waved as we walked through the entrance. Once the doors shut, Greg took my hand, and we walked to our prep room. It was much smaller than the one on Earth. In some ways, that was nice. I meant there wasn't enough room to pace.

I was helping Greg figure out how to keep his shoulder harness from slipping around when the flight crew coordinator came into our room.

"Lyndon and Brantley, correct?" We nodded.

"Excellent. Ready for your medical exams?" The coordinator moved forward and pulled a port on Lyndon's suit, then plugged in a small device that they had detached from their tablet. "New system. Uses the suit's biometrics and outputs, then measures them against the vitals from the departure check-in."

Greg and I looked at each other. My vitals were technically the only ones that changed, and Emory had added a note on my medical chart for the nausea medication they prescribed. The attending had signed off on it, so we hoped that would be all.

There were advantages to having multiple PhDs with a medical degree that specialized in dragon physiology. I didn't even know anything like that existed, though if I had asked the Alexander family, that's likely what they had as well.

A beep indicated that the tablet was done with Greg's exam. "All good," the coordinator said. "You're next." They waved the small interface at me after retrieving it from Greg's suit.

The coordinator plugged into my suit, and within moments, the tablet beeped. "Hmm, the diagnostic is detecting a rather large mass of almost a kilo." He pressed something on his tablet and the suit increased its pressure, and I gasped in surprise. Nothing that I hadn't felt before during lift-off, but it was definitely uncomfortable. "Sorry, I should have warned you."

They touched a few more buttons, and the suit eased up. "It's stationary. I'm concerned."

"What did you have for breakfast, Xav?" Greg asked, sounding a little annoyed, but what I felt from him was worry.

"Oh! Right. Yeah, I haven't been able to eat very well for the last two days, and once my meds kicked in, I couldn't stop eating any fruit I could get my hands on. I might have overdone it a little."

The coordinator frowned. "Your chart says you're on anti-nausea meds." He thumbed through a few screens. "Are you a puker?"

I shook my head. "Not really. Though I was told that disorientation sometimes happens for dragons, especially since we can't fly here and my anxiety was causing nausea, so I wasn't eating." If I could explain it, then maybe they wouldn't request imaging. If nothing came back on the images, as Denis and Emory suspected, a physical exam would be next. We'd be delayed and lose our seats on the shuttle home. That absolutely couldn't happen.

"Well, keep your vomit bag close. With that much food in your stomach, it might try to make a reappearance." We watched as they signed off on the tablet and pulled the interface from the port of my suit. "Have a safe trip. The flight assistant will check your suits on your way to the shuttle before you board."

"Thanks. Have a good day." I waved as they left. Greg and I glanced at each other. We didn't say anything, sharing a pointed look and the feeling of relief through our connection.

Two hours later, we were waiting for liftoff on the launch pad. I sat on Greg's right so we could hold hands. Once we were cruising back to Earth, the in-flight coordinator came to our seats.

"Looks like the two of you had a rough time on-base. I have in-flight chores assigned, but if anything is too difficult or you need to take a break, let me know. There's always folks too amped up to sit or sleep through their allotted times."

"Thank you," we both said. The pressure out of the gravity well was intense. I didn't puke, though my chest felt like it was bruised from the inside. None of my suit's sensors registered anything that would indicate internal bleeding. The egg felt intact from what I could sense. Greg had been in some pain from the pressure on his arm, but it subsided, too. Given that Earth's gravity was higher, it was a preview of what we might expect from reentry three days later.

We were a mess as the space craft rolled to a stop. It was the bumpy landing that finally caused me to vomit. Greg was in some pain, though his suit was helping in that department. Our pheromone connection wasn't making things any better. By the time we made it to our quarantine room, we were extremely exhausted.

Greg's mantra was as comforting as it was annoying. "Just a few more days," he kept saying, even as he passed out after a quick shower. We slept for the better part of a day. Ordered food when we woke up, and slept again. There were more questions about my "food baby" when I had another exam. The doctor was concerned there was some kind of blockage since he only felt the mass, but it didn't show up on any images or scans. And the blood work—which was difficult to take from a dragon, because there were only a few soft spots, one being our eyes, and the other being our groin—came back normal for a dragon that had recently went through an oviparity event. They cleared us to go home and gave me meds for constipation, telling me to follow up with our physician if that didn't help. If they only knew. I'd never been more happy to get on a transport in my entire life.

"We're almost there," Greg said. I took his hand, and we smiled at each other through the whole ride back to San Francisco.

WELCOME HOME

GREGOR

While everyone knew I lost my hand, we hadn't told anyone about Xavior being pregnant again. We thought that would be best left to discuss at home, away from any media attention, which there was some. We were heroes, after all, saving a renowned scientist and returning home wounded.

They filmed us meeting our twins and family at the transit station. More of the Brantley family had shown up for the occasion. Many of the same dragons I had met in Spain were standing there waiting for us. They formed a physical shield to separate our small family from shouts for comments and well-wishers.

Jordan organized transport back to the estate. Large passenger vehicles were waiting for us as we left the station. As we climbed in, the family divided up into groups. There were us, my parents, Xav's parents, and Catherine and Jordan in one vehicle, while everyone else climbed into the other two. Everett clung to me as much as I held onto him. Sasha kept pointing to my arm and making sad faces.

"It's alright Sasha. Papa is alright," Xavior said. He kept repeating the phrase to her as if he was trying to believe it himself.

She wasn't buying it, and neither was Everett. He was more careful than he'd ever been of me any other time I've held him. Dragons are fairly invincible, even at their age. I could only imagine what they were thinking and feeling. Though most of it was plain on their small faces. Xav and I traded worried glances the entire ride home. How much had we risked this time?

Losing my hand was one thing, but seeing our whelps distraught was causing a weird loop of misery for all of us.

Ransford turned slightly, looked at the four of us, and started singing a tune in a language I didn't recognize. When I glanced at Xavior, he was smiling slightly and singing the song quietly to Sasha. Everett took all of this in and visibly calmed, laying his head on my shoulder. Within another ten minutes, they were asleep in our arms.

I made eye contact with Ransford. "Thank you," I mouthed to him. He nodded and turned around. I looked at Xavior, noticing he had closed his eyes and was breathing easier as well.

No one asked questions, for which we were grateful. My parents were visibly upset. Xavior's parents were stoic. Faith and Trevor answered logistical questions we were too tired to answer ourselves. We had hugs and kisses from everyone before we escaped into Xavior's den. Once he shifted, the whelps did too and climbed onto Xavior as he settled into the nest. I imagined it would be awhile before the bed would make another appearance. Though I didn't mind sleeping in the nest with my family. I wouldn't be able to sleep anywhere else even if I tried.

Another day of relearning the basics of sleeping, eating, and visits to the bathroom seemed like paradise. By the third day, our families had sent queries via Jordan and Catherine.

While Jordan had called and left messages, Catherine showed up to examine my arm and take notes. "It shouldn't take more than a week to have a prosthetic printed and sent here for a fitting. The surgeon did very well and your nerve responses were good. With a little physical therapy, you should have the full use of your prosthetic in a month or less."

That seemed optimistic, but I would take it. "Thanks, Catherine. It'll be nice to do things with two hands again." I laughed, and she smiled, then glanced at Xavior.

"When was the last time he shifted?"

I shook my head. "He and the whelps have been in dragon mode since we came in here. Considering how much time he spent not being able to shift, I'm not surprised."

"If he doesn't shift in another day or so, then I'll worry." I frowned, and she picked up on it. Xavior wasn't paying attention to us while he played with the whelps. "Is there something else going on?"

"Um, yeah, actually. We need your help, but we would understand if you felt it would violate your code of ethics or just be too much to deal with."

"Help with what?" She asked, making concerned glances in Xavior's direction.

After I explained what happened and how Xavior was pregnant again, and who the parents were, she insisted on examining Xavior herself.

The whelps continued to play as Xavior rolled on his side and submitted to Doctor Alexander's examination. Once she was done, she gave us her assessment.

"While I detected some bruising, I didn't sense any bleeding or internal injuries. The egg seems to be in a good position and the fluid is still present." She turned to me. "I assume you haven't been able to check for the plug you mentioned since you came home?"

"Ah, no. I haven't. We've been occupied with other things." Primarily the whelps.

She nodded and bent to place her hands on Xavior's abdomen again. "It's there. I can sense it, though it would be better to see or feel its position." She caressed Xavior's side, sending a pulse of healing warmth through him. "We can do that later when you're more comfortable, Xavior."

He rumbled his agreement, and I did the same. "Sounds good."

"Okay, I'll leave the two of you alone for now. Let us know when you're ready, but don't wait too long. I know your parents are eager to see you." Xavior made an affirmative noise, then went back to playing with the whelps.

"Thank you, Catherine."

She touched my shoulder. "You're welcome, Greg. We'll make sure this turns out alright, just like last time."

"Hopefully not exactly like last time. Jordan might not make it."

Catherine laughed. "Gods and Goddesses, that fae can get himself into trouble."

I laughed too. It was true. Though I'm not sure what we would have done without Jordan and Catherine. They really were the whelp's godparents, in so many ways. We could never thank them enough for what they've done for us and our family, and with Jordan, actually thanking him wasn't a good idea. After Catherine left, and I watched my family play, I had another idea.

"Be right back, Xav."

I went to the small room off the main foyer from the entry where we kept towels, clothes, and various supplies. I dug around for a few minutes and found my glamoured tie. Knowing I was part dragon, and Xavior's mate, I wondered if the den would help me find something else Xavior had stashed somewhere.

Xavior had mentioned something about dragon scale armor in a conversation we had that seemed like a lifetime ago while we were waiting for the egg to hatch. It had come up when I asked if he had any other dragon histories written in English. And that had led to him mentioning the suit. He inherited it from one of his aunts with the story.

The aunt had removed some of her own scales and fashioned a suit for a warrior she wanted to protect, and was possibly in love with, but couldn't be with them because the warrior was already mated to another. When the warrior passed, her family returned the suit to Xavior's aunt. The suit had magical properties while his aunt was alive, but once she passed, the abilities had faded. It was still valuable, even to other dragons, as dragon scales were a durable lightweight material. Add to the fact that the suit was very rare and in good condition. Most suits like this didn't last long because they were often made from scales that were shed instead of removed, which didn't offer the same amount of protection.

"Dragon scale armor, dragon scale armor, dragon scale armor…" I chanted, while I reached for the same place my healing magic came from. Just as I was about to give up, the armor appeared in the hallway. "Holy shit, it worked!"

I walked out of the small storage room and touched the armor. It was in disrepair, as some of the leather was rotting, but it would have to do. If it didn't work, then all I would do was ruin a family heirloom. Hopefully, Xav would forgive me.

While the whelps weren't in mortal danger this time, my concern was having to heal every fifteen or thirty minutes because one of them gave me a cut that might be more serious than it looked when I was in my dragon guise.

I changed into shorts and a tank top, because it didn't matter this time if the clothing appeared in the glamour or not. Though mostly it was to protect myself from the armor. It was old, after all. I carefully took it off of the storage frame, then ran into a bit of a snag. It was hard to put this shit on one handed.

"Greg?"

He must have sensed my frustration as he came around the corner and saw me struggling with the armor.

"What are you doing, love?" He smiled and came over to me. "Where did you find this?"

"Your den brought it to me," I explained, excited about the experiment. "I was trying to surprise you and the whelps. I thought if I could give myself scales all over, and then use the tie, it might help protect my skin."

Xavior blinked. "That might actually work. I mean, it doesn't have the magic it had before, but the scales should protect you." He helped me put it on and fit the pieces to the right places. "Or it might be extra weight with the glamour and do nothing."

I caught his gaze, determined to see this through. "I want to try. Even if it doesn't work, then we tried it. I'm okay with that." I'd be disappointed, and we'd have to buy stock in whatever ingredients we needed to help Catherine make healing potions for us. Whatever the result, I would never stop trying for my whelps and Xavior.

"Actually, it's a great idea. I'm a little upset that I didn't think of it, considering I've had the armor around here for a while." He finished adjusting the suit pieces. "The twins were napping in the trees when I left to find you. I don't sense them moving around, so we probably have thirty minutes to give this a test run before they wake up." It was then that I realized Xavior was stark naked. He grinned as he caught my eyes roaming about the same time I realized I was admiring the view. "You make this work and we'll see how much we can actually do with it."

"Fuck, that would be amazing," I breathed out, already feeling the weight of the armor. If it did what I hoped it would, and not chaff, I would call it a success.

He looped the tie around my head, then helped put on the helmet. "Ready?" He conjured his phone from somewhere and started a timer. "The den should adjust to your size as you change. If it doesn't, I can modify it, though I suspect given what we know now, it's always had an affinity for you." He smiled. "Like you were meant to be here."

I leaned toward him and gave him a quick kiss. "That's because I was." I stepped back and used my right hand to trap the tie to my chest with a few fingers, then used my thumb and forefinger to turn the tie tack so that the glamour would work for five minutes.

The shift in perspective was instantaneous. The other thing I noticed immediately was that I had both of my hands, or paws rather. They worked, and I could stand on them with no pain. I flexed my left paw to show Xavior, amazed.

"That's because of the glamour. Even though your hand is missing, it can still sense your muscle movements and what should be there. Very similar to a prosthetic in some ways, though much more expensive. And glamours can fail at the exact wrong times."

I gave him an affirmative noise that amused him as he looked me over. "The image looks intact. Can you feel the armor?" I gave him a nod, then moved around. It was heavier, but nothing I couldn't handle for a little while.

"Now, how can we test whether your idea worked?" I flexed my paw and pointed to his and motioned for him to take a swipe at me. "Fuck, seriously? That was your plan?" I shrugged. Xavior sighed. "I'm not going to claw you. How about we start with a scratch?" I gave him another affirmative noise. If he couldn't scratch me, or draw blood, then it would stand up to two curious whelps.

Armored Solutions

Xavior

"By the elements, that worked." I had shifted a hand and scratched at Greg's newly formed glamour, and nothing happened. "Your vulnerable parts are still vulnerable, so be careful with those." I gave him a pat on his underbelly as I walked along his left side, then noticed his dick protruding.

"Can you feel where my hand is?" He gave an affirmative noise. I slid it closer to his groin, and he made a soft querying noise until I touched him. Then he flinched, pulled away slightly, then came back once he realized what I was doing. His whole reaction made me laugh.

"Feels different, doesn't it?" Another affirmative noise from Greg, with something like a delighted sigh, rumbled out of him. I wrapped as much of my hand around him as I could and made long strokes down his length. We had been way too into each other when he'd taken the potion for me to notice details. The length of him was a shimmering purple. The cilia moved and responded as I would expect. Greg involuntarily moved his hips.

The glamour was only as detailed as the image given to the creator. The scale armor and Greg's magic must have enhanced the glamour. Or that was the best explanation I could come up with that didn't have me wondering how Jordan knew such things. Jordan and I hadn't experimented like that when we were together.

When I let go of him to shift, Greg made a noise. I translated it to a slight disappointment until he realized I was offering more than a hand job. The hormones I took for this new pregnancy had made me horny, and it wasn't like my libido needed help. If we could make it quick, we could have some fun before the whelps woke up.

Just as Greg was mounting me, Everett cried out, looking for us. Greg froze, then backed off as his parental instincts kicked in and followed me back into the main part of my den. Everett cried again, then noticed Greg. He bounded out of the nest and to Greg with an alacrity born of excitement. To punctuate that, he called to his sister, and she poked her head up out of the nest and noticed the three of us.

It didn't take long before we were all playing together as they launched from the trees, using our backs as launching pads, until Greg's timer ran out.

When he shifted, the whelps cried, thinking the game was over. I glanced at Greg and he smiled. Elated that the whole thing had worked. The scales glowed slightly, likely from the effects of the glamour. The whelps cried out again, and Greg held up his hand to calm them. He fiddled with the tie tack again and within moments; he was my beautiful pearl dragon.

We played again, and I watched to make sure Greg was alright. At one point, I caught Sasha gliding toward a den exit that would take her outside. Instead of stopping her, I followed, and we ended up outside near the splash pads and the water features.

Sasha landed in the grass nearby and cried out. I wondered what her distress was until I noticed our entire family on the back lawn, some as bipeds, others as dragons. Glancing between them and Sasha, whose cry they couldn't have missed hearing, and froze. I didn't know how they would react to Greg in his enhanced glamour. My instincts were to pick up my whelp and go back inside. Greg bumped into me and dashed any hope of retreat with Everett perched on his head holding onto Greg's crown ridge while the little whelp flapped his wings in excitement at seeing the rest of the family.

Greg looked at me, making it clear he would follow my lead. I took a deep breath and moved forward. If Greg's glamour held, it would be a lucky break. I didn't know how long Greg had set it for this time, but at least he wouldn't be embarrassed when he shifted. Unlike humans, dragons didn't worry about nudity, which I knew Greg was realizing as he noticed how many of my family members hadn't shifted yet. His odd embarrassment was amusing, and smiles lit a good number of my family's faces, watching us approach as they picked up on his slight discomfort about it too.

Dragons and bipeds parted as we walked into the midst of them. There, in all their glory, were my parents. My father was proud and tall, his head held high. His green scales and wings glistened in the fading sun. My mother was carefully perched on his shoulder as small bursts of embers drifted off of her and died quickly. Her phoenix was half her height as a biped, but her wingspan was massive.

While we had done a naming ceremony, it was customary to introduce the whelps to the family at large. Greg and I had thought we would use the holidays as an excuse, either bringing more of my family here or returning to Spain. Plus, we wanted to wait for Denis and Emory. We also hadn't planned for Greg to be wearing a glamour either.

Greg projected calm, knowing we were in a potentially dangerous situation. I sniffed to see what the emotional state of the group was, and to my surprise, it was curiosity. In all the commotion, we hadn't told anyone about Greg's heritage. To me, Greg smelled like Greg. I had no idea what he smelled like to the rest of the group.

Faith stepped forward, nude, looking up at the both of us. I was a few meters taller than her as a dragon, and I still felt small among the others. Greg was larger than me, and my father was the tallest, at almost five meters. Trevor and Faith, when they were dragons, were the only ones close to my father's height. Trevor's obsidian scales absorbed and reflected the light, showing off undertones of purple and blue. Of the other family members, mostly Trevor and Faith's whelps, all of them had a mix of obsidian and green scales dotted with feathers. There were a few others. A light blue dragon I'd never met. A few dark red dragons too. I assumed one of those was Gavin's mate, Brice.

In the varied colors of dragons, Greg stood out. With the sunlight on him, he looked like an opal. Everett looked like a miniature version of Greg. A small jewel at the top of his crown ridge.

"Xavior, Gregor. We're all happy to have you home," Faith said. She turned to Greg. "You'll have to tell us, Gregor, how you've come to be one of us again. Did you take another transfiguration potion?"

Since we lost track of how much time Greg had left before the glamour wore off, I shifted to answer my sister. Sasha hopped on Greg and climbed up to sit next to her brother. If something was off, which was likely what prompted Faith's question, the whelps were picking up on it. Instinctively protecting Greg. The family wouldn't dare do something to him in front of our whelps. I noticed Lena was shifted and near Trevor, leaving Faith to perform her head of household duties.

"Our friend Jordan made a glamour to help us when the whelps were having difficulty shifting. When we saved my brother's life, he shared something remarkable with us . . ." I looked at Greg and smiled. He was calm and confident. I leaned on that more than ever right now.

"The Order of Saint George are themselves, dragons." I looked at Faith, my father, and my family. "They are locked inside their human-like bodies. We don't know why, or how, but I know this: the dragon you see before you is my true mate, the parent to our whelps, and my best friend. Nothing you say or do here today will change that."

Faith stepped forward and put her hand on my shoulder. "So dramatic."

"What?" I couldn't believe her reaction. Was I really overre-acting?

Faith laughed. "Do you seriously think we wouldn't under-stand, brother? We've already accepted him. It doesn't matter what he looks like, or whether he can shift. Gregor is part of this family as much as you and Denis. We would never forsake our own."

"Wait, wait." I held up my hands. "I mean, I'm happy, but I'm also confused. What does he smell like to you?"

Faith smiled. "He smells like your mate, you asshole." She hit my shoulder, and I flinched. Then she looked up at Greg and called out to him. "Is he always this dramatic around you?"

Greg chuffed, and the whelps copied him. I looked up at him and scowled. "Did you know about this?" He shook his head gently, because he knew the whelps were there. They chuffed again, delighted.

"If you're done, we were just about to see how far your property line extends. Want to lead the way?" Faith shifted and Lena crawled up her back before she and Trevor started off in a direction. My father nodded to me and turned to follow.

I looked up at Greg. "I guess we're going for a walk. You up for that?" He gave his agreement, and I shifted. The whelps transferred to me as we walked.

There was a time, long before we had biped features, when dragons roamed the earth. Much like the elephants in Africa and Asia. Families would move together, then break off along the way for any number of reasons. To create a new life; to give birth to it; to find a quiet place to take a last breath. We didn't roam like we used to, but every so often, we would come together and walk the mountains in Spain or the countryside in Britain. This was the first time my family had ever come to the United States and walked, honoring my home and my family.

Fifteen minutes into the walk. Greg stopped, and the glamour disappeared. I watched as he took off the helmet and walked to a tree, then sat under it. My family continued as I circled back to check on him. The whelps followed, shifting with me as we reached him. He looked tired.

"You alright?" I sat next to him as Everett sat next to us and Sasha snuggled up to Greg, fascinated by his armor.

"I'm fine. Mostly tired. The weight of the glamour and the scale armor adds up. If I hadn't done all of that endurance training, I would have collapsed long before the glamour wore off." Greg smiled, even though he was a sweaty mess. "Will your family be upset that we fell behind?"

I shook my head. "They won't mind. They'll walk in a long arch around the property and come back in an hour or two. It gives me time to make sure we have dinner ready. I'm sure Edward has it under control, but I'd feel better if I helped."

"That sounds like a good idea. Might need to have Jordan look at the tie. I think I wore it for too long." The armor looked alright, though the tie was now fused into the scales. Only the tie tack remained, sitting in the center of Greg's scale armored chest like a shiny silver button.

"You think we broke it?"

"I'm not sure. I'm afraid to find out."

Scared was more like it. He had been so happy as his dragon.

"Come on. We'll have Jordan look at it. If we broke it, maybe he can tell us how to fix it." What that would cost us, we didn't have a clue.

Greg frowned, then nodded. I stood, then reached down to help Greg stand. Everett climbed up onto my back while I bent over to pick up Sasha. Greg carried his helmet under his left arm, then offered his right hand to me and I took it. The walk back to the house wasn't too long and boosted my spirits considerably. "We should take walks more often."

Greg smiled at me and nodded in agreement. "We can make it our own family tradition."

"I'd like that."

SECRET SOCIETY

GREGOR

Two months went by in a whirl of family, laughter, and physical therapy. My new bionic hand was something else. I'd been working with a bio-mechanical therapist to make sure I could control my responses. Apparently, powerful impulses caused me to misjudge my strength or make it stop working all together. I'd had more of the latter, with one interesting moment of having sex with Xavior, as I held him up against the wall, my hand gave out just as I was about to finish. It caused me to slip as I tried to catch him and we ended up in a heap on the bathroom floor, laughing and shushing each other because we didn't want to wake the twins.

Each time I've had a blip, the nano connections adjusted, registering the failure and fixing the connective routines. It was a nice feature, but I wondered if anyone had died from a blip at the wrong moment. They recommend it not be used in high-pressure or strenuous situations reliably for at least two years.

If I was still a detective, I'd have to go through more extensive certifications before I could go back to active duty. As it was, to even register for stunt work again, I had a great deal of training ahead of me. While I prepared for that, Xavior worked on various projects and barely let anyone watch the whelps. The new pregnancy was progressing, but his moods were worse, and his cravings were odd at the best of times.

With Catherine's help, we continued to monitor Xavior. Jordan knew, too, in case Catherine needed his help. If things were still progressing well after this visit from Catherine, we were going to adjust our medical visits from every few days to once every two weeks.

"Your vitals are good. The egg feels like it's in a good position. The crystal structure isn't helping with the imaging much, but as long as I can measure progress manually, we'll be alright." She sighed. "Maybe when Emory and Denis finally arrive, they'll have something we can use for more accurate measurements." Catherine looked frustrated with herself for not being more precise. Xavior reached out to touch her hands as she removed them from his abdomen.

"You're doing the best you can." Xavior squeezed her hands gently and Jordan touched her shoulder. Catherine looked like she was about to burst into tears.

I looked at the three of them and realized it's more than Xavior's health she was concerned about. "Are you okay, Catherine?" I put my hand on top of her's and Xavior's.

She shrugged. Jordan spoke, answering my question. "We've been trying."

I knew what that meant, and I try to keep my emotions in check about it. It couldn't be easy to see Xavior pregnant again when they had tried so hard to accomplish the same thing.

Catherine squeezed our hands and let go. "It's alright. We'll know soon enough if this last time worked or not." She looked at me and smiled. "Your parents want to be involved. I've explained how mage families work with children, and they've been very receptive."

That had me curious, since I don't remember ever hearing about the makeup of mage families. "That sounds like my parents." I smiled. "They would want to do as much as they can for any child they were associated with. Jennifer was a teacher, after all."

"Yes, she mentioned that." Catherine smiled with genuine affection. "Mage families raise children together. No one parent handles everything. We all share turns in education, outings, parenting, and chores. As long as I lead my family, all the adults have a shared responsibility for any child in our family. This includes my children's children. The Alexanders have lived this way for some time. It's why most of us are physicians. We all learn from each other."

"Not all mage families function like yours?" I should have asked about it sooner. I assumed my parents would have asked those questions. It's comforting to know that if a sibling results from whatever ritual they are doing, everyone involved would care for them.

"Many do, but some are more archaic. More misogynistic. They push the less desirable duties off on younger members of the household. Especially the women. I've run into it more often when the head of the house is very traditional." Catherine shrugged. "I know everyone in my family would sooner bite their own tongue off than follow that kind of behavior." She grinned, and it was nearly feral.

It occurred to me, we never met anyone else in Catherine's family. "The next time we're in Spain, your whole family should come over for dinner. We should show them proper hospitality for occupying your time for so long."

"Oh, she hasn't been here the whole time." Jordan grinned. "Mages have this interesting mode of travel called phasing. It lets them travel ley lines between two nodes attuned to them."

It was the first I'd ever heard of it. Xavior was surprised and curious, which was something to note. It seemed he hadn't known that fact about mages either.

"On the nights we're not babysitting, she goes home, and I check on various projects. I'm slightly envious of her. It's much faster than the fae passages, and she can travel through bodies of water."

Xavior raised up on his elbows. He looked at all of us and then frowned. I could see and feel his obsession grabbing him.

"How many times have you tried the ritual?"

"Three," Catherine answered. I was blatantly not trying to think about it, but Xavior had latched onto something and wouldn't be deterred.

"Have you been using this node travel the whole time?" Xavior asked. Catherine and Jordan look at each other.

"La has cagado!" Catherine stood, clearly upset with herself. Jordan frowned.

I turned to Xavior. "Do you think it's been disrupting the ritual magic?" He smiled, then nodded. Through our connection, I knew he was absolutely pleased he likely solved the problem with the ritual not working as intended, but there was also concern for his friends overshadowing it.

"I don't know why I didn't think of it. It's very fragile magic. The ley lines would most certainly siphon it away when you traveled," Jordan said.

Catherine frowned. "It's never affected me before. I've node traveled thousands of times while I was pregnant."

Jordan reached for his partner and stopped her pacing. "Those were biological. This is magical, Cat. There is a distinction, even if it's a small one."

I reached for Xavior's hand and helped him sit up as I pushed to my feet. "Whatever we need to do, or however we can accommodate you both better, please let us know. We don't want to be a hardship to you, and you've both done so much for us already."

Catherine sighed. "We'll need to go back to España." She glanced up at Jordan. "The center of my power is there. If Xavior's right, I won't be able to travel for a month or two, at least not quickly. And if everything works, maybe not for a while after that."

"We're not tied to the estate here. Besides, the holidays are nearly here. We talked about Christmas with the whelps in Spain. Denis and Emory could meet us there if necessary," Xavior offered.

Catherine and Jordan looked at me, the expectation clear on their faces. "I don't think my parents would mind the trip, either. They had a lot of fun last year. If you'd like me to ask them, I can." Their relief was evident as Catherine left Jordan's side to give me a hug.

Jordon grasped my shoulder. "I would consider it a favor if you did so, Gregor."

My eyes widen. That was huge. And fortunate. "Since you put it that way. I might have something I need you to look at."

Jordan smirked. Looked me up and down, then smiled. "Need help already? You're so young. Did our dragon finally wear you down?"

I growled at Jordan, though somewhere in my head I knew it was a joke. "Ask him yourself if you're so curious."

There was a giggle like sound that drew my attention to Xavior, and he just grinned. Something about challenging Jordan had done it for him. Our connection was full of need, attraction, and unchecked lust.

I opened my mouth to say something and instead; he grabbed my hand and pulled me toward the suite's exit. "We'll talk more tomorrow. Give Greg a chance to talk with his parents. Consider the Spain thing a done deal. I'll make the arrangements." He dragged me out the door as we left Catherine and Jordan standing there. One with a curious look on her face, and the other with a smirk on his.

Once we were outside, and the door had closed, Xav's lips landed on mine. The kiss was passionate and had me hard within moments. Maybe I should pick a fight with the fae more often. Not a serious one, because I had no chance of winning. Though if mild verbal sparing was all it took to get this response, I'd risk it.

VIBRATIONS

XAVIOR

I broke away from Greg's lips long enough to drag him down the hall and into a linen closet. He closed and locked the door, clearly on the same page as me. Then was on him. My lips smashed against his, teeth nipping at his lips. We threw clothes on the floor, then I paused for ten seconds to toss a bunch of towels down.

He dropped to his knees, taking my throbbing dick in his mouth. Everything felt like I was on fire. His lips were pure magic as I threaded a hand through his hair, feeling his head bob on my cock and his tongue play along my shaft. It wasn't long before he had me groaning and I came down his throat. Panting, he looked up at me with a smile on his face while he swallowed a couple of times and licked his lips.

I loved our connection. It was so good to have a shorthand between us that backed up our body language. He knew I wasn't done, and by the state of his own dick, he wasn't either. "Lay down," I said.

One eyebrow raised, and I knew this was about to get inter-esting. Sometimes we fought for control. When Jordan's small verbal jab had pissed him off a little, dominance was flowing off him and into my brain like the best drug. With the hormone supplements I was taking, I couldn't help myself.

Greg had stayed on his knees. It prompted me to add a, "Please." Not a question, definitely a statement and a sign of respect Greg liked when I took the lead. Greg smiled and slowly put his ass on the towels. When I dropped myself onto his lap, he stopped me from grabbing his dick. Instead, he pulled me forward, using my hips to guide me and before I knew it, I was sitting on his face, the stubble and whiskers of his mustache and goatee pressed into my crack, as his nose touched my balls as his tongue dove into my hole. Both holes. "Fuck." I grabbed a rack of linens in front of me as Greg licked me from balls to rim and back again.

His finger slipped in, working me open, using his saliva to do it. I rode his face as if we'd never get another chance. When he moved his tongue from my rim to my seminal canal, the combination of his tongue in one place and his fingers in another had me grabbing at my dick, already hard again.

"Fuck, fuck, you keep doing that, and I'm going to come again."

All I heard in response was a soft chuckle as he reached for me with his left hand and wrapped it around my dick. Interesting thing about bionic tech. You could program it to do various things. Greg's hand vibrated softly as it pumped up and down on my cock. By the elements, I was a goner.

I bit down on a towel as he wrung my orgasm out of me. The fireworks behind my eyelids would have put any festival to shame. When he finally let go of me, moving me, changing our positions. I was face down and ass up before I realized it. He used his left hand, covered in my spunk, wiping it along my hole, mixing it with his spit.

He slowly pushed his dick in as I whined softly, begging for more. That's when he pressed his thumb into my canal and wrapped the rest of his right hand around my balls. I melted, relaxing until he slid inside of me. I felt his legs pressed against my ass. His left hand stayed on my lower back for a few strokes, vibrating, as he used it on us both.

Toys were always novelty things to me and never held my interest for long. Greg's new hand was everything. The more creative he got with it, the more I wanted it everywhere.

Just as I was on the verge of an orgasm, he stopped, pulled out, and moved me onto my back. He reached behind him and grabbed pillows off of the shelf and shoved them under my ass. "Fuck, you look amazing, Xav."

I looked like a beet with fluids all over me and a rounded stomach full of egg. Whatever he saw, it didn't matter. He loved me for it, and that's all that counted in my book. "Get back inside me before I make you."

He laughed. "So needy." He grinned. "I remember this from when you were first pregnant. You were insatiable. If it wasn't for my left hand, I don't know if I could keep up this time."

He very well could keep up, and I knew it. He put his hands behind my knees and pushed them back as much as it was comfortable for me to handle. When I grabbed my thighs, he let go of me and used his right hand to feed himself into my seminal canal.

"Fuck, fuck. You feel so good." He thrust into me a few times, then pulled out and pushed into my ass again. This was something he experimented with toward the end of the last pregnancy. This second one would give us plenty of practice.

"Which one are you going to come in?" I ask between each series of thrusts.

"Which one do you want it in?"

"Partner's choice." I didn't care as long as filled up one of them. Then later, we'd see if we could steal some time to fill up the other.

"The next time we have a weekend off, I'm going to take my time. Fill each one of your holes, starting with your mouth and working my way down from there." He pulled out and pushed into my canal.

"Fuck, Greg," I whispered.

"Then, I'm going to eat out each one. Make you come so hard you won't be able to walk or fly for at least a few hours." I laughed through tears and moans as he switched again and pressed into my ass.

When he put a vibrating thumb inside my canal and wrapped the rest of his hand around my balls while he thrust a little faster, I knew he was close. I held my legs open wider and moved my hips to feel everything he was giving me.

"I love you. Fuck, Xav. I love you," he said as he came inside me, continuing to thrust with each pulse of cum he embedded in me.

As he finished, he looked down at me and smiled, then moved his thumb, even while his dick was still semi-hard in my ass. "You want one more, love?"

I nodded. Fuck yes, I'd take one more. Who knows when we'd get to do anything again today. I needed everything I could get. His thumb vibrated at a slightly higher frequency as he thrust it in and out of my canal. I couldn't think, only feel as he massaged my balls and finger fucked me while he was still inside me. Each small thrust hit my gland, even as he tried to keep himself in my ass. I whimpered as he vibrated his thumb at an even higher rate against my balls and kept his fingers still. My toes curled as I shot cum all over my chest.

He smiled as he took his bionic hand away from my sensitive groin. Then he slipped out of my ass as he lowered my legs and bent over to lick the cum off my chest, working his way up until his lips met mine. I moaned softly as we shared my spend between us with each kiss.

I pulled him down to rest on top of me as we caught our breath. We were sticky and momentarily satisfied. "Five minutes, then we'll figure out how to clean up and find food."

Greg laughed. "Okay." And he kissed me again. Then I caught sight of his hair and laughed.

"Greg?" I grinned.

"Yes, love?" I was shaking with laughter while he smiled. "What's got you in stitches?"

"Your hair," I said with barely enough breath for him to make sense of the words.

He lifted his hand to his head and realized what had happened when his eyes widened in surprise. Apparently, his hand wasn't the only thing I came on. He laughed as he ran fingers through his hair, removing what he could, wiping it on the towels next to us. "Worth it."

I absolutely agreed and kissed him again.

IN RESIDENCE

GREGOR

The plan to move to Spain for the winter had gathered momentum. Organizing transportation and plane rides for various parts of the family was something Xavior excelled at, or rather, he and his staff did. Amid that, we'd finally gotten word of when Denis and Emory would arrive.

Their projects and lab spaces had to be handed off or shut down, and that took longer than expected. They put in for an extended leave, given Denis's accident. It meant that they would be with our family through the winter and the holidays. Emory was very much looking forward to the festivities after our stories.

The family still didn't know Emory was a unicorn. They had been very supportive when Denis finally told them about being a phoenix. In a way, I felt a kinship with Emory. There were very few things that could harm dragons. Fae, the Knights, and unicorns were at the top of the list. And maybe whales, if Xavior's stories were anything to go by.

Xavior wore loose clothing to hide the subtle changes he was already going through. We planned to keep it quiet until Denis and Emory could be here to explain things. He spent more time with the whelps and as a dragon. Being a dragon made him more comfortable with the pregnancy, and he explained it to me one night when he was desperate for more physical contact.

"My first pregnancy was uncomfortable toward the end because the egg was so big. This one makes me feel uneasy all the time and more tired. I think it's taking more magic to sustain itself than a normal dragon pregnancy."

I held him close and caressed his back. He sighed as scales rippled across his skin. "We have the batteries Emory gave us. Maybe we should use those to help you. Give you a boost. When Emory gets here, they can fill them again or make more."

Xavior pressed a kiss into my shoulder. "That's a good idea." His head moved to press his nose into my armpit. "I feel like I can manage the magical energy imbalance better as a dragon. There's more there for the embryo to take. The only time I seem to have a decent amount of energy as a biped is when I have a hormone rush, then I crash."

"Is that because of the med pod?" The small monitor and medication dispenser he came home with was still managing the pregnancy and likely sending updates to Denis and Emory.

"Probably." I could feel his lips curve into a smile against my skin. "Though I have to admit, I don't mind how we've handled it. Thank the elements for empty rooms and family around to help with the whelps."

I laughed softly. "I think everyone knows, anyway. It's not like we can easily remove that scent."

"They assume it's us reconnecting after so much time in a strange place and having the twins. They also know our relationship is very new. We have a lot of leeway right now because of that."

"That's good to know. I don't want to piss anyone off." I meant that too. Last thing I needed was someone in the family mad at me, or having to defend myself against a dragon. The consequences would be devastating if things went too far.

"We'd have to be extremely irresponsible for that to happen, I think. Plus, Faith would warn us if we were causing any hardship. There are over fifteen dragons and their various partners, of which most are dragons, and three whelps that are being spoiled. Everyone wants to see Denis and Emory too. Like I said, we have a lot of leeway."

A random thought occurred to me. "How in the world are you feeding everyone?" I knew how much Xavior could eat. Multiplied by fifteen dragons, that had to add up.

"All the waste being created, along with biomass from the gardens, supplemented with a hydroponics garden and a synthetic meat producer that both supply the estate, we've handled it fine. Though the staff was talking about sourcing our own replicated and synthetic meats. They already have a bakery. It would be a matter of expanding and modernizing the kitchen and building facilities to handle growing more things than we do already." He shrugged. "If it wasn't for dragon shit, we'd have to figure out how to borrow energy from various suppliers. So, essentially, our families and their guests are paying for themselves."

Xavior grinned, and I laughed. The miracle of dragon shit continued.

When Denis and Emory arrived, it wasn't by the local transport station. They were escorted via a line of vehicles that requested access to the estate. As soon as the gates opened, Edward alerted Xavior who then alerted the rest of the family in the house.

Apparently, the USEA had decided to forgo the press and the possible fanfare that might have resulted from Denis and Emory showing up at a local transport station. Our situation had been manageable, but they took it as a signal to take security precautions. Denis and Emory were valuable employees and vital to many of their programs. They wouldn't risk them again, even while they were on vacation.

The family had gathered on the front steps as the large vehicles pulled into the circle drive. They looked similar to the autonomous vehicles Xavior had rented for his parties, except these all had someone in the driver's seat. Maybe as security or precaution, I couldn't tell. When the first driver exited the vehicle, I could tell he was wearing a weapon. Which was a dead giveaway for a federal agent or agency relationship of some kind, though it was unusual for USEA to carry weapons. The officers that visited previously hadn't. It gave me a reason to worry. I glanced at Xavior and noticed the same concern when his gaze met mine. Denis and Emory were being treated like heads of state, which Xavior had at his parties, and even those individuals hadn't shown up with armed guards.

The armed driver opened the door to the rear compartment and Denis got out first, followed by Emory. Since it was Xavior's estate, and Faith was the head of the family, they moved first to greet them. I stayed back with my parents, holding Everett while Jennifer had Sasha. Trevor held onto Lena, too, though she was excited and talking Trevor's ear off. There was a ripple of tension in the crowd at the front door.

Words and handshakes were exchanged, and Denis nodded to the armed driver who got back in the vehicle. Moments later, the vehicles left. Then Denis and Xavior hugged, followed by Faith. Xavior offered a hug to Emory, who accepted, though it looked awkward, possibly because they knew they had an audience. Emory had been more open to shows of affection on the moonbase.

It made me briefly wonder about their relationship with Denis. Most of the couples here displayed a good deal of physical affection, whether it was a touch, a caress, or hugs and kisses. Holding hands was a very common sight, to the point when I refrained from my normal amount of touching Xav around our family last holiday season, to keep his glamour working until we revealed our surprise, they had wondered if something was wrong. It occurred to me that someone should warn Emory and Denis, so nosy dragons did not surprise them.

On moonbase, they often glanced at each other and smiled, but maintained a very professional atmosphere around everyone, including Xavior and me. It might take the couple time to relax in front of family, especially if they were worried about how the family would take to Emory and news of the pregnancy.

But for now, meeting everyone and getting settled for a few days was the plan. Then the family would leave as various endeavors took them back to their lives with plans for all of us to meet in again for the holidays.

I moved up to the small group with Everett, followed by my parents with Sasha, Xavior's parents, and Trevor with Lena. "Hello again, welcome home." I held out my left hand to Denis, and he took it.

"Well met, Gregor. I see your new prosthetic is working well. Fine craftsmanship. How are you handling the blips?"

"It's only been a few months, but I've only had one or two a week. Nothing serious. Only hand slips and such."

"Good to hear. I'm glad to see they've improved the design since I worked on it last."

It shouldn't have surprised me that Denis had designed the original. "Maybe we can talk about it later." I smiled. "For now, let me introduce you. This is Everett. And my parents Jennifer and Philip." Denis said a few polite hello's to my parents. I nodded toward the small biped Jennifer was holding. "And this is Sasha." Denis glanced between the two whelps.

"They're beautiful, Gregor." It was odd to hear Denis say anything was beautiful. It seemed less about the whelps themselves versus something Xavior and I had a hand in creating. Then he further surprised me as he held out his hands toward Everett. "May I?"

"Sure, if he's agreeable." I leaned Everett toward his uncle, and he looked at me, then back at Denis. The way Everett scrunched his face, I could tell he was trying to figure out why his other father was wearing a beard. He even looked at Xavior a time or two, concentrating their shared features.

After several long moments, he hesitantly reached out and Denis offered his fingers for the whelp to latch onto. Some kind of exchange happened between the two, and Everett leapt out of my arms toward Denis. He caught the whelp in mid-flight and brought him safely down again. Even with his lower half swaddled, Everett still used his upper body with little hinderance. "Most of the time, he doesn't wear anything. Clothing irritates his skin flaps. Never mind using diapers." The swaddling had come slightly undone, and I tried to wrap Everett up again to keep him warm while he clung to Denis.

"I see. I have to admit I'm curious about the webbing." He said, even as Everett grabbed his beard and pulled. Denis made a noise which attracted Emory, Xavior, and Faith's attention away from their quiet conversation. "Sorry, little one, that doesn't come off," Denis said.

A mild shock went through the group at his joke. Faith and Xavior looked especially surprised. Xavior broke first and laughed, which let everyone else laugh. Denis turned toward his brother and handed Everett off to him with a rarely seen smile.

"Come," Xavior said, wrapping a free arm around his brother's shoulders. "Lets meet everyone else and get you settled in." They walked back up the stairs with a very curious whelp as the rest of the extended dragon family welcomed more of their own.

CURE-ALLS

XAVIOR

With my brother and Emory safely settled at the estate, family life resumed at a casual pace. Denis and Emory were often invited to a meal or an outing on the grounds. They had declined leaving the estate, as more logistics were required for that, apparently. I hadn't realized Denis and Emory had become so important. We had quietly agreed to let things settle for a few days before we told everyone I was pregnant again.

While Denis and Emory were clearly excited about how well things seemed to be going with the pregnancy, I was struggling. I had no fucking clue how Trevor and Faith had ten whelps between them without being absolutely miserable all the time. Maybe it was the twenty or more years between whelps. I was bloody miserable. Pregnancy was for the birds or other dragons. Clearly, I wasn't meant to have the happy glow so many often talked about.

My second time through wasn't any more pleasant than the first so far. In some ways, it was worse. I was more irritable, tired, and felt bruised from the inside, both mentally and physically. Then my libido would kick in and give me a boost of energy.

While that part was enjoyable, the rest wasn't, and I was resenting the emotional swings my hormones were putting me through.

The random thought occurred to me while we were having dinner with my parents one night. My father hadn't ever carried any offspring, and never cautioned any of us against it. I often wondered if he wished he had. During his aging cycles, he stayed in his den and mother ran the house with help while he was "resting." I suspected it was for the sanity of the household in general, but my mother never said anything about it, even to this day.

Greg was understandably stressed too, but doing better than me by far. He was extremely accommodating, but even I found him unexpectedly annoying sometimes. That bothered the fuck out of me. This wasn't Greg's fault any more than it was mine. Thankfully, Greg had the armored suit now, which Jordan checked over after the tie merged with it. The suit had reinforced the spell work according to him, and if he had known about it, he would have used it instead of the tie. After we knew it was safe, Greg spent as much time as he could with us before he needed a break. Having him play dragon gave me space to breathe when I felt like my emotions were off balance.

Spending time with our whelps always brought me a measure of calm. They seemed extremely sensitive to my mood shifts, and I couldn't tell if it was pheromones they were picking up on or they were just really observant. Even if I approached them with smiles and a relaxed posture, if there was any hint of uneasiness, they clung and nuzzled me until my mood improved. After a few times, I approached my therapist to talk about other ways to deal with emotional surges around my whelps. The last thing I wanted was for them to worry about me. Their safety and mental health were more important, especially at this stage.

Every few days I cycled between only wanting my whelps near me to wanting Greg to rail me into a wall somewhere with whatever he could give me. I liked when he shifted back to his sweaty biped self. His scent was intoxicating, and another pleasant distraction for me until he went to shower. Unfortunately for us, we hadn't been able to try sex with his glamour suit. He was either too tired from playing with the twins after they went for a nap, or I was too tired. Our timing seemed to always be off, which added to my annoyance.

So, one morning, when Denis and Emory called Greg to see if they could visit, my anxiety spiked, and I growled at Greg for waking me up to ask.

"Could you give us a few more hours? Xavior isn't quite himself yet, and the whelps are still sleeping."

"Yeah . . ." He nodded. "I'll let him know. Maybe chat with Catherine if you get a chance this morning. She can bring you both up-to-date on things." Another pause. "Great. We'll see you after lunch then. Thanks. Bye."

The whelps were still nested under my wing. Greg always slept close to my head unless he was cold, which wasn't often. "How about I have breakfast brought to the den for us? I can see if the grandparents are interested in taking the whelps, and then we can have some time before you're prodded at?"

I perked up and gave him an affirmative sound. He rubbed my snout and kissed it before he disappeared toward the den exit.

After breakfast, my parents carted the whelps off for the rest of the day, and we found ourselves with some alone time. He was absolutely sweet, as usual, to the point of annoying, with the scent of his concern tickling my nose.

"So," he said as he sat near the end of my snout so I could see him. "What do you want to do with the rest of the morning?"

In answer, I summoned the glamour suit to my paw and gently set it down next to him. He chuckled.

"Your wish is my command." He stood, picked up the first piece of the suit, and pulled it on. When he shifted, I picked up desire and lust in the air. I wasn't sure if that was me or him, and I didn't care. We spent a few long moments, scent marking each other, before I presented myself with an obvious invitation.

Greg was never one to pass up an opportunity, unless interrupted. This time, he hurried to take up the place where I desired him. His initial thrust inward felt hard. I felt tight and tried to relax even as he adjusted his stance and moved his hips to make space. My tail thrashed along his side and back until he picked a pace that brought a low growl from my throat.

He was exceedingly careful with his claws. I think we both would have liked a bit of rougher play as dragons, but Greg wouldn't risk it without knowing whether or not a scratch would kill me. His grasp tightened, and I knew he was close. My legs shook from the effort to remain still. If this didn't satisfy me, I'd have us switch so we could have biped sex. At the moment, it was a nice warm up and I had no expectations for myself, other than wanting to see if we could use the suit for more than entertaining our whelps.

As Greg made quicker thrusts, I made encouraging noises. The slight movements eased muscles and let me relax some, which I appreciated. What happened next was a surprise for both of us. He let go, and we both felt his release. Pressing hard, he emptied himself into me and the magical pleasure immediately took effect. My stomach stopped cramping, I stopped feeling uncomfortable, and I hummed, enjoying the blissful effect of Greg's cum.

I didn't think too hard about it, enjoying the moment. It hadn't felt like this since before our first pregnancy. As Greg released my hindquarters, I pushed back to keep him inside and milk more of that sweet substance out of him. He indulged me for far longer than necessary. When we were through, I motioned with my head for him to lie next to me and he complied, our connection telling me he was also happily sated for the moment. I curled up next to him and slept more peacefully than I had in some time.

After our nap, I noticed two things: We had shifted, Greg had removed his armor at some point, and I felt comfortable for the first time in months. I was sure it had been his magical essence that had done the trick. All seemed right with my world as Greg moved closer to me and I nuzzled into him. Had we both suffered this whole time for lack of magic? I kissed him and kept kissing him until he moaned and then blinked at me as a smile formed on his face.

"Need something?" It came out in a mumbled mess and I still kissed him. "I sense you're feeling better. Everything okay?" He kissed me back, and I sighed, happily.

"Better than okay. I think your cum has the same magical properties with the suit as it did when you took the potion. It somehow made everything feel better. I don't have this dull ache, or constant tired-drained feeling. I slept better than I have since before I had the twins, and best of all, the tension in my abdomen is gone."

Greg grinned, then chuckled. "So you're saying my spunk is a cure-all?" He moved on top of me and nuzzled, kissing my jaw and neck.

"Your glamoured dragon spunk seems to be, yes." I cradled his face in my hands, running my fingers through his beard. "I know the suit is a pain. You put yourself through so much just for the whelps, would it be too much to ask..."

"Xav, you don't even have to ask. I had fun, and if it helps you get through this, I'm more than happy to wear the suit and stick my obscenely," he gave me a quick kiss. "Large," then another. "—Dick into you and fuck you every chance we get."

Our kiss went from teasing to intense and breathless in a blink before I pulled back a little. "You're amazing. Wonderful. Handsome. I love you, Gregor. I love you." The happiness I felt made me babble. He gave me more than I ever dreamed possible.

Later I when we met up with my sister and her husband for lunch without the whelps because, bless the elements, they were still with their grandparents, I quizzed her about how she and Trevor had managed having whelps.

"So you're telling me the whole reason the two of you can even stand to keep having whelps is sex magic?" It never occurred to me to ask since I hadn't planned on having whelps myself until I met Greg. Even Greg didn't ask when he quizzed Faith during the first pregnancy, because why would he?

They both nodded. "Faith is much better about it than me. I get to the last part and feel like I'm being torn in two, but then she works her magic, and I'm good for a few more days." Trevor grinned at Faith and she smiled back, giving him a quick kiss.

"You didn't know?" Faith asked. I shook my head.

"So you just dealt with it? All that soreness and pain?" Faith looked astonished, like I had done something she hadn't expected.

"Yes! Damn it. It would have been nice if someone had volunteered that information," I groused.

"In fairness, even if they had, there wasn't anything we could have done about it. We didn't have the potion, the glamour, or the suit," Greg pointed out.

I waved my hands in frustration. "But we had access to mages and other magic. We could have found a substitute or something. I was so fucking miserable. At least this time it won't be as bad."

Faith straightened in her chair. "What do you mean this time?" She set her juice down and looked at me. Fuck. We were going to wait for Denis and Emory before we said anything.

"Let's meet up with Denis and Emory after lunch and they can explain," I offered.

She looked me up and down. "What do Denis and Emory have to do with you being miserable?" Greg buried his face in his coffee cup as lunch turned quiet. "Fine, keep your secrets. I think I liked it better when you and Denis didn't talk to each other. At least then I knew everything."

Greg and I smiled at each other. Trevor hid a smile, and the conversation turned to less suggestive things, like figuring out where the best place was for a whelp playground.

PARENTAL ADVISORY

GREGOR

Catherine and Jordan's suite was doubling as an exam room with an audience. Denis and Emory had provided an imaging tool that aligned the crystals in the egg so that Catherine could examine the embryo, and conveniently show it to everyone on the holo display.

"So let me make sure I understand this," Faith said as she glanced between Xavior, Denis, and the holo screen. "This is your whelp." She pointed at Denis and Emory.

"Actually, it's a pegasus, or a foal rather, if that helps," Emory corrected.

Faith took a breath and continued. "And you both are the parents, along with Greg, because his dragon genetics were so much of a throwback that you could revive a whole species." Denis nodded. "Should I ask how you did this, considering there's no known magic on earth that can do such a thing?"

"Well, interesting that you should mention that, because it was a discovery Dawn made that helped us engineer the embryo. Your daughter is brilliant, Faith. Her techno-magical abilities are unprecedented."

Faith took in what Denis said, but didn't comment. Instead, she set her sights on Xavior and me. "And you both went along with this?" She looked at us like we were aiding and abetting a crime. Which might be the case, but the law was pretty fuzzy since they engineered the egg on Luna, and the gestation was taking place on Earth. We all hoped no one asked too many questions. Though we knew we'd have to tell our families, eventually.

"We want to tell the family I'm acting as a surrogate for Denis. Since the family knows he's a phoenix, it should make sense. We don't have to explain the particulars of how and what," said Xavior, in an effort to appease his sister.

"Did any of you think about how many questions there would be about a foal with wings?" Faith asked with a slight annoyance in her tone. "And what if they can't shift?"

"Happy accident?" I offered.

Faith glared at me. Trevor turned away and covered his mouth with his hand, stifling a laugh. She looked at all of us and then looked at Catherine. "Are you alright with this?"

"How we got here concerns me. However, as the head physician for this family, it's my duty to keep everyone healthy, including Xavior and the foal," Catherine said. "That should be the biggest concern right now. Everything else is secondary."

Catherine shut off the display, much to my relief. Xavior reached for my hand and I gave it to him, helping him sit up.

"So, what's your professional opinion?" Xavior asked, trying to refocus the group and move past the same conversations and concerns we had already answered for ourselves. Catherine was right. We were here now, and the health of Xavior and the foal were all that mattered.

"The foal looks healthy. Though I'm concerned about how much your magic and body are going to be drained by this second pregnancy so soon after having the twins."

"Would these help?" Xavior pulled out of his pocket the batteries that Emory had made for us.

"What are they?" Catherine asked as she took one small egg capsule in her hand.

Emory piped up and explained in great detail how they were charged and how they release magic upon contact with stomach acid.

"Have they been tested?" Catherine asked. That was a smart question. I hadn't thought to ask that, and I should have. I was more worried about Xavior arriving home in one piece.

"They have. Denis and I have used the prototypes several times, though originally we designed them as suppositories, since the rectal lining absorbs faster." Emory looked pleased with their explanation. "This model is an improved design. Xavior and Greg should be able to ingest them without issue."

"Xavior might, but I'm concern about Greg's reaction to complex magic." Catherine frowned. Everyone knew about the issue with the potion and how it almost killed me.

Jordan had moved away from Emory, eying the magical pills and them like he was afraid something might explode in his face. Emory being a unicorn was still a closely kept secret and the one piece of the puzzle no one asked about when they saw a pegasus embryo. Nor did the family point out that Emory didn't smell any different from Denis. Xavior and I were the only ones that knew Denis and Emory were using some kind of magic to mask Emory's true nature. Though I would bet Jordan might sense the amount of magic they had. Like could recognize like in this small a room. Even if they assumed Emory was a very talented Equine shifter, they were mostly right.

"If you take it," Jordan put his hand on my shoulder. "Don't wear the glamour at the same time. Especially now that it's embedded in the scale suit."

"I think that's sound advice. I'm not trying to have a repeat of what happened with the potion." Xavior squeezed my hand to reassure me.

Emory shrugged and added their assessment of the situation. "The battery should disburse the same amount of magic that dragon ejaculate does. We originally designed them with that specific application in mind."

Which, if I understood what Emory was saying, they had designed the magical batteries as a kind of sex toy for Denis and them. I tried very hard not to blush and probably failed. It also meant that Denis knew dragons had magic laced ejaculate, too. By the look on Xavior's face, he was drawing the same conclusions as I had. He looked surprised, then annoyed that he was the last one to know why dragons had magical ejaculate in the first place. Never mind that it was a perk dragons could enjoy even without a pregnancy involved. It also meant that Denis and Emory did, in fact, have sex, and apparently enjoyed it enough to make toys for each other.

Everyone in the room shared a knowing look, likely because they all came to the same conclusion I had about the little batteries.

I felt a flush of heat creep further up my neck as Emory focused on me. "You should find that your own ejaculate will produce similar effects after you ingest the battery." There were double takes all around and my blush blossomed across my face, likely bright-red enough to have done a fae proud.

"Well, I assume your med pod would alert us to when I might require a magical supplement, yes?" Xavior asked Denis and Emory.

"Certainly," Denis responded. "We've taken the liberty of modifying the system to use Earth based communication to alert you via your phone so that you can take action immediately. The only thing we couldn't store in the med pod was supplemental magic. The batteries solve that problem nicely."

Xavior and I exchanged a look. "You thought ahead," Xavior said, stating the obvious but calling out how premeditated it looked to both of us. Given the looks being exchanged between everyone else, they were having the same thoughts.

"We expected, based on previous experiments, that there might be a need," Emory said. "We prepared for this as much as possible, for a successful outcome over the years we have attempted to produce an offspring. Besides, it gave me ample reason to study dragon sexual physiology and mating practices, which was helpful for other reasons." They smiled slightly before it disappeared into the stoic face they usually wore, confirming way more than I wanted to know about Denis and Emory. Everyone else looked amused on some level. If I didn't know any better, I'd say it was Emory's attempt at telling a joke. Though they continued as if they hadn't said anything amusing at all.

"Xavior, your health and safety are paramount. We couldn't attempt this without you, and your life is more important than our offspring. While we have taken risks," Emory glanced at their mate. "Denis and I refused to endanger your life any more than necessary. The monitor also has the option to terminate the pregnancy if it becomes life threatening."

They really had thought of everything that might be necessary or go wrong. The care and concern Denis and Emory had shown through this entire process was much more than I ever expected, given what Xavior had told me about his brother. Maybe it had started out as a selfish endeavor on the couple's part, but at the moment, it was hard not to empathize, considering how much Xav and I went through to have the twins.

"Thank you for everything you've done so far. It's appreciated," said Xavior. His honest sincerity wove through our connection. He knew they had his best interest at heart. I appreciated that too. No fetus was ever worth the life of a parent. Especially not one with twins and a mate. I'm glad they understood that.

"May I have access to the monitor?" Catherine looked at Denis and Emory. Having Catherine as an objective observer would definitely help reassure everyone involved.

"Absolutely. We'll set up a secure link so you can monitor, send notifications, and take actions as well. As Xavior's physician, we want your expert opinion," Denis said.

"Well," Xavior interrupted. "If show-and-tell is over. We should probably find our parents and talk to them about all this. Besides, I'm starving, and I want to see my whelps." Xavior stood after that declaration and headed for the door. I followed him, and didn't look back to see who came along with us as I reached for Xavior's hand again and we walked to the playroom where our parents were entertaining the whelps.

HARBINGER

GREGOR

When dragons put their minds to having something done, things can move pretty quickly. Within days of us discussing it, parts for a large playground set had shown up at the estate. Between Xavior, Faith, Trevor, me and other family members that hadn't left yet, we'd put the whole play set together in two days, including the protective surface that would cushion them if they fell. Denis and Emory stayed inside, continuing to acclimate.

The location was a pleasant spot near the trees for the shade they provided. It was also the only clearing that was close enough to the house without having to tear up part of the garden. The whelps had watched the progress from the sidelines, with our parents keeping an eye on them. They played, ate, and napped in the shade of the nearby trees as we finished up.

The next morning, we ate breakfast as a large group, and everyone dressed casually to spend the morning playing with the whelps on the new set. As we headed toward the door, we were all chatting away about what the whelps might try first. Xavior opened the front door, and from there, our morning descended into chaos.

Individuals dressed in military uniforms armed with large caliber rifles pointed them at Xavior, then me, as we were pulled out of the entryway to the circle drive and put on our knees. Fear shot through me as I worried for everyone else and repeatedly yelled: "Close the door!"

They listened, thankfully, as I heard the large door slam shut. I knew there was security around the estate, especially around the house. Whoever these people were would have to lay siege to it to get inside.

"This is private property! You're trespassing!" Xavior yelled as they cuffed him. They weren't normal cuffs. They dampened any abilities he had. I felt him wince. Then our connection quieted, which alarmed me. I hadn't realized how much our connection was part magic until it was gone.

Xavior glanced at me as my wide-eyed look met his. "We'll be okay." I don't know if I believed what I said, and I had no idea if Xavior believed me, either. He nodded in response. Then I was roughly shoved into cuffs, the same model as Xavior's. The connection to my magic faded and left a hollow space. Had it always been there? These were unlike the nanite bands that had only dampened our abilities when we'd been in the isolation bubble. I glanced at Xavior, willing us both to stay calm. Raids like this were so rare, it couldn't be legal. "Who authorized this intrusion?" I asked, putting as much authority in my voice as possible.

"Wouldn't you like to know, Gregor." The woman who spoke walked through the wall of personnel that had surrounded us. "It so happens that your dragon here has a warrant. He's being extradited to France to stand trial."

She was as tall as I remembered, though her hair was shorter, with more gray in it that made the light brown even lighter. Her back was straight as she carried herself with a confidence, staring at Xavior and me with steel-blue eyes demanding that those around her obey. It was her eyes I remembered most. I glared at her.

"Yes, I know what you've been up to. The entire world does after you saved his brother, that so-called scientist. So noble."

She said with disdain as she glanced at my arm. "I thought I taught you better than that."

"What you taught me and what I'm capable of are two different things."

"I can see that." She glanced between us. "Still, I have a warrant. You and your partner are welcome to fight me if you'd like. I would relish the challenge." I was sure she would. All these years without doing the one thing she was trained to do? She had to have jumped at the chance to come after us. Whoever offered it to her knew what they were doing.

"What warrant? What am I being charged with?" Xavior asked. It was a good question. After everything we'd been through, this was a nightmare come to life.

"The death of Bianca Cooper," she said.

Xavior growled. "Those charges were dropped."

"Yes. Here in the U.S. but in France, they were filed on behalf of the Lafayette family. We were contacted to execute the warrant."

"No." I found my voice, and the woman turned toward me.

"What did you say to me?" she asked as she turned to face me. The surrounding personnel twitched with bridled anticipation. She stilled them with one motion of her hand.

"No. You can't take him." If she wanted a fight, she'd have one. There was no way I'd let her leave with Xavior.

She laughed softly. "What makes you think you have any say in this?"

"He's pregnant. And by law, you can't carry out a warrant against a pregnant dragon, no matter where it originated from. He's protected."

The shock that floated across her face gave me a small thrill. Not only because she knew I was right, but because she had to have known who fathered the offspring. Which was technically true, though the other two parents were inside. I gambled that the information about our twins wasn't common knowledge. Besides, I was still right. Xav was pregnant and by law, she couldn't do shit.

Whatever my face looked like, my mother backed up a step, which put a knowing smirk on my face. Only when Xavior's worried voice reached my ear did I realize he might not know what was going on. "Greg?"

"Xavior, say hello to my mother, Narissa."

She glanced between the two of us and sighed. Xavior remained quiet. "You're an embarrassment to the Order, Gregor. I'm ashamed you've come to this. Mating with a dragon. How could you?"

"I'm an embarrassment? Are you fucking kidding me?" I got my legs under me and stood. Her goons grabbed me, but they didn't force me back to my knees. They stopped jostling me when she gave them another wave of her hand. "You have the gall to come here on some kind of flimsy extradition warrant and say I'm an embarrassment? You threw me out! I can't be an embarrassment to something I'm no longer part of. So uncuff us, and get the fuck off our property."

She flinched. That small tell thrilled me. She had no idea who I was now, and that gave me more power over her than I realized. Though I could see it in her eyes that she thought I was bluffing and she even smiled as her gaze locked with mine. "I want proof, now. Or he's coming with me."

Practically on cue, Catherine came out of the house. I'm certain our family had been listening via security feeds to the whole drama playing out in the driveway. They pointed guns at her and she held up a tablet. "You asked for proof. Xavior is my patient. I have scans. I'm also the matriarch of the Alexander family." Catherine's voice carried over the group, her soft accent becoming more pronounced as she spoke. "The Lafayette family has no jurisdiction in the United States. They would need to contact a local mage family in the area to take any legal action. If they had taken those steps, Xavior's lawyer would have been contacted first, and he could have saved you the trip. Here." She held out the device to my mother.

Narissa's gaze only left mine for a moment to take the tablet from Catherine. "How do I know you haven't falsified this data?" Narissa asked as she looked it over.

"If you have an anti-tamper device, you can check the tablet. You can also see there are several weeks' worth of data from a monitoring device." I prayed that even someone as knowledgeable as my mother about dragon physiology wouldn't recognize the fact that the fetus lacked features in the right proportions to be a dragon.

My mother looked over the data and handed the tablet back to Narissa. "Uncuff them." No one moved for a moment, obviously stunned at the reversal of their leader's decision. "Now!" They moved quickly after that.

It was a gratifying moment. So much so I got in her face, determined to make a point. "You ever come here again with your goon squad, I'll make sure you'll regret it."

She smiled, then sighed. "Maybe you are my son after all." That chilled me to my bones as I watched her back off and move her people down the drive with merely a nod. Then a portal opened. They walked through it and disappeared.

Catherine narrowed her eyes. "That was a mage portal. Someone was definitely helping them breach security. They wouldn't have been able to come inside the wards otherwise."

Xavior took my hand and squeezed it. "Are you okay?" he asked.

I turned to look at him. "Shouldn't I be asking you that question?" I moved closer and pressed my forehead to his, as I took a breath to calm my heart before it beat right out of my chest.

He brushed his nose along mine. The small action making me smile, reminding me of how dragons commonly show affection. "She had no idea how many other dragons were here. If she had wanted to start a war, we could have given her one."

"She's not worth the effort." I tugged at our hands, moving us back toward the door. Our connection finally reassert itself, and my hands tingled with a sudden feeling of magic. Maybe I needed to practice more. An overwhelming need to learn what else I could be capable of came from a burning desire to protect my family. I wouldn't let her surprise us like that again if I could help it. "Let's make sure everyone else is okay."

While telling my mother about the pregnancy was the last thing I wanted to do, it worked. She couldn't touch us for at least eight months. It was time enough to get Renard involved to stop whatever this new plot was to accuse Xavior. If I'd had time, I might have seen what face she would have made when I told her the Knights were originally dragons just to watch her horrid house of cards fall around her. But that would have to wait for another day.

We went inside and everyone began hugging us. They gave our whelps back to us and they clung to our chests. My dad came up to us and touched our arms.

"Don't underestimate her. She's patient and will wait for another opportunity," Philip said. We nodded, and he left it at that. The rest of the day was subdued as overall security was double checked and the wards around the estate were reinforced by Catherine, Jordan, and Emory.

The current plan was to keep everyone safe inside the building until we could assess this current threat. With that many dragons unable to go outside, and only one pregnant dragon's pheromones to keep the peace, everyone decided it was best to forgo a formal dinner until there was more breathing room. The staff set up a buffet for everyone to eat from throughout the day and late into the evening.

Later that night, Xavior and I talked after the whelps went to sleep.

"What did you sense from her?" I asked, afraid to know what he felt, what he saw, and what stress it might have caused to the foal, even though Denis had checked him over and Xavior's monitor hadn't shown any issues.

"She is not a good person, Greg. Egotistical and Narcissistic. She really thought it was her duty to bring me to justice as if it was a divine right."

I kissed him and sighed. "I wish you hadn't met her at all."

Xavior shrugged and moved closer to me, burying his nose in my armpit. "Option B involved a lot of murder and I wasn't up for it. I am pregnant, after all."

He looked up at me and we grinned at each other and kissed some more before we fell asleep in each other's arms.

The next morning, some members of the family gathered for breakfast, and instead of cheerful talk about the new playground, we talked about the Order and what to do next.

Catherine spoke first. "I contacted the local mage family, the Petersons. They have reached out to the North American council to see what they can do about this family in France not going through proper channels."

Xavior nodded. "It could be another tactic from the Cooper family. There were news stories that the Envoy had stepped down shortly after he heard my case. They haven't announced his replacement. It's possible the coven is still trying to finish what they started."

"I have an old family contact I can reach out to and see what information they have about this situation. Hunter groups stay loosely connected," I said. Plus, there was my sister. I didn't want to think about her being involved with Mother again. She had even said she'd cut her off after she was thrown out of the Order, too. We were only starting to really reconnect. I wanted to believe her, but I wouldn't stop pressing for more answers, regardless of whether Katie was involved or not. "We should probably contact Renard, too."

"I took the liberty of reaching out to my brother last night. He will be in touch to gather more information later today," Ransford said. While none of us liked the situation, I had the impression there was a lava flow just under the surface of Ransford's skin. Yet he remained calm, especially when Corley touched him. I wondered if her influence was a manifestation of their pheromone connection, or the longevity of their relationship.

"Will this disrupt plans for Spain?" Faith asked.

"No," I responded. "They can't hold us here or restrict our movements. They don't even have legal standing. If they try to come after us with the whole family in residence, we would be within our rights to handle them accordingly."

It was damn near a declaration of war on the Order, which gave me another idea. "I'll reach out to our contacts in Rome and make them aware of the situation. They might have internal investigators that could deal with it as well."

"You've been in contact with the Order in Rome?" Philip asked.

So much had happened it was hard to remember who knew. "Ah yeah." I sighed, feeling guilty for not telling my parents. "Technically, I have an offer from them to re-certify as a Knight of the Order through the branch in Rome. I haven't taken them up on it." The dragons around the table were quiet, sharing looks of concern between each other.

"If you know the enemy and know yourself, you need not fear the result of a hundred battles," Denis quoted. Emory nodded in agreement.

"You've read, Sun Tzu?" Trevor asked.

"Philosophy and science share kinship. Understanding one can often lead to answers in the other," Denis replied. "Understanding how the Order works in Rome is to our advantage."

It occurred to me as I sipped my coffee that Denis wasn't concerned so much about the Knights individually, but what they represented. They were technically a lost family of dragons. Did the Order know that? How dangerous would they be if they discovered that their ability was tied to latent dragon DNA? While I knew my mother and maybe other local groups likely didn't know, the Order in Rome was the first. With the church's resources, it was entirely possible they knew and kept it a secret.

If the sects of the Order became embroiled in an internal civil war, what might happen to them or any dragons caught in the middle? My gaze met Xavior's. It wasn't my life or his we were risking any longer by communicating with the Order in Rome. Whatever we did, we'd have to tread lightly to protect our families.

Damn my mother and her whole ideology to hell. I sighed, rubbed a hand across my face, and set down my cup. "We've done what we can for now and we'll coordinate any more efforts moving forward. We don't want to make decisions with only half-baked hunches and circumstantial evidence."

Xavior smiled at me. The rest of the family was staring, waiting. I met their gazes and then looked at Xavior again. He smiled and cleared his throat. "Well then, what would you like us to do first, Gregor?"

Oh. Shit. I looked around at everyone again and took a breath. "Okay then. Let's start with Renard, then work down the list from official lines of query to less official and more dangerous. No one should risk themselves to get information. My mother's dangerous, yes, but she still plays by the rules. That's to our advantage. Let's use that while we can."

There were nods of agreement around the table and breakfast continued as the topic turned to other things like the replicated meat, and where Xavior purchased his coffee.

We spent the rest of the morning on the newly made playground watching three small whelps play their hearts out. There were plenty of pictures and laughs. We breathed a little easier now that the security had been updated. But even I could tell that there was a small undercurrent of worry among the adults.

Regardless of what the Coopers or my mother planned, they wouldn't be allowed to harm our families, of that much I was certain.

SISTERLY SUPPORT

GREGOR

It was a few weeks before I tried calling Katie. There were two things I wanted from her and I needed to see her, not just hear her voice, in order to decide what to do next. I used Xavior's office setup in our suite to call.

Three pings sounded before Katie acknowledged the holo vid call and answered with her mobile.

"Greg! Hey brother. How are things?" She was standing in a kitchen and someone was moving behind her. There was a towel tucked over her shoulder.

"Making dinner?"

"Yeah. Elena is making something fun that she picked up traveling, which I still suck at pronouncing, so I'm not even going to try."

Someone, possibly Elena, yelled the name, "Arrumadinho!"

We laughed and tried to repeat it, but failed. "What is it?"

"An appetizer made with meat, beans, and a vinaigrette which looks like pico de gallo to me but doesn't taste like it," Katie said. "The name comes from how it's arranged on the plate or how you put it together."

There was a slight pause in the conversation, and Katie frowned. "Seriously, what's up? Your giving detective face."

Shit. "Yeah, that's fair. Can we talk in private?"

Katie nodded. "Be right back, babe."

Two things became three in that moment, because Katie was right, I was in detective mode. I saw the door close behind her as she turned to sit on the bed in the room she entered.

"Okay, spill."

"When's the last time you talked with Mother?"

Katie frowned harder. "What the fuck kind of question is that?"

"Katie." My hand covered my mouth, making me focus on being silent. I needed her to answer the question. The silence went on for some time until she sighed and finally told me.

"Fuck, Greg, I haven't talked to her in years. I don't even know if she knows I exist."

She was still in shock that I even asked the question. The voice analyzer flashed me a notification and said she was telling the truth. I felt guilty for using it without telling her. The silence went on for a few more beats, then I dropped my hand to speak.

"She was here. On the estate grounds. She threatened to drag Xavior to France on an extradition warrant."

"Jesus." Katie looked away, then down at her shoes, then back at me. "Is everyone okay?"

I took a breath and relaxed a little. "Yeah. We're alright. Shaken, though. She got through some pretty heavy security."

"How?"

"A mage portal from what we could tell."

"Mages? That's new. She's not one to rely on heavy magic like that."

"It surprised me too."

We listened to each other breathe, taking in the information. I watched Katie's face as she thought about what happened. We were all trained hunters. She knew Mother as well as I did. "It's sounds desperate, or it was a show of dominance. She wanted you to know that she could get to you, and Xavior."

"Well, we know. We're following up with several contacts here."

"How did you get her to back off?" Her frown turned flat, and her brow furrowed. She knew as well as I did that our mother didn't just back off, but she also followed the rules.

"I told her Xav's pregnant."

"And she believed that?"

"Not only did she believe it, but she told me she was disappointed in me, too." I grinned. It was small at first, but Katie laughed and I joined her. Once the ironic laughter faded, an anger lit in her eyes.

"Fuck, she has some nerve." She caught my gaze. "I understand now why you wanted to know if I had contact with her."

I acknowledged that statement with a nod. "It bought us some time, but I don't know how much." I wanted to trust Katie with more of the truth. Hopefully, at some point, I could. Right now, I couldn't. Things were too raw and vulnerable. And the last thing I needed was our mother deciding to go after Katie to get to me or Xavior.

"Hopefully, it's enough to take care of whatever warrant she thinks she has. It's got to be legit. She wouldn't have tried to execute it otherwise. Though the way she violated security measures makes me think she knew there was a clock she was trying to beat."

"That makes sense." We had mostly come to that conclusion as well. It was good to talk about it with someone who didn't think I was paranoid or wouldn't take the risk seriously. Though the dragons around me were very much taking it seriously. "At the risk of really pissing you off, can I ask another question?"

"Given the circumstances, you shouldn't be worried about pissing me off."

"Hey. I care about you. We didn't survive our mother and reconnect all these years later only to let her destroy our relationship." Which was true. I had to believe that Katie would forgive me given the circumstances, as she said, but there was also a chance she wouldn't.

"Greg. You're the only one that even wanted a relationship with me. Our father—"

"Step father," I corrected, because Neil was definitely not my father. I probably didn't have to point that out, but I felt the distinction was necessary.

"Right." She paused a moment, then continued. "Neil wouldn't stand up to her, not even for Trish and Little Neil."

I sighed. Protecting the younger two was something Katie and I had agreed to do from the very beginning. They didn't have the Knight's marker, but they went through the same training we did. Mother didn't care that they weren't technically Knights. She treated us the same, unfortunately.

"They followed his example, even after we spend most of our childhoods protecting them," said Katie. "I know we were a lot older than them, but I hoped we could all trust each other."

That stung. If circumstances had been different, maybe I would have had some kind of relationship with our younger siblings. Our siblings knew us. We had reached out to both of them. They answered with silence. Given they still lived close and visited Mother's estate, it made me think they wanted their inheritance more than us, and that hurt, too. But neither Katie nor I could do anything about that.

"They're adults now. Like us, they have to make their own choices. Maybe someday they'll come around."

She smiled. "Maybe." Katie took a deep breath and let it out. "Now, what was your question?"

I glanced around before I finally asked it, looking Katie in the eyes. "How much do you know about your traveling partner?"

Katie laughed. Looked at me, then laughed harder.

"Okay, that wasn't the reaction I thought you'd have. What am I missing?"

Katie grinned. "Elena is a dragon, too."

My grin matched my sisters. "No, shit?"

"No shit, bro. She even knows what I am and is alright with it. She has an older brother who is protective of her. Apparently, she told him, and he basically hates my guts."

"Damn. Family drama already. It's only been a few months. You're moving pretty fast."

"In that we are very much alike, mister with two kids."

"Guilty."

We talked a little longer, and then Katie had to go. Elena was done with dinner. "Listen before you go, just know I love you and if you need anything, reach out. And the invitation to visit is still open."

Katie paused from standing and sat back down. "Do you think that's smart?"

"What do you mean?"

"If mother is sniffing around, I don't want Elena anywhere near her."

I frowned. "You're serious?"

"Dead serious." She frowned too. "I love you, but maybe we should wait. Just until all this blows over."

I couldn't fault her logic there. It was clearly a risk I hadn't considered, mostly because I didn't know Elena.

"Maybe we can figure out a way you can protect Elena, too. Like I can with Xavior." I wondered if I could get Denis to make another ring.

"I'm not giving anyone a sample of my blood, Greg. End of story."

"Katie."

"No, I'm not doing it." She sighed. "I'm glad you and Xavior have a good relationship, but I don't know him like you do. I can't risk it. Not with mother having mages involved."

She had me there. Xavior hadn't been honest with me about the blood sample or the ring, even though it had saved him and his brother. We eventually resolved that point of contention. Thus far, the ring has worked. Thankfully.

Plus, there were mages that could do some pretty terrible things with blood if they had access, the right circumstances, and motivation. From her perspective, she wasn't wrong. Then there was Catherine and her family, whom I trusted with our lives. Not to mention Jordan. While Katie didn't know everything, her viewpoint wasn't likely to change with more information.

"If you change your mind—"

"I'll let you know." She tried to smile, but it didn't light up her eyes like it usually did. "In the meantime, stay safe. I love you, Greg."

"You too, Katie. Love you."

I shut down the call and sat there staring at the holo device on the desk, hoping with all my heart that it wasn't the last time Katie and I would talk.

THE PREMIERE

XAVIOR

"We're at the London premiere of the sequel to . . ."

The flashing lights were more than I wanted to deal with, especially in my state. Though the chance to wear the dress I had made for the first premiere was too much to pass up.

Greg was in a tux that showed off the Brantley house colors, which matched the colors of my dress or robes, or large swaths of cloth, depending on your point of view. It came with a small half jacket with puffs of material that drifted off my shoulders and tights—mostly for modesty's sake. The whole idea was to make it look like I was floating on a cloud. Greg called it my cherub robes, which I rather liked, and so had Jael. Maybe a naughty cherub. I even had a gold circlet on my head to complete the image. I never much understood the idea of baby angels. Then again, human religions had some rather fanciful notions.

Jordan and Catherine were just ahead of us since we all arrived in the same car. He had upgraded to a suit with color. This time, it was a deep red and had splashes of orange and black from head to toe. Even his hair had dashes of color to make it look like flames surrounded him, especially since his skin was constantly displaying shades of pink and red. It gave him a halo effect, which was only outshined by his smile and the adoration he had for Catherine, who was wearing a burgundy colored dress that played with all her curves, including the large belly bump that was present.

For them, it was a time of anticipation and commitment. With their child, Jordan could keep his consort position indefinitely. Antiquated as the practice was, I was happy for them, and specifically for him. He deserved to find the happiness he once had, especially since I couldn't return the full measure of his feelings for me. He was still our friend, and my best friend. His happiness meant a lot to me, and I was glad he could find someone he cared about so deeply.

Once we were through the media gauntlet, Greg stopped us and pulled me to the side. "Still feeling alright?"

I nodded. "So far, so good. The lights were a lot. Been a while since I was on a red carpet for one of our movies."

"Yeah. I've adjusted to it since the sets are always bright, even for the night scenes."

"And here I thought it would be the imagers that were annoying." Greg pulled me in for a hug and a kiss. We stayed like that for a moment more before Jordan found us.

"Catherine wanted me to find you and make sure everything is alright. She's sitting at our table."

"Everything's fine." Greg held me closer, then glanced at me. "Ready to go in?"

"Ready as I'll ever be."

Jordan smiled, "After you." We headed in and found Catherine waiting. The look of concern on her face was endearing. While she was our family physician, we'd quickly become friends, commiserating over body changes, cravings, and sleepless nights. She reached out to touch my hand, and I took hers up and pressed a quick kiss to her knuckles.

"Everything alright?" she asked.

"Nothing amiss for the moment. I'm hoping I can make it through the whole movie without a bathroom break."

She laughed. "That makes two of us." The movie was nearly three hours long, and neither Catherine nor I made it through the first thirty minutes.

I enjoyed watching what I saw of it. The effects were so well done; it was hard to pick out Greg's work as stunt person. In the last movie, he had been a stunt double for one of the secondary characters. The second movie focused on that character and gave Greg a bigger challenge. So while I knew most of the fight scenes and athletic abilities were likely his, it wasn't his face on the screen.

After the movie, Jordan went to an after party while the rest of us returned to my sister's place north of London. Faith and Trevor had offered to whelp sit while we were at the premiere. Having a familiar place to stay always helped.

"Did Denis and Emory say when they were joining us?" Catherine asked.

"They should head back from Geneva tonight or tomorrow. Apparently, vacations aren't exactly vacations for those two. They've been advising on several projects, even though they aren't directly involved. I pointed out that they both needed to stick close," I said.

Catherine shrugged. "They're able to check on everything with the monitor. I'm able to see them logged into the data stream. I'd like to think it's their way of dealing with their anticipation and anxiety without bothering you all the time."

That had been a slight problem in the beginning. If it wasn't Denis, it was Emory checking on me. Along with the gifts, which were normal for dragon culture. At first, the gifts were practical, but as I showed more, the gifts became more extravagant, and included Greg, too. They were everything from the latest gadgets to things they had invented to make us more comfortable. At one point, they had an entire bedroom set delivered to the estate. That's when Greg and I sat down to talk with them about boundaries.

"The monitor system has saved our sanity. We understood how anxious they are, but needed breathing room." Greg said.

"How often are they accessing it?" I asked.

"Oh, they don't just access it, it's streaming them data in real time." Catherine smiled as I sighed. "I wouldn't be surprised if it gave them GPS updates as well. They'll probably know you're in labor before you do."

Greg put his hand on my leg. He had probably picked up on my annoyance. I remembered being annoyed at just about everything during this part of my last pregnancy, too. "They're trying to make sure you and the fetus are safe. Denis doesn't want to lose you again," Greg said. The reminder soothed my annoyance somewhat, and I leaned toward Greg to give him a kiss.

Denis and I had spent a lot of time talking about the past, what I remembered, and what he remembered or had written about it. I filled in as much as I could for him. Some things were still difficult, but mostly, we were trying very hard to be brothers again. As we continued to talk, he smiled more, though seriousness was still his default. We fought less and tried to understand each other. The safe old habits of distance and silence died hard, much to our mutual annoyance. Greg arbitrated at first, then even he became annoyed with our antics and put us in a room with our therapist, Dr. Grayson, who was not only a shifter, but an empath too.

I put my hand on Greg's, "I get it, I do. Though I'll be happy when this is all over. I'm done with carrying eggs. If it hadn't been for the suit and the batteries, I'd be even more of a bitch than I am right now." That got the desired laugh. I wanted to lighten the mood.

Greg's personal magic had increased with every use of either Jordan's magic, or Emory's. While everyone, including Greg, was delighted with his increased magical abilities, I wasn't so sure. Magic was mostly neutral. It was the individual that changed it. The more he used magic, the more I worried about what it might cost him. Then again, maybe I was worrying over nothing.

"Well, if you need a top off, let me know. The twins should be asleep by the time we get back to your sister's place," Greg grinned.

"Did you just joke about sex in front of Catherine?" I was proud and surprised. "And you're not even blushing!" Though the moment the words left my mouth, a creep of red dotted his cheeks as I sniffed his slight embarrassment because I pointed it out. All he did in response was shrug.

"Well, I, for one, am glad he feels like he can come out of his shell, even a little. Give it another five or ten years and he'll be a hedonist like the rest of us," said Catherine.

We laughed, and Greg blushed more. "Oh, he might not talk about it, but he's more hedonist than anyone knows." I picked his hand up off my leg and turned it to kiss his palm.

"And there's the line." Greg moved his hand to clasp mine and bring it back to his lap. Catherine laughed, amused by us, and by how far Greg had opened up around her and Jordan. I kept most of our activities between us unless he wanted to share. Thus far, the more daring of our exploits remained unknown to our closest friends, though I was prompted to share a few times. They made many speculations about our sex life. None of which we confirmed unless Greg was comfortable with it. He had boundaries, and I respected them until he decided otherwise.

"I love you." I leaned into him, and he wrapped an arm around my shoulders and kissed my forehead.

"Love you too," he whispered. The rest of the ride was quiet as we watched the rain fall outside the vehicle's windows.

Later, ensconced in a suite in my sister's house, with the twins in an adjoining room, Greg took the time to put compost logs in the fireplace and have me light it. We settled in front of the fire in our boxers, my back to his front, and his hands on my belly. My scales shimmered in the light just under the surface of my skin.

"We should take a walk on the grounds tomorrow before Emory and Denis arrive."

"That's a good idea."

He kissed the back of my neck, and I gave him a little moan for his effort. "Is there anything you need?" he asked.

I chuckled, "Just you, like this . . . and maybe a hot choco-late?"

"In the middle of summer?"

"I know, I know. Maybe it's a craving? I've been thinking about hot chocolate all night. And a fruit smoothie. With honey. Um, and peanut butter with apples."

"That's new."

"Is it?"

"You've never asked for fruit before. Did you eat enough at dinner?"

"Yeah. I had a massive salad with half a replicated chicken on it."

Greg shrugged, then pushed me forward a little so he could crawl out from behind me. I put my hands down and grabbed one of the large floor pillows to keep myself propped up.

"I'll see what I can find in the kitchen." He grabbed his robe from the bed and walked toward the door. I watched him as he turned and gave me a smile, his fierce pride and happiness scenting the room before he left on his errand.

As he opened the door, he nearly ran into a tray on the floor. He looked down, then back at me. "Your sister doesn't have house staff, does she?"

"No, not really. Not like my estate. She has a cleaning service and a cook, but only during the day. Why? What's that on the floor?"

He picked it up and brought it inside. "It's everything you asked for, on a silver platter, literally." He brought it over and set it down next to me, and my mouth watered.

I picked up the hot chocolate first and sipped it. There were two on the tray. "Are you going to drink yours?"

"Is someone listening to us? How did everything you asked for show up like we ordered room service?"

"I'm not sure." After biting into an apple, I immediately want-ed five more. I was poised to take another bite when we heard soft thumps hit the bed, then the floor behind us as the round objects rolled off onto the floor.

Greg stood and went to pick up one of the stray apples. "Did you want more apples?"

There were exactly five apples scattered around the room. I counted as Greg picked up each one and brought them back to me. "Yes, but I didn't expect them to come from thin air."

"You think it's a ghost?"

"My sister's place hasn't had hostile ghosts for a century or more..."

"What?" I ignored Greg's shock. Trevor and Faith had an agreement with the ghosts that lived in their home. They wouldn't have bothered us unless they thought the there was some kind of danger.

"... besides, ghosts can't manifest things that are real. They would be illusions; fake. You wouldn't have been able to pick them up. Taste one."

Greg bit into one apple, and his eyes widened. "This is the best apple I've ever had, I think." He glanced at it, surprised. "It reminds me of the pies Mom makes sometimes."

"Oh yeah, Jennifer makes fantastic pies. And cookies. Her lemon-ginger shortbread cookies are epic."

"Yeah." Greg smiled. "I miss them too."

Moments later, on one of the nearby tables, a plate of cookies and two glasses of lemonade appeared as if Jennifer had dropped them off herself. Greg and I looked at each other, amazed and a little scared. The monitor beeped, and a few moments later, Greg's phone started ringing.

He went to get it while I munched on apples, content and warm next to the fire.

"Hello?" he said. "No, everything's fine, as far as we know. Yes, the monitor beeped, but it always beeps when it's doing something. Magical drain? Just a second."

Greg put the call on speaker, and Emory's voice filled the room. "The data is showing that Xavior has a large amount of magical energy that's cycling through his system. Have either of you experienced anything?"

We looked at each other, then Greg explained the random food items showing up.

Emory made a noise like a cross between a surprised sound and a whinny. "They're manifesting! This is marvelous. Denis, the fetus is manifesting!"

"What does that mean, exactly?" Greg asked.

"It's harmless, but it's an indicator that they have developed their own magic. It's very common for my species."

"Wait, I thought we were having a pegasus?" I interjected.

"We are, but they are part dragon, and part unicorn. We weren't sure if they would develop elemental magic or raw magic. Unlike dragons, unicorns can access their magic before they emerge from the parent. Sometimes the parent and the fetus can work in tandem, combining their magic." Emory was very excited.

Then Denis spoke. "Did you do something to trigger the fetus's magic?"

"No," Greg shrugged, and I continued. "We came home from the premiere, checked on the whelps, made a fire. We were enjoying it when things appeared."

"During the summer?" Denis sounded surprised.

"It's London, Denis, it's raining outside. It seemed sensible."

"You didn't think that was strange, Greg?" Denis asked.

"I have no basis for strange any more. Though I asked about the hot chocolate he wanted."

"How close are you to the fire, Xavior?" Denis asked.

"Half a meter, maybe less? Nothing I haven't done before. The whelps liked it well enough."

"Of course," Emory said.

"Yes. That would explain it," Denis replied.

"You want to clue us in over here?" I asked.

"Fire is a powerful element in your family. It's likely the conduit through which the fetus is creating magic," Emory said.

"So, no going near fires any more?" Greg said.

I couldn't bring myself to even think about it. It was one of the few things that relaxed me that didn't require physical activity. And the larger I became, the less I wanted to move. If the fetus reacted to fire, would it react to water the same way? I sighed, lamenting that floating in the pool probably wouldn't be an option, either.

"No, it should be fine. However, you'll want to limit desires and wishes while near a fire so the fetus doesn't use up their magic. They need it to continue developing," Emory replied.

After another ten minutes of back and forth with Denis and Emory, they let us know they would arrive at Faith and Trevor's house tomorrow evening. We wished them well, ended the call, then reluctantly moved away from the fire. Once out of the fire's light, I noticed my belly shimmered with a light of its own, then quickly dimmed. How I hadn't noticed that my skin was glowing was a shock to both of us.

"Okay." Greg bit into one of the shortbread cookies as he came to sit next to me after I moved to lie on the bed. He looked like he was weighing what to say next while he was chewing. No one could accuse Greg of not being thoughtful. "We'll get through this. Only a month left, tops, right?" I groaned and laid back on the bed as he took another bite of cookie. "These are exactly how I remember them," he said as he looked at the cookie in his hand before finishing it and dusting the crumbs off his hands. "That's wild. You must have one hell of a memory to have an exact flavor profile."

"Jennifer gave me the recipe. I have it memorized."

Greg glanced at me. "How many times did you make her cookies?"

"Before we moved in together?" I looked up at him. He smiled and shook his head. "I wanted to impress your parents."

"Xavior," he leaned over to kiss me, the taste of shortbread cookies on his lips. "I love you," he said, then showed me other ways in which he loved me before we both drifted off into a peaceful sleep.

IMPORTANT EVENTS IN HISTORY

MAGICAL SPECIES PACT OF 1452

As trade and expansion became more prevalent, territorial wars and colonization became more commonplace. While harvesting parts of magical beings had always been unseemly, the trade and expansion of different empires pushed it into high gear. It was at this point that the Council of Elders, the wisest and oldest magical beings in Europe, came together to create the Magical Species Pact to protect magical beings or anyone that used magic. The pact made magical beings inert or non-magical upon death. If any part of the being was magical, it would render any magic that part or person carried inert. It effectively enforced tolerance between species that shared the same continent.

What they did not understand at the time was how this would affect beings with regenerative powers, such as phoenixes. Magical species that go through a cycle of renewal, such as phoenixes, have a duality of power as their death generates magic that causes a rebirth, allowing the individual to keep their magical abilities, whatever those were. There's been some side effects attributed to the pact, as phoenixes have reported issues with memory loss since its enactment.

Nor was death magic taken into account. Of the number of elders that were represented by the council, very few had any domain over the dead or undead. This was the loophole that allowed Joseph Florentine to thrive.

NECROMANTIC WAR: 1873 TO 1878 (THE NECRO WAR)

The major theater of war was in Europe and the Prussia Empire, though it spilled over into parts of the Russian Empire as well. Joseph Florentine had been an exceptional necromancer who rose to power in the mid-1800s. His platform centered upon allowing magic users the rights and freedoms to use magic as they pleased. He and his followers wanted to abolish the Magical Species Pact created by the Council of Elders to protect magic users. Florentine considered it the height of hubris that one of the most powerful groups of magical beings in Europe had forced magic users on that continent into the pact.

It took many magical species, including necromancers, vampires, and non-magical species (mostly humans) to fight off Florentine's forces.

ABOUT THE AUTHOR

M.L. Eaden works by day in the tech industry, but at night, she reads books, writes stories, throws axes, and is an avid gamer with a current addiction to Azul. Originally from the sunflower state, she migrated to one with a lone star—and more sun. She tries desperately to keep up with two adorable cattle dogs that still act like they are five instead of the seniors their vet says they are.

There are more great things to find at mleaden.com – blogs, reviews, and her latest newsletter. Sign up today @ mleaden.com and receive a free downloadable short story!

ALSO BY M.L. EADEN

You can find more books from the
Mythical Desires Universe at:
mleaden.com/books

Or sign up for the newsletter:
mleaden.substack.com